CRUSH

BOSTON BRAWLERS BOOK 3

JUNE WINTERS

BRYNN CONLEY

"Okay, here we are!" I said, forcing a cheer as I plated the last meal I'd ever cook for the Gibson family. "It's Eloise's favorite: meatball lasagna."

Eloise eagerly clutched a kid's fork in her tiny hand. "Mmm!"

"Eloise, what do you say to Brynn for cooking you your favorite meal?" Mrs. Gibson asked.

"Thank you, Miss Brynn."

"You're very welcome, Eloise!"

Mrs. Gibson wore a bittersweet smile. "Last night, Dan and I were talking about all the little things we'll miss about having you around—"

Her husband finished her sentence. "But especially your cooking."

"Oh, you guys. Careful, you might make me cry."

"Bless your heart," Mrs. Gibson said.

I watched Eloise shovel a bite of lasagna into her mouth. I wasn't sure if she understood that I wouldn't be her nanny anymore; every time it came up, she seemed oblivious or disinterested. I couldn't blame her. Kids have different ways of dealing with things. And I was the only nanny she'd known the past two years. Who knew what she could possibly be thinking?

It's never easy moving on from a family. But when Mr. Gibson received the unexpected news that he was being laid off from his architecture firm, I became an expense the family couldn't afford. There was no doubt in my mind that Mr. Gibson would quickly find another job and the family would rebound. Still, I felt awful for them to go through the stress of losing a job. And while I shared the pain of losing a job—because I was losing *my* job too, after all—at least I didn't have a family of my own that depended on me. Just Pickles, my cat.

Gotta look on the bright side, right?

The worst part about losing my job was that my time with little Eloise was being cut short. Okay—'little Eloise' wasn't actually so little anymore. But it's hard not to think of her as the darling little dumpling she was when I first started two years ago. Eloise is four and a half now, and is the sort of well-mannered, well-spoken child that makes life very, very easy for a nanny. *Too* easy, maybe—maybe I would've had a little more job security if she were an absolute hellion. Ha ha. Just kidding. No one wants that. She's adorable and I'm going to miss her a lot.

While Mr. Gibson's layoff came as a surprise, the truth was, I *was* expecting to be cut loose in a few short months anyhow. From day one, the plan was that once Eloise started preschool, my time as the Gibson family nanny would come to an end.

Originally, that timeline fit me just fine because I have an affinity for babies. That's what I like about being a nanny—I can help people raise their babies while they're so friggin' cute, right up until they're old enough to start school, and then I can move on to another family to start the process all over again.

But not having those last few months to come to terms with leaving the Gibsons—well, I guess I felt like I was robbed of closure. It came so suddenly.

Just like the first time around.

Life has a funny way of kicking you again and again until you get the message, I guess. But I'm still trying to figure out what the message actually *is*.

After dinner, it was the regular routine: I washed the pots and pans and cleaned the kitchen and made a little small talk before I left their home for good.

"So what are you up to tonight, Brynn?" Mrs. Gibson asked.

"I've got dinner plans with the guy I've been seeing," I said.

"Oh, fun! The paramedic?"

I nodded. "The one and only. Brad."

"You've been seeing each other for a couple months now, haven't you? Are things gettin' a little serious?" she asked in a teasing tone.

"God ..." I croaked out an anxious laugh.

Were things getting serious? I was already torturing myself with an internal back-and-forth about the right time to have 'the talk' with Brad. Mrs. Gibson's prodding seemed like a hint from the universe that it was indeed time to tell him.

I gulped. "Maybe? I don't know."

"You seem so nervous!"

I spun the wedding band around and around on my ring finger. Or rather, I spun the part of my finger where the wedding band *used* to be. Old habits die hard.

"That's because I *am* nervous," I said.

"Brynn Conley," she began with a grin, "I did not have you pegged as a commitment-phobe."

"*I'm* not," I said. It was always the guys that couldn't handle the commitment. But I didn't really want to get into all that right now. "Anyway. Who knows. We'll see how things go."

Mr. Gibson—who had stood by with an uncomfortable leer while his wife talked to me about my dating life—suddenly stepped forward. "Well, Brynn, it was a pleasure. We'd be more than happy to give you a reference, so don't hesitate to let us know if you need one."

"A *glowing* reference," Mrs. Gibson added.

"Thank you both so much. I really appreciate that."

"Seriously," Mr. Gibson added, "whether you need a reference for another nanny job, or a real job, just let me know and I'd be glad to put in the good word."

His wife discreetly pinched his arm and quietly reprimanded him. "*Honey! That was rude!*"

I knew what he meant, but a small piece of me was always a little perturbed when someone implied that nannying wasn't a '*real*' job—whatever that phrase even meant in the first place. Wasn't a real job *any* job that paid the bills? Or did I have to be chained to a desk and working a nine-to-six schedule before I was officially worthy of someone's respect?

And call me crazy, but nannying is the most meaningful job I've ever had.

To his credit, Mr. Gibson looked thoroughly embarrassed. His cheeks went red and he stammered. "I, uh—I didn't mean anything by that, Brynn. I'm sorry that sounded rude."

"Oh, it's fine. I know what you meant." My smile put him at ease. "Anyway, I should get going."

I hugged them both, and then it was time to say goodbye to the little one.

Only Eloise didn't want to say goodbye—she crawled under the couch and refused to come out instead.

"If you don't say bye to Brynn now, you'll never see her again!" Eloise's mom warned her.

With a heartbroken bawl, Eloise climbed out from under the couch, ran into my arms, and hugged me so tight I thought she'd never let go.

"Miss Bryyyyyyyyynn!" she wailed, sobbing. "Don't go!"

Yeah, that'll break your heart.

Darn. I'd managed to hold it together all night until that very moment, but now the tears started to trickle.

"Aw, sweetheart!" I said with a sniffle. "I'll still visit you, okay? I promise."

After her parents pried the little girl off of me, I made it out the door and hurried to my car.

Whew. That was tough.

2

SHEA ELLIS

There was a time—still seems like yesterday—when, after I made it home from the hockey game, I was mobbed at the door by my three adoring children. I'll never forget the way those kids looked up at *Daddy* with these huge, disbelieving eyes. Because *I* was the same guy they'd just watched on television: the captain of the Boston Brawlers. Their very own Daddy was a hero in real life.

These days, now that my kids were a little more grown up? Well, things were a bit different.

I sighed as I climbed out of my car, shut the automatic garage door behind me and stepped into the house. The living room was pitch-black, but some weirdo music was loudly playing on the sound system.

Huh. Strange.

"Hello? I'm home," I called out to nobody, my hand sliding along the wall until I found the light switch.

I flicked on the light. And had a dagger plunged straight in my heart.

Sitting in total darkness, and on complete opposite ends of

the sofa—*guilty much?*—was my fourteen-year-old daughter, Chloe, and a shaggy-haired boy in baggy clothes.

"Who's this? What's going on in here?" I asked sternly.

"Nothing!" Chloe barked.

"Nothing, huh." I stole a peek at my wristwatch. It was 10:30 at night. I walked over to the stereo and killed the music. "It's almost your bedtime, Chloe."

She groaned.

I stepped behind the couch and clapped a heavy hand on the boy's shoulder. "Aren't you going to introduce me to your friend?"

"His name is Adam," Chloe said, adopting that timeless teen affect—the one that sounds like, '*Ugh, oh my God, Dad, you are so embarrassing me right now!*'

This Adam character looked like he was a couple grades older than Chloe. I gritted my teeth and extended my hand for a shake. "Hi, Adam. I'm Mr. Ellis."

Gulping loudly, Adam stuck out his limp, quivering hand. I gave his hand a good squeeze. Not hard enough that he'd yelp out in pain ... but hard enough to let him know that he was dealing with an overprotective, hockey-playing father.

"H-hi, Mr. Ellis," he said, quivering like a nervous puppy. "It's nice to meet you."

"Oh, I bet it is." I chuckled as I pulled him off the couch and to his feet. "Well, Chloe, it's a school night, so I think it's time for Adam to go home."

Chloe folded her arms. "Da~d ...!"

I pulled my car keys from my pocket and jangled them. "Come with me, Adam. I'll give you a ride."

"I got my ride already." He raised a skateboard into the air. "Right here."

"Oh, I can't let you skate home so late, Adam. It's dark out. Wouldn't be safe. Plus, I think we need to have a little chat."

"Okay," he said in surrender. "T-thank you, Mr. Ellis."

I set my hand on the back of Adam's scrawny neck and guided the trembling teen to the door. Chloe watched with arms folded.

"Me and you are going to have a little chat of our own when I get back," I told her.

"Whatever." With an exaggerated eye-roll, Chloe stamped off to her bedroom.

———

After getting to know Adam a little better—and giving him a good grilling about his intentions with my daughter—I came home for good.

First, I found the nanny, Estel, asleep in the den. She was wrapped up in a blanket with a knitting project in her lap and the TV droning in the background.

Asleep again?

I touched her shoulder. "*Pst.* Estel. Hey. Wake up."

With a smack of her lips, Estel woke. "Oh! Hello there, Shea, I was just resting my eyes for a minute."

Yeah, I'm sure.

"Listen, Estel. I caught Chloe with a boy. Unsupervised."

"Oh—Adam, you mean?"

"Wait, you knew he was here?"

"Yes."

"And you left them alone?"

"He seems like a nice boy. They weren't up to anything bad," Estel said. "Er, they *weren't*, were they?"

I sighed. "I don't know. I found them in the living room with the lights off. I don't know what they were up to—my mind won't even *begin* to let me go there—but I can't imagine it was good."

Estel waved her hand at me as if all this were no big deal. "Oh, Shea. You know how teens are these days."

I didn't know *what* Estel was trying to imply about what that twerp was trying to do with my daughter, but my insides revolted at the mere suggestion of something inappropriate.

"No, Estel, I don't."

She gave a shrug.

"Where are the boys?" I asked, even though I figured I knew the answer.

"Downstairs, I'd imagine."

I left Estel and made my way downstairs. Sure enough, my ten-year-old twins, Cameron and Nicholas, were embroiled in a fierce game of one-on-one inside the soundproofed confines of their indoor rink.

Years ago, when it became obvious that the boys loved hockey as much as their dad—and were destroying lamps and breaking windows with their indoor roughhousing—I paid a pretty penny to have this modern marvel built. The floor was made of synthetic ice, so they could skate on it with real ice skates. It's not the same feeling as skating on real ice, but it's as close as you can get to the real thing. The rink also had a net, boards, glass, a scoreboard, and even a little penalty box to sit in. Best of all, the entire thing was soundproof and virtually indestructible, so the boys can shoot and hit in there all day long and not break anything or make a huge ruckus.

I slipped on my skates, opened the door to the rink, and entered the boys' world. The air in their rink was hot and humid and hard to breathe. Thankfully, they didn't truly *stink* yet ... that would still be in the years to come.

"Hey, boys! Really worked up a sweat in here, eh?"

They were both red faced, and their arms and necks glistened with sweat. "Hey, Dad!" they said at the same time, but neither turned to look—their game was too heated. Cam was intent on trying to deke and dangle his way around Nick, but Nick's defense was rock-solid.

I glided over and helped Nick out, lifting Cam's stick into the air so Nick could snatch the unprotected puck away.

"*DAD!*" Cam shrieked.

And when Nick raced away with the puck and roofed it into the empty net and threw his arms into the air to celebrate his victory, Cam *really* let me have it.

"Great! Thanks a *lot*, Dad! That was game point! What'd you have to do that for?!"

With a frown, I ruffled his hair. "Aw, I'm sorry, bud. I didn't know your game was so serious. I was just messing around. But it *is* your bedtime, anyway." I scooped up the loose puck and tried to get back on his good side. "Hey, Cam. One last shot. Lemme see that one-timer."

With a fire in his eyes, Cam set up, stick cocked and ready to release.

"Call it first," I said.

"Crossbar," he said without hesitation.

I feathered a pass right into Cam's wheelhouse. He channeled that fury into his release and blasted the puck off his blade. A cannon of a shot caromed right off his target, the crossbar, with a loud iron *clang*.

I gave my son a clap on the back. "Nice shot there, buddy." He certainly didn't get it from me—his shot might *already* be heavier and more accurate than mine.

"Yeah, yeah," Cam mumbled, still a little incensed at his dad.

"How was the game, Dad?" Nick asked.

"We lost." I paused. "You boys didn't watch, I take it?"

"Nope," they said at the same time.

I wasn't surprised. These days, my sons weren't even fans of my team. It sucks, but I guess it's just a part of watching your kids grow up. They were Chicago fans instead. Their favorite players? Jonathan Toews and Patrick Kane, of course. Last time we played Chicago, I met with Kaner and Toewser after the game and asked them to autograph a stick for my boys.

Yeah, it's a little embarrassing for a vet like me to tell some younger guy that *he's* my son's favorite player. But whatever. They were both classy about it. And when I gave those sticks to the twins, the look in their eyes made it all worth it.

"So if you weren't watching the game, what were you up to instead?" I asked.

They looked at each other, then me.

Cam shrugged. "We've been down here."

"Wait, you've been down here the entire time? Since I *left*?"

They nodded.

"Did you boys do your homework?"

Their heads hung low and they toed at the fake ice.

"Did you eat dinner, at least?"

"Estel told us we could eat when we're ready," Nick said.

"So that's a no." I sighed. "You boys gotta eat if you want to grow big and strong. How many times do I have to tell you? Nutrition is just as important as practice and training. Head upstairs and eat some dinner. Then do your homework."

"But the food Estel makes is so gross!" Cam whined.

"Yeah, we hate her cooking," Nick added.

I shrugged. "You gotta eat, boys."

The boys grumbled as they coasted off the ice.

———

The dreaded talk with Chloe was next.

I went to her bedroom. Aggressive music blared so loudly from her speakers, the bass made the floor and walls shake.

For God's sake. I should've soundproofed her room instead of that rink.

"Chloe!" I yelled, knocking on her door. She didn't answer, so I knocked harder and louder. She couldn't hear a thing over her music.

When she still didn't answer the door, I didn't have a choice—I turned the knob and entered her room.

The domain of a rebellious teen girl: walls painted radioactive green, pictures of her friends that she'd glued to the wall (*sigh*), posters of bands and movies and teen heartthrobs taped from floor to ceiling. I'd never let Chloe know it, but every time I entered this place, I was a little intimidated by a world I can't possibly understand.

Chloe finally saw me standing in her doorway. Her face twisted with outrage and she flung her iPad aside. She killed the music and started ranting, arms waving in the air.

"*Dad!* You can't just barge in here like that! Ever hear of a thing called *privacy*?!"

"Ever hear of the volume knob? I tried knocking but you couldn't hear me over this death metal."

"It's *not* death metal, Dad. You really think I'd listen to *death metal*? Who do you even think I am? Do you even know me at *all*?"

I pinched the bridge of my nose. "I'm not a music expert, Chloe. I like jazz and country."

"Uuuugh." Her head rolled back and she let out an exasperated howl. I guess I couldn't have possibly said anything more offensive to a teenage girl. "Don't remind me."

"Look, if you can't hear me banging on your door, your music is too loud."

She rolled her eyes. "All you care about is *rules* this, *rules* that. You never let me do anything."

"Listen." I took a seat on her bed and patted the spot next to me. "Come here." The moody teen made me wait a beat before she reluctantly made her way over, her head and shoulders swaying with an unbelievable amount of sass. "Maybe I do have a lot of rules. But that's because you're still a child—"

She groaned at that word.

"Okay, fine, you're a *teen*. But legally, you're still a minor, got it? And that means I'm responsible for your care. And that means you have to follow my rules. And Chloe, you *know* the rules. You know you're not supposed to have friends here past nine o'clock. And you know you're not allowed to be unsupervised with boys."

"We *weren't* unsupervised. Estel knows that Adam was over. I even introduced her to him."

"Right. But I found Estel asleep in the den, so she wasn't really watching you, was she? Which means you were unsupervised."

"So what? Now it's *my* job to make sure the nanny stays awake? I don't think so! Besides, me and Adam could've snuck up to my bedroom if we really wanted to be *'unsupervised'* so badly."

The nuclear level of sarcasm she slathered on that word, 'unsupervised'—and the fact that it was obviously code for something else in her mind—made my throat clench.

No no no, not my baby girl.

"Just obey the rules, Chloe. I don't think I'm asking a whole heck of a lot here. Okay? Are we good?"

"Yeah. Sure. Whatever."

Sometimes, a dad has to settle for a sarcastic *whatever*.

"So is that *all* you wanted to talk to me about or what?" she asked, her eyes flicking towards the door—an obvious hint that it was time for Dad to hit the road.

"Do you always have to be this sarcastic?" I asked.

Chloe groaned, her head making an exaggerated roll around her shoulders.

Right. Wrong question to ask a teen.

"Forget it. Listen, I actually did want to ask you something."

"What?"

"The Brawlers' season ends in two months."

"And?"

"Well, just like every other year, the team is throwing the end-of-the-year gala. It's the team's last bit of fun before the play-offs begin and the real grind begins." I patted her thigh. "I was hoping you'd go as my date again this year?"

She let out a deep sigh. "Oh, God. Not *this* again."

I reared back, both surprised and maybe even a little hurt. "But you went with me last year."

And every year since the divorce.

"Yeah, and every year I've been mortified on the inside. Like, *who* decides to bring their daughter as their date? No one else, Dad, only you! The other players bring their wives and girl-friends! Do you have any idea how *weird* it is to be your date? Besides, I'm too old for it. It's not cute anymore, it's just creepy. Everyone's looking at us and laughing."

I made a sour face. "They're not laughing at us, sweetheart. They think you're adorable."

"*That's* weird too. I'm not 'adorable' anymore and I don't want to go, Dad."

Hurt, I slapped my palms on my knees. "Well. Fine. Can't make you do anything you don't want to do." I sat up and made a beeline for the door. "Don't stay up too late."

"Dad ..." She sighed with a hint of remorse.

"Goodnight, Chloe."

I made my way back downstairs, where Estel was gathering up her things. She was getting ready to head home.

"Listen, Estel. I don't think this is going to work out anymore."

"Huh." Estel took a second to let that sink in. "You sure, Shea?"

"Yeah."

"Well, okay. Do you need time to find a replacement first or anything ...?"

"No, I think I'll just pay you the last of what I owe you."

"Okay."

I have to admit, I wasn't entirely sure about firing Estel. I was expecting her to plead to keep her job, or at least ask what went wrong, and maybe I'd reconsider. But the fact that she didn't even try to fight for her job told me all I needed to know.

The search for a decent nanny continues.

3

———

BRYNN

Brad the paramedic was excitedly telling me all the gory details of his day that *probably* weren't appropriate for a dinner date. Luckily for him, I was having a hard time hearing the actual words coming out of his mouth—I was engaged in an epic debate.

Should I tell him?

God, Brad looks so young.

He is *so young.*

There's no way he'll be ready to hear this.

But how much longer am I willing to invest in a guy if he can't even talk about kids?

Indecision: it's enough to drive a person crazy.

I tuned in right at the tail end of Brad's spiel. "Anyway, that was *my* day trying in vain to save some poor guy's life. Pretty crazy turn of events, eh?"

"Yeah, um, sounds like it."

Brad gave a sturdy shrug. His features were so boyish and young—he was only two years younger than me but could've looked *five* years younger if not for his sleek, military-style haircut. He wore a high and tight, with the sides of his head shaved, and only a shock of hair at the top.

"Enough about me, though," he said, wiping a hand through the air. "So now that you're moving on from the Gibsons, what are *you* going to do?"

"Er? What am I going to do about what?"

"I mean, maybe you'll want to take some time off? Rethink things, maybe?"

"Rethink *what* things?" I asked, genuinely confused.

"I don't know." Brad took a gulp of his beer. "Maybe you'd like to go back to being a personal trainer? Or maybe you'd like to go to school and study something else? I mean, you don't really think you'll be a nanny forever, do you?"

Oh. Is that what this is about? What's up with people being judgmental about my job today?

"I probably could be a nanny forever," I said, and I'll readily admit that I might have sounded a tad bit defensive. "Would that really be a problem for you?"

Brad realized he'd stuck his foot in his mouth. "Hey, I'm not saying it's *bad* to be a nanny or anything like that."

Yet everyone seems to want to imply it, I thought to myself.

"And I can tell you're a badass nanny, Brynn. I'm just trying to say that it must get old, taking care of other people's crotch-spawn."

"It has its ups and downs," I offered quietly.

A spark glinted in Brad's eyes. "Yeah, I can see that. You get all the joys of being a parent, but at the end of the day, you get to go home to some peace and quiet."

I forced a smile. "Yeah. It's really great."

I twirled my fork and took the last bite of my fettuccine Alfredo.

Brad shook his head with awe as I pushed the empty plate

aside. "Man, it never fails to impress me how much food a little girl like you can put away."

"Little girl …?" I muttered, taken aback.

"Look, I didn't mean anything by that either." Brad rolled his eyes. "Sheesh, Brynn. I feel like I'm walking on eggshells around you tonight. What's with you?"

He was losing his patience with me, and the worst part was, I couldn't blame him. He had no idea that he was picking at old scabs of mine.

But he'll know if you tell him. It's the only hope you've got.

I reached across the table and grabbed his hand. "I'm sorry, Brad. I think I'm stressed out because of my job situation," I said. Which wasn't a lie, it just wasn't exactly the whole truth, either. "Can we talk about something else?"

"Sure. I understand." He nodded. "How 'bout another round of speed dating, then?"

Speed dating: that was what Brad liked to call his habit of asking me a succession of random questions. And although I thought this game of his was a little cheesy, this time, it was a welcome distraction.

He drummed his fingers on the table. "Okay, so: favorite sport?"

"That's easy. Cross country. I was something of a track star in high school—"

Brad interrupted, wagging his finger. "No, that doesn't count. I meant *team* sport."

"Hockey then, I guess."

He reared back. "Hockey? No shit? Are you a Brawlers fan?"

"Once upon a time," I answered. "It's not like I watch their games ever. I just grew up watching hockey to try to fit in with my older brothers."

"Oh. That's cool. What's your favorite part about hockey— lemme guess, it's the fights, right?"

"I dunno." I gave a coy shrug. "The hot guys?"

Brad rolled his eyes. "That's such a chick reason to like a sport."

I fired back. "Reminder: my first answer was cross country, but you wouldn't accept it because you said it wasn't a team sport. Which is such a *bro* thing to say, because cross country absolutely is a team sport."

We bantered back and forth and I started to let myself have a good time. Brad's speed dating was the medicine I needed to stop obsessing over *the right time* to tell him—at least for now.

After dessert, Brad paid the bill, we hopped in his truck and he drove me back to my apartment. In the cab of his truck, we kissed, and he asked if he could come up with me.

With a heart nervously skipping in my chest, I told him yes.

———

Pickles greeted us at the door, *miiiao.*

"Can I get you something to drink?" I asked Brad, my voice wavering. "Wine? Whiskey?"

"Sure. Whiskey would be great," he said as he plopped onto my couch.

"Whiskey for two, then," I said.

I'm not a big fan of liquor, but I figured I'd need the courage.

I poured the two glasses in the kitchen and took a second to breathe and find my center.

My friends have always told me that I should wait before I have 'the talk' with any guy that is even slightly promising. Their theory is that I should let him fall in love with me before I tell him the truth. But I've already experienced that, in a way. And in the end, the years we spent together didn't mean a thing to my ex-husband, Michael.

So why keep it a secret any longer than I have to? If Brad's the type of guy that's going to bolt, then I can't stop him, he's going to bolt. Better to let him know sooner, before *I'm* the one who ends up falling in love with someone who can't give me what I need.

And call me old-fashioned, but I won't sleep with someone unless I think we've got a future together. Sex just screws with my head. Especially after everything I've been through.

I returned to the living room, drinks in hand. I sat next to Brad and gave him his whiskey.

"Cheers," he said, our tumblers coming together with a *clink*.

We both took a sip.

"You look gorgeous tonight, by the way," he said, his voice lusty.

His hand went to my face. He stroked my cheek, readying me for the kiss. But when he leaned forward, I shied away.

Brad chuckled. "You kissed me in the truck, but now you won't? What's wrong, Brynn?"

"I'm just—" I stammered. "I'm sorry. I'm nervous. It's been a long time for me."

"We can take things slow. Just like we have been."

"Thank you." I rested my head against his shoulder.

Brad put his arm around me, and we sat in the comfortable silence, quietly sipping our whiskeys. On the inside, he was probably wondering what the hell he was doing with an obvious nutcase who hadn't given him anything in the two months we'd dated.

I felt so awful, but I just didn't have the strength to tell him yet. It seemed so crazy, so out of left field! But I knew if I didn't tell him, I wasn't being true to myself, and I'd only continue to act weird and flaky.

Eventually, Brad tried to kiss me again.

This time, I didn't pull away. Our lips met, and we shared a long, soft kiss.

But it was only a matter of time before Brad started to kiss me hungrier, deeper, and his hand began to travel down my side. His hand glided over my hip and he traced his fingertips up and down my thighs, always moving closer to my crotch.

"Brad," I said, gently pushing his arm away. "Wait."

He tried to hide his growing impatience behind a chuckle. "What is it now?"

I twisted a lock of hair around my finger. There really wasn't an easy way to bring it up without sounding crazy.

"I like you, Brad."

"I like you too," he said, although his tone seemed to ask, *so why can't we fuck?*

"God, there's no way easy to do this but to just come out and say it." I paused. "Brad, how do you feel about kids?"

He nearly spit his whiskey out before howling with laughter. "And here I thought I was moving too fast for *you*. Kids? Really? That's what's bothering you? Maybe we should pump the brakes a little before we start talking about kids."

I slithered out from under his arm. "Look, I know it's weird to have a talk about kids this early. And trust me, this isn't my way of telling you that I'm ready to get knocked up after a handful of dates."

"*Whew,*" he said, comically tugging at his collar.

"But I'm serious, Brad. Before we waste each other's time, I need an answer. So, do you want to have kids?"

He looked at me as if I were insane. And hey, maybe I was.

"Wow. This is seriously happening? You really need to know *right now* if I want to have kids someday?"

I nodded.

"Jesus," he huffed. "I dunno. Yeah, maybe? I guess I do. Why? Do you?"

"I *do*, but I might not get the chance."

Brad chuckled. "You're how old? Twenty-seven? Hey, I get it, the clock is starting to tick for you, but you've still got plenty of time, Brynn. Women are having babies later and later these days."

"That's not what I meant." I shook my head. "I'm infertile, Brad."

The jokey smile finally left his face. "You're wha'?"

"I'm infertile. That's why I was asking if you want kids someday. Because if you do, there's a good chance I won't be able to give them to you. Most likely, we'd have to adopt, but now I'm *really* getting ahead of myself ..."

"Shit. I'm uh, I'm so sorry, Brynn." Brad's eyes darted around the room. "You have a diagnosis?"

"Hypothalamic amenorrhea," I said.

One of the nice things about Brad being a paramedic was that, for once, I didn't have to explain my condition to a guy. He heard it, processed it, and shook his head.

"Well, HA, that's usually temporary, right?"

"That's what they say. But it's been years now, and the doctors aren't sure. They say there's a good chance it won't ever happen."

He frowned. "Damn. What's the story?"

I sighed. "It's a long story."

He nodded.

And I was saddled with the realization that I had *definitely* murdered the mood. Brad didn't want to kiss me or grope me so much after I laid that one on him—what was I thinking? Even if he truly didn't want kids, there was no way anything steamy was happening between us tonight.

I shook my head. "I'm sorry to drop that on you. Dating is kind of a strange, emotional thing for me now. I've been burned in the past because of my condition."

"Well, I uh, I don't know what to say, Brynn."

"You don't have to say anything. You can take some time and

think about it. I like you, Brad, and that's why I had to tell you before things went any further. I'd feel dishonest if I didn't tell you sooner."

"Right on."

Yeah. Right on.

The mood was dead, but Brad stuck it out with me for a little while longer, checking his wristwatch every so often. After twenty minutes on the dot, he finished his drink, stood and announced that he'd had a great night, but he needed to head back home.

I showed him to the door. I had a funny feeling in my heart that this was the last time I'd see Brad again. The crazy part was that I couldn't even be *mad* at the guy, because a true sleaze would be the type to stick around and say anything just to get laid.

That didn't make it hurt any less, though.

I climbed into bed but my mind just wouldn't let me sleep. With nothing else to do, I pulled out my laptop, and Pickles kept me company while I browsed the agency site for a new nanny job.

4

SHEA

Last night, after I fired Estel, I posted an ad on the nanny website. I had half-a-dozen responses overnight, and so I spent the rest of my morning responding to the nannies' emails. I needed someone who was available immediately—ideally, someone who could start as soon as tonight.

The site I use is sort of like Craigslist, but for nannies. If you need a nanny, you post an ad describing what you're looking for, and all the potential nannies out there can find it and respond to it. All the candidates come vetted by the agency, which runs background checks on them and everything; that way they won't hook you up with any psychos or drug dealers.

Not having a psycho in charge of raising my kids is obviously a good thing—and you know who else I try to avoid when I'm looking to hire a nanny? Brawlers fans. That's why I don't put a single word in my ad that could tip anyone off about who I actually am or what I do for a living.

And that's also why I interview the nannies someplace public before I introduce them to my kids. That way, if I happen to end up with a sports-obsessed nut who knows who I am, they won't know where we live.

If I sound paranoid about it, well, I have my reasons. Let's just say that I spent too much of my life with someone who called themselves a fan.

Anyway, only one nanny who responded was available to start tomorrow and was willing to meet me in the morning for an interview. While I rushed out the door for the team skate, we traded a few back-and-forth messages trying to figure out when and where we could meet for a quick interview.

In fact, I was still texting with her when I walked into the Brawlers' noisy dressing room—which proved to be an error in judgment on my part. My teammates started in on me immediately.

"Hey, everybody, look! Boomer got a smartphone!" someone shouted.

Boomer. That was the nickname the boys came up for me once I announced my impending retirement—as in, Baby Boomer. Never mind the fact that I'm a member of Generation X; my teammates will never let facts get in the way of a good gag.

Radar piped up, doing his best grumbly imitation of me. "Ahhh, you damn kids today. Can't walk anywhere without your nose buried in that phone, can you? Keep your head up, kid!" He shook an angry, old-man fist in the air.

I pocketed my phone, but the boys weren't done with the ribbing.

Lance, our star offensive player, butted in next. "After *all* the shit you've given us about limiting our 'screen time,' I never thought I'd see the day you'd walk in here texting, Boomer."

"Yeah, yeah. Don't get too used to it."

Lance tapped his chin. "But for you to be texting, it must be something important. Could it be? Is our captain finally ready to start dating again?"

"Yeah, right." My bachelor days were a distant memory, and everyone knew it.

But Lance rushed over in a fit of excitement and jumped on my back. You'd think that now that Lance had a wife and baby daughter at home, those two girls would keep him busy and he'd have a little less of that wild energy of his ... but nope. He's still the same Lance. A big damn kid himself.

"*Oof,*" I grunted, staggering under Lance's weight.

"Who you textin', Boomer?" Lance teased, all 205 pounds of him hanging from around my neck. "It's a girl, isn't it? Admit it! You're finally back in the game! So what's her name?"

"Would you get the hell off me?" I said, choking.

"Not until you tell me her nam—"

I gave a powerful shrug of my shoulder and bucked Lance off my back like a bronco. He hit the carpet with a *thud.*

"I forget her damn name."

"So it *is* a girl." Lance picked himself off the floor and dusted off his hands. "And you don't even remember her name? Boomer, you dog! I didn't know you had it in you!"

"I told you, it's nothing like that." I took a seat at my stall. I stripped off my suit and started changing into my gear.

"So who is she?" Lance asked. He just wouldn't let it go.

"You really want to know?" I asked Lance.

The whole room answered, *"Yes!"*

"She's a nanny, alright? I'm interviewing a new nanny for the kids."

The room deflated with a defeated groan.

"Sorry to disappoint," I said, "but I told you it was nothing."

"*Another* nanny?" Radar asked. "Didn't you just hire a new one a few months back?"

I sighed. "Yeah. Estel. I felt bad for letting her go, but she just couldn't keep up with the kids."

"Your nanny's name was *Estel*?" Quinton Brooks shouted from across the room, his interest apparently piqued. Brooksy is my cranky defense partner, and an even bigger pain in the ass to play against than me. "And you're wondering why Estel couldn't keep up with three young kids?"

Ilya, our Russian goalie and resident ball-buster, leered at me. "Maybe try to find a nanny closer to your children's age, rather than your own," he joked in his thick and broken accent.

The room burst into an uproar. It didn't matter if the goaltender's insult wasn't all that funny in itself—his accent automatically made everything that came out of his mouth sound a hundred times funnier. Besides, my age—I'm thirty-seven, by the way—was the ol' reliable joke that never failed to earn a chuckle around the room.

"Ha ha. Hilarious," I said when the laughter started to wind down. I stepped into my skates and laced them up. "For your information, Ilya, I think the nanny I'm meeting is younger, based on her resume."

"Ooh," Radar cooed. "Class of '72, then? Is she more of a Marilyn than an Estel?"

The room cracked up all over again.

"Class of '72?" another teammate asked incredulously. "Whoa there, what do you think Boomer is, a cradle-robber?"

"Actually, that's a good idea," Lance said, butting in. "Maybe Boomer will hire some hot teen nanny? Some girl he can't keep his hands off of?"

"*Teen* nanny? I'm thirty-seven, Lance. Do you have any idea how dumb the stuff is that comes out of your mouth?" I slipped the practice jersey over my shoulder pads. "You guys are so dumb. Young, dumb, and full of cum. Jesus, I don't miss being a twenty-something who can only think about getting laid."

"So what *do* you think about?" Ilya asked.

"Yeah, Boomer, tell us what we have to look forward to when we're all dinosaurs like you," someone else in the peanut gallery said.

"Winning the Cup," I answered, and my tone fell deadly serious, whether I'd meant for it or not. The effect was the same regardless: the room had fallen silent, and all eyes were on me. Play time was over.

"All I can think about is winning that Cup before I retire," I continued. "Two more months. That's all I've got left. And now that you guys are finally married and done with your man-whoring days, we've got the best shot we've had in years. Yet we keep screwing around and dropping stinkers like we did last night."

Twenty blank faces looked back at me. These were the kids I'd spent so much time mentoring, until they matured into grown men—married men, with good wives that helped keep their lives together and their home in order. *Radar and Lance especially.* In a way, it was kind of funny that I helped *them* find the thing I never could.

But whatever. I'm past the point of caring about that.

I tapped my stick on the floor. "Now let's go hit the ice and put in a hard day's work."

————

Coach kept us on the ice longer than scheduled. He hadn't liked the way we lost our game last night, either. Too many guys looked like they'd mentally checked out and were going through the motions.

So, to end the practice, he bag-skated us—a punishment where the players have to skate from goal line to goal line, over and over, until we've skated so many laps that our bodies start to quit.

When Coach decided that we'd finally atoned for our sins and told us to hit the showers, more than a few guys were bent over clutching at their side-stitch. My teammates dragged their sorry bodies off the ice.

But I skated off the ice upright and with a smile on my face.

I might be *old,* as all these young guns are always so quick to remind me, but I take my conditioning seriously.

When I made it back from the shower, I heard my cell phone's chime. I swung my locker door open, rooted through my bag, and snatched up my phone.

It was the nanny. She'd sent me a few messages during our bag skate: *"Hi! I'm here." "Where are you?" "Hello? Mr. Ellis?"*

I hoped she hadn't left. My thumbs busily tapped away at my screen, composing a message. "Running behind, but I'll be there soon. Sorry. My work thing ran a little long."

"No problem. How do you take your coffee?" She punctuated the question with a wink.

"Black. But coffee's supposed to be my treat."

I was interviewing her for the job, after all.

"Don't worry about it," she replied. *"It'll be easier to find me this way. I'll be the girl sitting by herself with two cups of coffee."*

"Okay, I'll see you soon."

I was the first Brawler dressed and ready to go. I slung my briefcase over my shoulder and waved at my team. "See you later tonight, boys."

They moaned and groaned their goodbyes as I stepped through the door. I chuckled at their banter, which faded as I made my way down the hall:

"How the hell is Boomer still standing?"

"Beats me. I feel like I'm about to die."

"We gotta ask the old man for his gym routine."

"What's the point? We all know you wouldn't stick to it, you lazy bastard!"

"Hey, screw you!"

———

I hurried through the arena, fetched my car in the parking lot, and rushed across town to the cafe in Charlestown.

My hair was still damp from my post-practice shower when I parked the car on the curb. I made my way to the cafe, doing my best to hide the shooting pain that stabbed through my ankle with every step.

I know what you're thinking. And don't get me wrong: I'm *fit*, as in my physical conditioning is great, but that doesn't mean I've got some miracle body that can withstand the aging process. I'm still thirty-seven, and my body's breaking down. My ankle has been a thorn in my side for the past few years, and lately, it has only gotten worse—not that I'd ever let anyone know it. If it wasn't bothering me so damn bad, I probably wouldn't have to retire.

Anyway, I pushed the cafe door open and looked around. At mid-morning, the place was mostly empty. A few younger people sat staring into their laptops and phones. An elderly couple stared out the window, people-watching.

And then, towards the back, I saw her. Or rather, I saw *a* girl sitting by herself with two coffee cups.

Oh, hell no, I thought to myself. *Please tell me that's not her.*

She'd been sitting upright, watching the door with an inviting smile. Through the cafe's large windows, the morning sun fell on her flawlessly radiant skin. She'd done her ash blonde hair up, into a tight bun, and it glowed like a halo around her head.

This ain't gonna work, I thought to myself as I walked up to her. I hoped this was a mix-up, that I had the wrong girl. I hoped that *this* girl was on a coffee date with her boyfriend, and he happened to run to the bathroom right before I entered, which would explain the second cup of coffee.

Because this girl? She was too young. Too pretty. Too blonde. Too *perfect.*

My kids would eat her alive. Chloe especially. This innocent, beautiful blonde girl represented everything that little *rebel without a cause* hated about the world—and she'd derive some sick joy out of torturing the nanny to her wits' end.

And if Lance and the boys saw that I hired her, I'd never hear the end of their sleeping-with-the-nanny jokes.

But she went through the trouble of meeting with me, and I owed her an interview at the very least.

With a sigh, I stepped forward to meet her.

5

BRYNN

The last sliver of the late-morning sun shimmered through the cafe's wall of windows. I'd grabbed a cozy table for two towards the rear of the cafe, against a brick wall. A golden sunbeam stretched towards my table and fell on my arms and legs, warming my skin.

And I sat in that cafe by myself, waiting and waiting.

I'd almost given up on our meeting altogether, but Mr. Ellis finally texted me right when I was ready to leave. So I gave him another hour. If he didn't show within that time period, *screw it,* I'd walk.

I sat with two paper cups of coffee in front of me. Mine, a latte. His, a black coffee.

Okay, so Mr. Ellis likes his coffee black. That's something, I thought to myself.

It was really the most I knew about my prospective employer. Because the truth was, I had no idea who I was meeting—only that his name was 'Mr. Ellis.'

It was easy to picture this Mr. Ellis as a rich, self-important jerk. Maybe a hotshot lawyer or radiologist. Some type of busi-nessman whose time was *clearly* a lot more valuable than a lowly nanny's time.

Lord knows, it wouldn't be the first time I interviewed for someone like that.

The longer Mr. Ellis kept me waiting, the more I started to doubt this whole thing. Why did this guy need to find a nanny on such short notice anyway? How many kids did he have? How old were they? Why didn't he include that information in his ad? Why did he need someone to start working *tonight,* and why did he seem so secretive?

And really, who meets at a *cafe?* It's not like we were internet strangers trying to date each other. Did we really have to meet someplace 'safe'?

I'll be honest—all the secrecy and lack of information was a little creepy. Not that I thought I was being catfished or anything, but ... well ... the thought did cross my mind. I guess you can never be too careful, right?

Sitting in the cafe, I double-checked my purse to make sure I still had that little spray can of mace.

Whew. Still there.

Just then, the cafe door opened. My eyes shot up, my warm and professional smile snapping right into place just in case it was Mr. Ellis that came walking through the door.

A towering man—I'd guess he stood six-foot-five, at least—lumbered into the cafe. His walk wasn't exactly easy. He had the strut of a man who'd put his body through hell to make a living —not *broken down,* exactly, but the worn walk of a warrior. Accomplished, yet maybe a little tired.

Which was surprising, considering how fit and muscular he *clearly* was beneath his expensive suit.

He took off his sunglasses. With a strong chin and a rugged jawline, he was a dashing man, and he looked a lot younger than his walk seemed to imply.

A hush came over the cafe's patrons, as if we were all in the presence of a movie star. Everyone stopped and stared at him. A few people even pointed at him and whispered.

Should I know who this guy is? I wondered.

I had to admit, he *did* look important. And honestly ...? Kinda hot, for an older guy.

I didn't think he was *my* super self-important Mr. Ellis, though. Or maybe I just didn't want to believe it could be him— because I'd never, ever thought that any of the fathers I worked for were hot. Frankly, I never wanted to be in that situation, either.

Tall movie star guy looked around the shop, then spotted me. And he kept staring in my direction.

No way. You can't be serious.

Then he started walking towards me.

Oh no.

I felt my practiced smile fade from my lips. With every step he took toward me, my heart pounded harder.

"Two coffee cups," he said, snapping me from my trance.

"E-excuse me?" I nearly whimpered.

"I forgot your name." He pointed at the cups in front of me. "But you're the girl I texted with, right? You're interviewing for the nanny job?"

"Right," I stammered nervously. "I'm Brynn."

"Okay, Brynn." He spoke curtly and with a gruff, growly voice that he tried to keep low. "I'm Shea."

Mr. Ellis's first name was Shea. Something about that name seemed so deeply, *strangely* familiar, but I was too woozy to place it.

Mr. Ellis stuck out his hand. I gave him mine and stared, entranced, at the sight of his hand completely swallowing mine up whole. My tiny hand was gone, lost somewhere inside that firm but gentle pocket of meat and muscle.

"Mind if I sit?" he asked, his voice as coarse as the salt-and-pepper stubble that covered his jaw.

"Of course not, Mr. Ellis."

"Just call me Shea," he said as he peeled his suit jacket off his shoulders and sat opposite me.

Now I wished I'd picked a booth to sit at—with his hulking frame, his enormous arms and mountainous shoulders, he made the 'cozy' wooden table look ridiculous. Like a circus elephant trying to balance on a tiny platform.

"Will do, Shea."

He opened his briefcase and rifled through his organizing dividers. He flipped through papers, looking for something that he couldn't find. Through his dress shirt, hard lines and mounds of muscle flexed and swelled with his movements. The sight begged for my eyes, but I refused to give in.

Stay professional, dummy.

Eventually, Shea looked up at me, stumped. "Huh. I know I printed off your resume, but I must've left it at home."

"Here. I have extra." Thankful I'd come prepared, I slid a copy across the table to him.

"Thanks."

Silently, Shea studied my resume. And I studied him. His hair was wet and dark, but I could still see the striking glints of gray running through it. Handsome lines were etched into the skin around his slate-gray eyes—which didn't make him look *old* so much as it did wise.

He was a very attractive man. When Shea finally looked up from my resume, my eyes instinctively and nervously darted away.

Obvious much?

"So you've been nannying for five years," he said, "and you've been with three families in that time."

"That's right."

"Pretty good history." He bobbed his head. "You used to be a personal trainer?"

I smiled. "Yeah."

"Interesting." For whatever reason, that bit of info seemed to make him think. "How'd you like that?"

"I liked it a lot."

"Why'd you get into nannying?"

"I guess I felt the calling," I said, forcing a cheerful smile.

There was no way in hell I'd ever drop the *real* story on someone in an interview.

He looked at my resume again, and the hint of a frown surfaced. "The kids you've nannied have all been on the younger side, I see."

"Yeah, I really love taking care of the little ones."

I figured Shea had young ones at home himself, but he gave a head shake. "Hm. Mine aren't so little."

"Tell me about them," I said—since that's how these interviews *usually* went.

"Okay. I've got three. The oldest is my fourteen-year-old daughter, Chloe. She's currently knee-deep in that whole 'rebellious teen' phase, and I can't say or do anything without somehow embarrassing her."

I frowned with sympathy. "Oh gosh, that's such a tough age."

"You're telling me. Then there's my twins, Nick and Cam. They're ten years old, and so they're a lot less trouble than Chloe ... but they're a heck of a lot more physically destructive."

"Twins! You're so lucky. Are they fraternal or identical?"

"Sure am. They're fraternal."

"And how are they so destructive?"

"Ever meet a ten-year-old boy?" Shea asked with a laugh. "Their schedule is a lot more demanding than Chloe's, too. Chloe likes to be left alone and do her own thing. But the boys are both pretty serious about their hockey careers. They play on the same travel squad. So, before school, they need to be driven to their 6 AM practice."

Hockey careers? I wondered. That was a weird way to phrase it—almost as if there was a legitimate chance that they would have a *future* in hockey—rather than just saying his sons were passionate about the sport.

"Sounds like you've got a handful," I said.

Honestly, I didn't think I was cut out for the job. It sounded like Shea needed someone who had experience with busy and possibly difficult kids, *and* could effortlessly juggle jam-packed schedules. Could I do that? Maybe, but I wasn't exactly confident. Would Chloe even listen to me? I was only thirteen years older than her, after all. In the eyes of a rebellious teen girl, what authority could I possibly have?

"And is it just you at home, or ...?" I asked, trailing off, my eyes instinctively darting to his ring finger. It was bare.

"Just me. I'm divorced."

"Oh, I'm sorry."

"Don't be. When I'm on a business trip, the kids stay at their mother's. When I'm home, they'll be with me, and that's when I need a nanny."

"I see. Do you travel a lot?"

"Quite a bit, yes—several times per month. Some trips are long, but most are only a few days long. So I'm looking for a nanny who's willing to live with us for about half the year."

"Oh, wow, I didn't know you needed a live-in nanny." He'd left *that* part out of his ad, too. I started to think that Shea just wasn't very good at this whole 'finding a nanny' thing.

"Would that be a problem?" he asked, one brow arching.

I didn't have a good reason why it would be—except for Pickles.

"Um, well, I have a cat?" I stammered, and maybe a small

part of me was hoping that Pickles *would* get me eliminated from Shea's consideration.

But Shea gave a shrug. "That'd be fine. Chloe loves cats."

"Great," I said with a gulp. I started to wonder what kind of job he had where he had to travel several times a month. "Sounds like you're always traveling. May I ask what you do for a living?"

Shea waved a hand. "Oh, it doesn't matter. I'm about to retire in a few months anyway."

Doesn't matter? Retire?

Why was this guy so cagey and weird with all his answers? And how old was he in the first place? He definitely didn't look old enough to be retiring. He must've been more successful than I realized.

But Shea butted in before I could ask any questions.

"Listen, Brynn. You seem like a nice girl." He looked at my resume again and gave a small shake of his head. "You've got a good resume, too. But I'll be honest. I'm not sure you're what I'm looking for."

Which was funny, because a moment ago, I thought I would've been fine with hearing that. But something about being told you don't have what it takes only makes you want to prove the person wrong.

"Why not?" I asked defiantly, suddenly determined to change his mind.

"You'd be perfect if you had experience with kids the same age as mine," Shea said as someone walked by our table. "But the kids have never had a nanny as young as you. Honestly, I'm worried that they wouldn't listen to you, that you'd get taken advantage of—"

Shea stopped talking, because that stranger who'd walked past our table actually came to a complete stop. He hovered over us, looking at Shea and listening in, until his intrusive presence had to be addressed.

Shea looked up at him, mildly annoyed. "Do you mind?"

The grown man looked and sounded jittery. "Hi! I'm sorry to bother you, Shea, but I'm a huge fan. Got time for a selfie?" The fan held his cell phone out, at the ready to snap a selfie of the two men together.

Wait a minute. What?

The wheels in my head started to turn.

Shea ... Ellis. Shea Ellis.

Oh my God.

Shea Ellis.

Before Shea could even give an answer to that fan, time froze for me and I was engulfed in a flood of memories: I remembered those painful preteen and early teen years, when all I wanted to do was fit in and hang out with my older brothers. They were in high school, and so funny and interesting—I just wanted to be around them! I remembered all those evenings we spent hanging out in the den, watching the hockey game, their favorite sport.

And I remembered that no matter how much I wanted to fit in with them, I knew I'd never be worthy. I remembered the sting of their teasing. *"Haha, Brynn, you don't know a thing about hockey. You can't even name three players on the Brawlers, can you? Can you?! Go ahead, try! Let's hear it if you lo~ove hockey as much as you claim you do!"*

I'd try, but sure enough, I couldn't. No, I didn't *really* care about hockey—I just wanted to be around my cool older brothers! Why didn't they understand that? Why'd they have to make me feel bad for looking up to them? Why'd they make me have to go through this whole charade of proving how much I liked hockey?

And then I remembered something else: their excitement

when a fresh-faced rookie joined the Brawlers. He was a young, hulking defenseman that my brothers lovingly referred to as "a horse." Big, fast, strong and hard working. They were sure that he'd lead the Brawlers to glory.

His name, of course, was Shea Ellis.

And since I copied my brothers, Shea became my favorite player, too. But while my brothers idolized Shea for his hockey prowess, I liked him for another reason entirely.

I thought he was cute. *So* cute. He was my first crush, actually.

Back in those innocent days, something about having a crush felt *wrong.* So my crush was my dirty little secret. Of course, my brothers figured it out in a hurry—and that became another reason to tease me, another piece of evidence that I wasn't a *real* hockey fan.

I denied it all, of course.

I denied it, even as I taped Shea's poster to my wall, painted my lips with lipstick I stole from my mom, and covered Shea's cute face with bright red smooches.

And now here, back in the real world? I was sitting right across from him. Shea Ellis. My first crush—from baby-faced rookie, to handsome hockey hunk all set to retire—and here he was, interviewing *me* to be the nanny of his kids. It was so absurd, so unreal! In moments like those, you realize how magical life can be.

Time resumed from its standstill.

The stranger jumped into action without waiting to get permission from Shea to take the selfie. "It'll only take a second, Shea, thanks a lot." The fan put his arms around the hockey player's shoulders and invaded Shea's personal space, cheek-to-cheek, his outstretched arm now holding the phone across the table and invading *my* personal space.

The grimace on Shea's face told me that he didn't appreciate the situation but accepted it as one that came with his fame. But *I* didn't have to accept it. Nor did I like it very much when the fan's knuckles brushed against the side of my head as he tried to find the perfect angle, as if I didn't exist.

I snatched the phone away from the fan before he could snap the picture.

"Hey, what the hell, lady?" the fan barked. "Gimme back my phone!"

"Excuse me," I said, shutting off the camera, "but we were having a private talk before you interrupted. And you never even got Shea's permission for a picture."

"But it'll only take a second!"

"No," Shea said firmly. "She's right. It's not a good time. No selfie."

I gave the fan his phone back.

"Wow," the fan huffed. "Never knew you were such a dick, Shea. You just lost a huge fan."

We watched as the fan scurried away, out the door and across the street.

"Unbelievable," I said. "Do fans approach you in public like that a lot?"

"Here and there. Usually, they're polite about it, but every once in a while you get a guy like that." Shea's eyes glittered at me, and he leaned forward over the table. "But you just laid down the law on that guy, Brynn. I liked that."

I gave a confident smile and moved in for the kill. "Anyway, Shea, before that guy interrupted, you were telling me that I'm not a good fit for the job."

He chuckled. "I was?"

"You sure were."

"Look. I won't lie. My kids are a handful, and I'm a little worried that you've only got experience with young children. But if you think you're up for it, I'll at least give you a shot."

"I'm up for it."

"Great. I've got a game tonight, which means you'll be on your own once the kids come home from school. Can you make it by three o'clock?"

"Sure can."

"Good, then I'll have some time to show you around before I have to leave. Don't worry about staying the night just yet. We'll start you off slow—and make sure my kids don't drive you up the wall."

I laughed. "Sounds good! I'm your girl."

He smiled. "Good to hear."

6

———

SHEA

I held the door open for Brynn as we left the cafe.

"Thank you," she said with a smile so warm it could melt an old, grizzled heart like mine.

Yeah, I wasn't sure about her when I first sat down for that interview. But she'd won me over, especially with the way she handled that overzealous fan. That took me by surprise—I didn't think she had it in her. And frankly, I figured the kids could use someone like that after Estel let them get away with bending the rules.

But Brynn? She didn't seem like a pushover.

She had spunk. And sass. And smarts.

And *beauty*. Not that looks ought to matter when choosing a nanny for my kids. But fuck me, it sure was easy to catch myself staring at her.

Most importantly, she didn't make a big deal out of me being a hockey player. She didn't even ask me about it. And she *had* to have known after that guy asked for a selfie.

"Okay, so I'll see you in a few hours," Brynn said as we parted ways.

But I didn't want to leave her just yet. I wanted to find a way to keep her by my side. Reaching into my pocket, I found my car key fob and pressed the unlock button. My Bentley Bentayga, parked right in front, beeped at us.

"Need a lift?" I asked casually.

"Ooh," she giggled, almost teasingly. "Thanks for offering, but I drove myself. But hey, nice ride, Shea."

I felt like I'd been caught, somehow. Like she'd seen right through my lame attempt at impressing her. Jesus, how old was I again? I was as hopelessly lost with women as I ever was.

I shook it off. "Just making sure. I'll see you soon."

"Bye!"

———

Back at home, I had some time to kill before the game. Instead of my usual pre-game routine—a big lunch followed by a nap— I found myself picking up the house, so Brynn wouldn't think the Ellises lived like a pack of wild animals.

And then I cleaned myself up, shaving away my scruff.

On game days, I have to be at the rink before the kids even make it home from school. So I texted the kids to let them know that they could expect to find a new nanny when they got home from school. I told them to be on their best behavior so they wouldn't scare her off.

By the time I'd finished, Brynn was at the door.

"Hi, Shea!" she said cheerily.

She'd changed from her interview attire into something a little more casual—blue jeans and a black frilly blouse. They weren't revealing items, but I could tell that the girl had a heck of a figure.

I waved her in, fighting off the urge to sneak a peek at her butt as she stepped past me.

Control yourself, you old dog. She catches you doing that, and you're done. You're no better than all those sex-crazed boys on the team.

Brynn looked around the house, eyes wide. "Wow, your place is beautiful."

After the moment with my Bentley, I figured to play it humble. "It's a mess right now, but thanks. Let me show you around."

I gave Brynn the tour and let her know some of the house rules so none of the kids could pull any fast ones on the new nanny.

"No matter what Chloe tells you, she's not allowed to go out with friends until she's finished her homework."

"Okay."

"The twins need to do their homework before they play hockey, too. Because once they set foot in that rink, they won't come out until it's bedtime. Oh, and make sure they actually stop to eat dinner, too."

"Ha. Noted."

"If Chloe has any boys over, they're not allowed to be unsupervised. No closed doors or anything like that. She was pushing the envelope on that rule with the last nanny."

Brynn tilted her head at me. "Does Chloe have a boyfriend?"

I raised my hands. "Boyfr—she better not!"

She covered her mouth and giggled. "Oh, no."

"What?"

"Nothing, nothing. I get it. It must be hard to watch your girl grow up, that's all."

"Ugh ..." I put the thought out of my mind and grabbed my bag of gear. It was almost time for me to go.

"Do the kids know I'll be here?" Brynn asked.

"I sent them a text, so they should know by the time they get home."

"Great."

"Anything else you need to know?"

"If anything comes up, I'll give you a call."

She walked with me to the door. I turned around to give her a smile, and my eyes swept over her one last time. "Okay, Brynn. Good luck tonight."

She patted my arm. "Thanks. And good luck to *you*, Captain."

I climbed into my car and smiled.

Hope the kids don't give her a hard time.

———

I must've still been smiling when I made it to the arena, because the second I walked through the dressing room door, the boys started giving me shit.

"Look who just walked through the door! It's Mr. Sunshine!"

"Can you stop making that face, Boomer? I'm not used to seeing it and now I'm scared."

"Yeah, Shea, you're awfully smiley there."

"I am not," I said, my scowl going back into place.

"Ah, now that's more like it," Radar said with a laugh. "So what's gotten into you?"

I threw my bag into my locker and took a seat at my stall. "Nothing."

"You sure?" Lance asked, leaning into me. "You sure it doesn't have anything to do with that *hot teen nanny* you were meeting up with earlier?"

The room went *ooooooh* as the boys remembered our talk from earlier, and everyone cracked up and all agreed that the hot nanny was *definitely* the reason I was in such a good mood. They bantered and speculated over how long it would be before I was banging the nanny.

"Idiots," I grumbled.

But then it occurred to me that actually, they were *sort of* right for once.

"Okay, yeah, I'm smiling because of the nanny," I admitted. "But *not* because I want to sleep with her, you horny toads. Only because I'm impressed with how she handles herself." I told them the story about the fan who barged in our interview wanting a selfie, and how she'd sent the guy packing. "So, yeah, I think it's going to work out."

"I bet it will work out," someone joked, *wink wink.*

"Har har," I answered.

"How old is she?" someone else asked.

"Um ... twenty? Maybe?"

The room went, "*Oooooh.*"

"Not that it matters," I said, "because that's *way* too young for me and I'm not interested."

"Is she hot?" someone asked.

"Seriously, what kind of question is that?" I huffed.

"A pretty simple one, Boomer," someone else answered. "So why won't you answer it?"

I rolled my eyes. "She's attractive, yes, but I don't see what that has to do with anything. She has a great resume and a real can-do attitude."

"Sounds like a good fit," Ilya began, and I braced myself for the punchline that I knew was coming. "The hot nanny has a can-do attitude ... and Boomer has a *wants-to-do* attitude!"

The room burst into laughter.

Okay, I'll admit it, I laughed too. But only because it was so absurd.

"You guys are ridiculous," I said at last. "Now can we stop with the nanny jokes and start talking about game strategy or what?"

"*Aye-aye, Captain ...*"

7

——————

BRYNN

After a second's lull, the towering hockey player lingered in the open doorway, giving me a small smile. "Okay, Brynn. Good luck tonight."

I almost wondered if he wanted a hug before he left—but jeez, wouldn't that be a little awkward for us both? I patted his arm instead.

"Thanks. And good luck to *you*, Captain."

He walked through the door and into the garage. I heard his car start with an aggressive growl, and then the mechanical *whirr* as his car backed down the driveway.

That was it. Shea Ellis was off to do his thing as a real-life superhero.

And I was officially on my own. Home alone in a freakin' *mansion* owned by the Boston Brawlers captain. I couldn't wait to tell my brothers!

The house that hockey built was palatial. I'd expected as much when he gave me the address in Brookline. But I still couldn't believe I was actually here—in the house of hockey badass, Shea Ellis. *My very first crush.* He was still totally handsome, too.

But obviously, that didn't matter to me anymore. I was only his nanny—and acting like a creeper fangirl was the fastest way to get fired from this sweet gig.

Anyway, I had a job to do, and some time to kill. So I retraced the tour Shea had just given me, walking from room to room and gathering what other clues I could about the family.

In the living room, I stopped and studied the framed pictures of Shea and his three kids.

During our interview, Shea had said that Cam and Nick weren't identical twins. Could've fooled me! The young boys didn't look a lot like Shea yet, but they sure looked like each other. I hoped it would be easier to tell the boys apart in person, because at least in the photographs, I couldn't see much differ-ence. They both beamed with bright-eyed smiles and wore their chestnut brown hair buzzed short. They were handsome, athletic, and happy-looking boys. I was sure that the girls in their grade went crazy for them. I chuckled, imagining the metric ton of heartbreak that those twins would surely cause in a handful of years ...

Then there was Chloe. She had lovely curls of strawberry blonde hair. She had her father's same mouth, nose and eyes. She was a beautiful girl, no doubt, but seeing her transforma-tion into those turbulent teen years pained my heart. Her style and appearance changed from one picture to the next. Her posture grew guarded and clumsy, like she didn't know what the heck she was supposed to do with those limbs that seemed to grow longer and lankier by the day. Her smile faded, until she stopped smiling in photographs entirely. An insecure loathing began to fill her eyes. God, puberty was the worst, wasn't it?

Don't worry, sweetheart. You'll find yourself and get through it.

I continued my tour.

As luxurious as Shea's house was, it was almost obvious that a single dad ruled here. Not that it looked like a bachelor pad or was messy or anything like that—but the décor definitely lacked a certain warmth that made a house feel like a *home*. There wasn't much decoration or artwork to liven the space up. Instead, each room seemed to be furnished with only the bare essentials, so it wouldn't feel empty. Beyond that, the poor guy didn't know what to do with his place.

Until you set foot in the basement, that is.

Calling the basement a *Man Cave* wouldn't do it justice. This was more of a *Man Deep Underground Military Base*. Hockey memorabilia from Shea's storied hockey career covered every wall, every nook and cranny: blown-up pictures of Shea and his teammates in action, framed jerseys from the various teams he'd served on, a glass display box filled with pucks from his career milestones, a huge assortment of sticks, all the various knick-knacks he'd picked up during a decade and a half of a pro career, a Ping Pong table, a Foosball table, a full entertainment system, a humongous sectional couch, a mini-bar ...

Then, down the hall, there was the indoor gym.

And one door down from that, the indoor *rink*.

No wonder Chloe's having a rough go of it, I thought to myself. *She's probably feeling suffocated by all this masculine energy.*

Just then, there was a thunderous barrage of footsteps that came barreling down the stairs. The excited banter of two young boys echoed down the stairway.

When the twins emerged at the bottom of the stairs, they saw me and immediately stopped dead in their tracks. Their eyes were big but their expressions blank.

"Hi guys!" I said. "I'm Brynn, the new nanny."

Their shy, boyish gazes dropped to the floor. "Hi," they said at the same time.

"How was school?"

"Good," they said quietly.

"Wait, your dad *did* send you a text letting you know about me, right?"

They nodded.

Whew. Small relief.

"Okay, help me out," I said. "Who's Cam and who's Nick?"

"I'm Cam," the one on the right said in a small but serious voice.

"Nick," the other one said.

"Nice to meet you boys." I shook their hands. "I'll probably have to keep asking you that question until I can tell you two apart."

"Oh, that's easy," Nick said, finally smiling and showing some personality. "Cam's got the bigger nose."

Cam gave his brother a playful shove. "Yeah, and Nick's got an ugly scar right under his eyebrow."

"Yeah, I got a big scar—'cause *you* can't keep your stick down!"

I watched as the twins started arguing with each other over who had the worse on-ice habits. It was as if I wasn't even standing there anymore, which was probably why they weren't so shy anymore. Soon, they challenged each other to a game of one-on-one and went marching past me, ready to solve their dispute in their indoor rink.

I folded my arms and called after them. "Boys?"

They turned back, remembering me.

"What?" Nick asked.

"Do you have homework?"

Their sheepish silence said it all.

"Your dad told me you have to finish *all* your homework before you play hockey."

Cam huffed. "But Estel never made us do *any* of our homework."

"Sorry, boys." I shook my head and pointed upstairs. "Your dad was very clear about what he expected from you two. You can play hockey after your homework is done."

"Aw, man ..."

The twins trudged back upstairs, and I followed them.

———

I was chopping onions and listening to music when a voice from behind scared me and nearly made me slice the tip of my finger off.

"Who the hell are you?"

I set my knife down and turned around. It was Chloe. She had her arms folded over her chest, and her eyes were narrowed at me with suspicion. Streaks of faded pink and blue ran through her shoulder-length hair.

"I'm Brynn, the new nanny. You must be Chloe."

"New nanny?" Her face soured, like my story stank. "Since when do we have a new nanny? Dad didn't say anything about that. What happened to Estel?"

"I don't know about Estel, but your dad was supposed to send you a text to let you know to expect me. Didn't you get it?"

Chloe rolled her eyes. "Oh, so *first*, I get in trouble for using my phone during class and Dad flips his shit and grounds me for a week. But *now* he sends me text messages during school hours and expects me to be reading them? *Nice* double standard, Dad."

I frowned. "Sorry, Chloe. All I know is that your dad told me that he'd send you a text. Your brothers got it."

Chloe checked her phone and read the message aloud. " 'Hi kids. Just a heads-up, tonight we're having a new nanny come by. Her name is Brynn. Please be on your best behavior for her. Love Dad.' " Chloe shrugged. "I guess you're legit after all."

"Thanks." I chuckled. "Would you like a snack?"

Chloe slunk into the bar stool at the kitchen island. "Sure, I guess."

I made her a dish of carrots, celery sticks, and hummus. "So how was school, Chloe?"

"Awful."

"Really? Why?"

"I hate it. School's such a stupid waste of time. Year after year, they teach us the same three topics, again and again and again. I thought high school would be different, but it's not! How many more times can I learn about the Civil War or the American Revolution? I *get it* already. I mean, really! And the worst part is, I know I'll *never* need to know this stuff in the real world. Or, take something like geometry. I mean, *proofs?* Really? Will I *ever* need to use proofs in the real world, or am I just bashing my head against the wall trying to understand this nonsense?"

She waited for my answer. So I thought about it. And I thought about giving her a measured answer from my perspective. Something like, *'well, realistically, you probably won't use much geometry in your day to day life—but it's still a great way to develop logical and deductive abilities, which will serve you in untold ways during the course of your life!'*

But then I remembered how, when I was a teen, it drove me nuts that adults would use their *enlightened perspective* to justify all your suffering from their comfortable distance.

"I sucked at geometry too," I said with a laugh. "I only passed by the skin of my teeth. And I wasn't a bad student otherwise. But geometry? That was the one and only subject that I ever got a D in. Anyway, to answer your question, no, you'll probably never need geometry."

She smiled from ear to ear. "Ah-*ha!* I *knew* it!"

"Well, hold on, you *might* need geometry if you go on to study engineering or architecture or something like that."

Chloe gave an apathetic shrug. "I can't see that ever happening, 'cause I suck so bad at math."

"So which subjects do you like?"

"Art." She paused. "English, I guess."

"Are you an artist?"

"Artist," she said with a scoff. Her eyes rolled, not at me, but at herself. "I like to draw, but I'm not very good."

"You'll have to show me your drawings sometime!"

Chloe's expression grew heavy. "No way. I'm way too bad to show anybody."

"Aw, I doubt that. Besides, you should see my attempts at drawing. That'd build your confidence in a hurry."

Chloe laughed a tiny laugh. She swirled a celery stick around in the hummus, then looked up at me gravely. Guilt was in her eyes.

"What's wrong?" I asked.

"Did Dad say anything about Estel?" She lowered her voice. "Did I get her fired?"

I frowned, wishing there was some way I could reassure her. "Sorry, Chloe, but I don't know anything about Estel or what happened with her."

Chloe let out a sigh and told me her story from last night: she had a boy over, Adam. Adam was one of the popular boys at school. For that reason, their paths never really crossed until this year, when they got put together in French class and started talking to each other. Just the other day, Adam asked if she wanted to hang out after school, and so she invited him over, but when Shea came home, he 'caught' them hanging out together and immediately leaped to some serious conclusions. But really, they were only listening to *Radiohead* together—Adam's favorite band—with the lights off.

"So today in French class, Adam told me that when Dad drove him home, he gave him this absolutely *crazy* speech about all the things he expects from someone who wants to date his daughter. Like, *totally* embarrassing stuff: he needs to have a job, and always dress up nice, always refer to my dad as 'Mr. Ellis,' never ever drink alcohol, always have me home on time after dates—the list kept going on and on! But we've only hung out *once* and I can guarantee you that Adam doesn't want to date me. I'm so embarrassed by the whole thing."

Chloe inhaled a long, deep breath.

"And if *that's* why Estel got fired, because I hung out with Adam, I'm going to feel really, really shitty about it."

I touched her arm. "Aw, Chloe. It sounds like a misunderstanding. I doubt your Dad would've fired Estel over one small incident like that alone. It's not your fault, okay?"

"Yeah, okay," she mumbled, staring at the floor. When she looked up at me again, her mood had changed. "Hey, Brynn."

"What's up?"

"Just so you know, I'm going to hang out with my friend Nicole in a little bit," she said with shifty eyes.

"After your homework's done, you mean?" I asked as I picked up my knife and went back to chopping onions.

Her jaw fell. "But it's all geometry proofs! Which I won't even need in real life. You even said so yourself, remember?"

I chuckled. "Yes, but before you can forget everything you've ever learned in geometry, you need to actually pass the class."

"Hmpf." Chloe shook her head, but she still wore a grin. "Even if I only pass with a D?"

I grinned, too. "Even if you only pass with a D."

Chloe quietly watched as I continued my prep cooking.

"Hey, Brynn."

"Yeah?"

"Are you going to move in with us like Estel and the other nannies did?"

I smiled. "If your dad wants to keep me around, yeah."

"Well, I hope he does."

"Then you better get crackin' on those proofs, girl."

"Okay, okay. Fine." She slid off her stool and took her backpack to her room.

8

SHEA

Sure, hockey's a violent sport. Just not quite like it used to be.
These days, fighting is frowned upon, which has had a
series of unintended consequences on the game. There used to
be a code in hockey. A respect among warriors. Back in the day,
when you threw an objectionable hit, you had someone from
the other team wanting to square off with you. You had to fight
to clear your name and restore balance to the game.

Afraid of getting your face caved in by that hulking enforcer?
Then maybe you should think twice before you slew-foot our
star player.

That might sound primitive to most people, but I don't care.
That was the type of hockey I grew up playing. And you know
what? It was a system that worked. It kept guys honest. The
game felt calmer, safer, less on-edge than it does today.

But nature abhors a vacuum. And now that fighting is
frowned upon, there's a new breed of player in the league: the
pest. He's a guy who skates around the ice, running his mouth
all night, throwing sneaky elbows to the face, butt-ends to the
ribs, cheap shots behind the play, you name it. All when the ref
isn't looking, of course. And he will *never* answer the bell,

because the fact that he doesn't fight only pisses the opposition off more, which works out just *great* for him.

I've watched the game change a lot over the years. I've had to rein in my style of game, just like the other tough guys have, and let things slide that we never would've let slide ten or, hell, even just five years ago.

Seeing Brynn snatch the phone away from that rude fan reminded me of that fact. There was a time when I was younger, meaner, and I didn't take any shit on the ice from anybody.

I'm not sure when I started to lose that edge. I suppose it didn't happen all at once. Instead it happened slowly, day by day. Age had something to do with it too, I'm sure. Seeing this game as my *career* rather than my *dream* played a big part too. Whatever the exact cause was—somewhere down the line, it happened.

Tonight, though, I wasn't going to stand for it.

And the goalie is the one guy on the team that I will *not* let you mess with.

So when our goalie, Ilya, pounced on a loose puck to freeze the play, and Kevin Kasdorf kept whacking at Ilya's hands to try to make him lose the puck—even *after* the ref blew the whistle—we had a serious problem.

Kasdorf is the Calgary Fire's resident shit-stirrer. The exact sort of gutless clown that I just described to a tee. And I'd already warned him about his extracurricular activities too many times to count tonight.

It was time to take out the garbage.

I dropped my shoulder and, with an explosive step forward, powered my momentum straight through Kasdorf's sternum. It was a hard hit, and Kasdorf would've hit the ice regardless—but the way he turned into a rag doll, arms and legs flailing as his limp body sailed through the air, was so shameful it turned my stomach. It didn't matter to him if he looked weak; all he cared about was selling the call. Not a shred of self-respect in that kid's body.

Pathetic.

Kasdorf's teammates grabbed hold of me, and we pushed and shoved, trading gloved shots to the face. Desperate to restore order, the refs blew their whistles again, loud and long and shrill.

Kasdorf acted like I'd really rung his bell. He slowly staggered to his knees—until he realized that neither ref had signaled for a penalty against me. Then, the pissy little bastard *suddenly* made a miraculous recovery. He jumped up to his skates and rushed over to the closest ref, angrily screeching about how I should've gotten a penalty for hitting him after the whistle.

I broke free from the scrum and coasted by Kasdorf. "We can settle this right now, Kasdorf."

But fighting wasn't an option for him and we both knew it. He ignored me, pleading his case to the refs instead.

"You can dish it out but you can't take it, eh Kasdorf? You'd rather run to Mommy and Daddy and let them solve all your problems?"

That finally got his attention. "Look at you, Grandpa! You're really movin' tonight! Did the doctor tweak your meds? Haven't seen you with this much pep in your step since '02!"

"Talk is cheap, Kasdorf. Drop the gloves and let's go."

He cackled. "You're not worth my time, Ellis. The game has passed you by."

My nostrils flared. "Big talk from a plug who won't fight."

"I won't fight a geriatric, no. That's elder abuse." He threw his head back and laughed. "Hey, Ellis, just curious, how's your ex-wife doing? How are the kids?"

I didn't know what the hell he knew—or *thought* he knew—about my family. But frankly, I didn't give a shit. He'd lit my damned fuse and I chugged towards the bastard like a runaway train.

Kasdorf's eyes grew wide and a look of pure *'oh shit'* spread across his smarmy face. He ducked, putting the referee's body between us as a shield. I threw my gloves to the ice, reaching over the ref with my bare hands, and grabbed hold of Kasdorf's jersey. The ref tried to push me away, but I was too furious to be stopped. I shoved the ref out of the way and wrestled Kasdorf away from his protection.

Pulling Kasdorf by the jersey, we glided into open ice where we could trade punches without refs or teammates getting in the way. Kasdorf grappled my arms, trying to prevent me from getting a hand free to fight with.

"Hey hey hey!" Kasdorf barked. "I don't wanna fight!"

I yanked and tugged, trying to work my arms free so we could finally square off and have a fair fight.

"Drop 'em, Kasdorf—"

Pop.

My head shot back, recoiling from a sudden blunt force.

In one fast motion, Kasdorf had thrown his gloves off and socked me right on the eye. It stunned me. It shouldn't have—I should've known that the punk would never square off and agree to a fair fight.

A stream of warmth ran down my face. I was cut, and the metallic taste of blood trickled onto my lips.

Kasdorf wasn't going to wait for me to regain my wits before he started swinging again, either.

"Yeah yeah yeah!" he whooped as his fist slammed into my jaw. Another fist deflected off the side of my helmet. Another caught me square on the chin.

Shit.

This was going badly.

I had to stop the onslaught.

I charged forward and bear-hugged Kasdorf to tie up his arms. There, the same battle played out again: two men trying to free their arms. Only this time, I was a lot more pissed.

Thinking the fight had run its course, the refs rushed in and tried to split us up.

"Yep! We're done here!" Kasdorf encouraged them, hoping he could squeak out a win on a dirty fight.

"No!" I roared at the refs. "Back off!"

Out of respect to a veteran player, the refs backed away.

"Hey!" Kasdorf yelled, imploring the refs to come back. "Where the hell are you idiots going? Fight's over! Get this fucking guy off me already!"

"You wanna fight dirty, Kasdorf? 'Cause I can do that, too."

"No no no!"

I grabbed hold of Kasdorf's collar and yanked his jersey over his head. With his face covered, he never saw the series of haymakers coming. With each punch that impacted Kasdorf's obscured face, the Boston crowd roared louder.

When I felt Kasdorf's knees go weak, I knew he was done. I let go, dumped the pest to the ice, and skated to the penalty box to a raucous ovation.

———

After a hard-fought win, every guy in that room will be smiling from to ear. Euphoria bursts from our hearts and souls. There's this sense that *all is right in the world,* that the forces of good have finally conquered over evil.

It's one hell of an addictive drug.

Once we're back in that room and the sweat-soaked gear starts to come off, the oral history of the game begins—the story of every goal, every picture-perfect pass, every key shot block and cutting insult on the ice is retold and relived to a howling chorus of laughter.

Tonight, though, all the boys wanted to talk about was my fight.

"That was some sweet old-time hockey out there, Boomer!"

"Kasdorf finally got a dose of his own medicine."

"I didn't hear a fuckin' peep out of Kasdorf's beak the rest of the game, by the way. The little shit was on his best behavior after that!"

"How'd it feel, Shea?"

It'd taken twenty-two stitches to close the gash above my eye, and my puffy, busted-open knuckles were currently throbbing against a bag of ice. But all that said?

"Pretty damn good," I said with a grin. "Might not feel so good tomorrow."

"You fed that rat-fucker his lunch," Lance said. "Actually, you were throwing your weight around all game long. Every time I saw someone land a big hit, I looked up and saw ol' Boomer standing over some poor dude he just clobbered. What got into you tonight, anyway?"

I shrugged. "Don't know. Something about that team just rubs me the wrong way. I hate 'em. It's Kasdorf, mostly."

Everyone grunted in agreement.

"Oh yeah."

"Guy's a fuckin' coward."

"Fuck him."

"Um, hello," Ilya said as he peeled off his sweat-soaked goalie equipment. "Boomer hires a hot nanny and suddenly plays like he's twenty years old again. And people believe this is only a coincidence?"

"Aaaaaah!" everyone sang, as the topic of the day reemerged once more.

"Not this again," I said, but I couldn't hide my smile. Because there was *some* truth to that after all, wasn't there? Yeah, I had some small hopes that Brynn would work out as our nanny. And so maybe I happened to play a little more inspired tonight. So what?

"See! He's smiling! He knows it's true!" Ilya said, pointing a finger.

"So how hot is she, anyway?" Brooksy asked.

I peeled off the last of my sweaty clothes and wrapped a towel around my bare mid-section. "You guys seriously won't give it up, will you?"

"Nope. Not until you tell us," Ilya said.

"Is she a seven? An eight? Jesus, is she a *nine*?" Brooksy asked.

"Sorry. I'm not going to rate my nanny." I made for the showers, leaving the bozos behind. "Can't believe I even have to say those words."

"Just make a move on her, Shea!" someone called after me.

"Yeah, she'll go for you!" someone else yelled.

I rolled my eyes.

If only things were so simple.

9

BRYNN

It was just before 11:00 PM when I heard the throaty growl of Shea's car pull into the garage.

The hockey player stepped through the door, looking a lot worse for wear than when he'd left. A swirl of blue and purple bruises marked the places where his face had been mashed. An inch or two of black sutures held the skin above his eye together. Dried blood lingered in his eyebrow.

Looking at him made my stomach flutter—and I must've not been doing a very good job of hiding the effects his visage had on my insides.

"That bad, eh?" he asked, his smile fading.

"Sorry," I said, cringing. "It physically pains me to look at you."

"Ah. Words every man wants to hear," he chuckled. "So how'd it go tonight, Brynn? You don't look anything like me, so that's a good sign."

I laughed. "The kids were great. Everyone finished their homework first thing. Chloe hung out with her friend Nicole, and she made it home by curfew. The boys spent the night practicing."

"Huh. So where are they now?"

"Oh, everyone's showered and in their bedrooms."

Shea checked his watch. "In bed before 11:00. Not bad, Brynn."

I gestured at his eye. "Does it hurt?"

He took a seat at the kitchen table. "Nah."

"It was awfully tense in here during that fight of yours," I said. "Nick and Cam went nuts once you managed to pull the jersey over that guy's face and started to really sock him."

Shea looked startled. "Wait, the boys watched the game?"

"Of course! Don't they always?"

"No." Shea lowered his voice. "Their favorite team is Chicago."

That came as a surprise. "What's their tie to Chicago?"

"Beats me. One day, they woke up and decided that their favorite players are Toews and Kane. I guess they wanted to root for players that aren't their dad."

I laid my hand on his shoulder. "Aw. That must be tough."

He gave a small laugh. "I figure it's part of them having to grow up and become their own men. Right? That's what I tell myself, anyway."

I smiled at him, although I felt more like frowning. I didn't know what to say. "Are you hungry? I made you a plate. I'll heat it up."

"Starved. But you didn't have to do that."

"I think it's important for a family to eat together," I said as I punched numbers into the microwave keypad. "And if someone can't be there during dinner, they should have a plate waiting for them when they get home. Food keeps a family together, you know?"

"I guess so. I miss a lot of meals since I'm always on the road."

"It breaks my heart that so many families don't eat together these days—or worse, when they're eating in total silence because they're all staring into their phones."

"Don't even get me started on the phones," Shea said, shaking his head. "But wait. Are you telling me that you actually got my kids to sit at the same table and eat dinner together?"

I grinned. "Maybe they're just showing off for the new nanny."

"I'll be damned. Hey, while that food's heating up, I'm going to say goodnight to the kids." He paused with a wicked grin. "Or the impostors pretending to be my kids, that is."

———

Shea's plate was waiting for him when he returned, wisps of steam rising from his dinner—which was seared chicken with a creamy lemon sauce; golden potatoes mashed to a fluff; and bright green, garlicky string beans.

"Wow, Brynn. This looks like a feast."

"I hope you like it."

He smiled at me. "The kids sure had glowing reviews."

"I'm glad to hear that," I said. One of the things I enjoyed most was cooking a meal that people loved—nothing made me happier feeling like I'd nourished their heart and soul.

"Oh my *God*," Shea gushed after taking the first bite of chicken. "This is delicious, Brynn." Eagerly, he sampled the potatoes next, and then the green beans. His eyes rolled back in his head and he went *mmmmm*. "You know, I'm really glad the twins loved your meal."

"Why's that?"

"I've had a hard time getting them to understand how much they need to eat."

"W-why?" I asked. Shea was wandering dangerously close to

a sensitive topic to me—the only question was if he somehow knew about it.

"Because they're growing boys," Shea said. "Growing boys who are very physically active and want to play pro hockey like their old man."

Oh, I thought with a breath of relief. *That makes sense.*

"Are they that good? To go pro?" I asked.

"Sure. But honestly, it's not how good you are, it's how bad you want it. And these days, everyone starts their kids earlier and earlier with strength and conditioning programs, and specialized diets, and so on."

"Oh, wow. That's a lot for a ten-year-old."

"I agree. Don't get the wrong idea—I'm not pushing them into it. I think hockey's supposed to be fun for the kids. But I want them to understand that if they're serious about going pro, they're right at the age they need to start weight training, getting those movements down, and eating big." He shrugged. "At the *very* least, they need to eat more so they can gain mass. They're a little undersized for their Atom league."

"That's a little surprising, considering their father's genetics."

Shea laughed and almost choked on his bite. "Yeah, right?"

"Careful, don't choke. Half of Boston would want me dead if I killed their hockey captain."

Shea had a devilish spark in his eye. "Ah hell, they'd get over it. I'm retiring at the end of the year, anyway."

"Shea! Don't talk like that."

"Did you play any sports growing up?"

I hesitated. "Cross country. If you think that counts as a sport, anyway."

"I absolutely do."

I smiled at him. "Good."

"Speaking of good?" Shea took another big bite of chicken

and swallowed it down. "This is amazing. Can I fire you as my nanny, and then rehire you as my personal chef?"

I laughed. "No, you can't do that."

He flashed an indignant smile. "Why not?"

"Because that's not the job I interviewed for."

"You'd rather raise my kids?"

"Yes."

Shea shrugged. "Works for me, as long as you still cook."

"I will. But don't go building me up in your mind thinking that I'm some gourmet chef or you're going to end up disappointed."

"I doubt that," he said. I could've sworn I saw his eyes flash up and down my body for the briefest of seconds.

I watched the hockey player inhale his meal. Sure, I loved feeding people—but something about feeding an athlete, someone who made a living off of his physical prowess, made it doubly satisfying. I couldn't stop smiling as I watched him excitedly finish his meal.

Then his plate was empty, and Shea ran off to the fridge and got seconds.

"Aren't you going to heat that up?" I asked as he hurried back to his seat with a plate of cold food.

"I can't wait that long. This is too good," he said. "You know, Brynn, I almost feel sorry for the guy who ends up marrying you."

"Excuse me?"

"If you feed your husband like this every day of his life, the poor guy is going to blow up like a blimp, and then you're going to leave him for someone younger and hotter."

"Hey, *I* didn't make you get seconds." I laughed and slapped at his shoulder. It was hard and round with muscle. "You scared me, by the way. I thought you were going to say something *way* worse."

"Like what?"

"I don't know! Something mean."

"I know I probably looked it during that fight, but I swear, I'm not a mean guy." The wise wrinkles around Shea's eyes curled up with a smile. "Just do me a favor, Brynn. When you do decide to get married? Make sure you marry a guy you can trust."

"That's a little easier said than done, isn't it?"

"Yeah, but trust me, you want to make sure. Hell, hire a PI to follow the guy around before you tie the knot. That's what I recommend."

"A *PI!*" I howled. "Little over the top, don't you think?"

"Better to be safe than sorry. Trust me, divorce is a total pain in the ass. A constant cloud of stress that hangs over you for a year, if not longer, until it's finally over."

I stifled a cynical laugh. "Build me a time machine, then, and I'll take your advice and marry someone else this time around."

"Huh?" The baffled look told me that Shea had missed my point.

"I'm divorced too, Shea."

He nearly choked on his food a second time. "You? *You're* divorced? Seriously?"

"Sure am."

He waved his hand at me. "Bull. I don't believe it. You're not old enough to be married, let alone divorced."

"Whatever." I rolled my eyes. "I was nineteen when my first serious boyfriend, Michael, proposed to me. I said 'yes.' Then I said 'yes' to a divorce when I was twenty-two."

"So that was what, a week ago?" Shea asked with a playful twinkle in his eye.

"Oh, *ha ha*. I guess I'll take that as a compliment. But no, that was five years ago."

Shea's jaw dropped. "Wait. You're twenty-seven!?"

"Hey, you can do math! Whoever said athletes were dumb jocks?" I patted Shea's shoulder again, but this time I let my fingers linger on his taut muscle for just a second longer. The chiseled ridges were such an alluring sensation beneath my fingers—part of me wanted to run my fingertips through the crevices and valleys of his muscle. But I didn't, of course.

"I never would've guessed you were that old," Shea said.

I squinted at the salt-and-pepper hockey player who was my childhood crush once upon a time. "Are you calling me old now?"

"Trust me—no. All I'm saying is, you look great for your age. Besides, you're young, *I'm* old."

"You're only ten years older than me, aren't you? Thirty-seven isn't that old at all."

"Yeah, but remember how I make my living. Those are ten *hard* years of hockey, of plane rides and hotel beds, of fights and hits and injuries ..." Shea shook his head. "Never mind all that. I still can't believe you're divorced."

"Why's that so hard to believe?"

"Because you're—" Whatever Shea was about to say, he thought better of it and caught his tongue. "Well—because! It just is. That's all."

"Wow, Shea," I teased, "you're a real wordsmith."

"That's why I make the big bucks playing hockey, and not writing poetry," he teased right back.

But after a pause, the athlete decided he had more to say.

"Anyway," he began quietly, "what I meant was, look, you're smart. You're beautiful. I don't even know you all that well, but I can tell you're fun to be around. You seem like the type of girl that a guy would crawl through hell and back to keep."

Is Shea Ellis flirting with me? I wondered, my pulse racing in my neck. *But he can't be flirting with me. I don't deserve his attention.*

"Yeah, well," I muttered, "I'd think a wife would crawl

through hell and back to keep her hockey-playing husband, too."

"That's what you'd think. Especially because, when I met her, she said she was my biggest fan."

"That's, er, funny," I croaked. *Uh oh. Definitely can't let this guy find out about my teen crush, or he'll never forgive me.*

Shea lowered his voice. "I don't like to talk bad of the kids' mom. But let's just say that was the first of many lies that she told me."

I frowned. "Sorry to hear it. Marriage sucks."

"Yeah," Shea agreed. "Love sucks even worse."

I frowned. It made me sad that he thought that way. But I guess I couldn't blame him. His wife had obviously hurt him.

"Enough heavy shit," Shea said. "Can I ask you a question?"

"Sure."

"Why'd you quit personal training?"

It was like Shea sucked the air right out of my lungs. Was I really that transparent? Could Shea see right through me, and knew to ask all the questions that cut to the core of my being? I panicked, not knowing what to say or do.

But before I could figure out how to answer, Shea spoke again.

"I mean, nanny, personal trainer—they seem like two dramatically different life pursuits, you know?"

I managed to catch my breath. *Relax, Brynn! He doesn't know anything about you.*

"Oh, well, you'd be surprised," I said. "In one job, you have to hold hands with babies, teach them how to walk, and make them do things that they simply don't want to do, period. And the other job, of course, is nannying."

Shea burst out into a fit of laughter so loud I worried he might wake the kids. "Brynn, that was savage! I love it!"

I smiled. "Glad you liked it."

"Hey, Brynn."

"Yeah?"

"I know I hired you to be a nanny, and not a chef or a personal trainer. But if you ever manage to get the twins into the gym and show them a thing or two, I'd really appreciate it. Of course, if you feel like you're twisting their arms to get them to pump iron, then don't worry about it. And only if you have the time to do it."

"But wait, Shea." I paused for dramatic effect. "I still haven't told you if I want this job or not."

The hockey player looked like I'd just broken his heart.

"Wha'?" he muttered.

I felt terrible immediately. I put my hand on his. "Aw, it was only a joke! I was feeling feisty, I'm sorry. I'd love to be your nanny, if you still want me. And if the boys are up for it, I'd be happy to show them some things in the gym, too."

He smiled at me and shook his head in disbelief. "I'm starting to think that you might be a little sarcastic, aren't you?"

"Maybe a touch."

"Uh-huh. I'll have to remember that."

Shea's plate was empty. I looked at my watch. "Oh, yikes. It's getting late. I should go."

10

SHEA

Until Brynn, I never realized how empty this house has felt since the divorce. Really, since a few years before the divorce—but whatever. The point is, I'd forgotten what it was like to come home from a game and have someone to talk to.

Sure, I could talk to my kids, and I could talk to the other nannies. But that's not really the same thing. What I mean is, it's been a while since I've had someone to *truly* talk to. Someone to laugh with. Someone to tell jokes with. Someone who could make *me* laugh. Someone I can't help but look at—

Jesus, I thought, *are the boys right? Do I seriously have a little thing for the nanny?*

Maybe. Maybe not. It was hard to tell. I hadn't felt anything for a woman in a long time—not since my heart was broken. Truth be told, I didn't think I *was* capable of feeling anything for a woman anymore. I thought once you had your heart broken badly enough the first time around, you'd never let yourself be vulnerable like that again.

What the hell are you talking about? I thought to myself. *You don't know anything about her. All you know is that she seems like a real good fit for the kids.*

Still, I couldn't deny it—when Brynn checked her watch and frowned, I knew it was time for her to go, but I wished she could stay.

"Oh, yikes. It's getting late. I should go," she said.

"If it's too late, you're more than welcome to stay in the guest room."

"Thanks, but I can't. I need to feed Pickles."

"Right. The cat." I bobbed my head. "Let me walk you to your car."

"Walk me to my car?" She laughed, eyeing me strangely. "I'm parked right there in the driveway."

"I know, but it's your first night and it's dark outside. And I want you to feel safe."

Okay, yeah, there wasn't much of a threat in our gated Brookline community. But I couldn't help but offer it anyway. Maybe part of me wanted to wring every last second out of our time together, too.

"Knock yourself out, then," she said with a laugh.

She gathered up her things. I walked her outside—slowly, side by side, letting my forearm sometimes brush against hers. Even a small touch like that felt so nice. God, it'd been so long.

It was unseasonably warm for a late winter night in Boston. Spring was on the way, and a damp, earthy aroma filled the air as the warming soil woke from its winter freeze. Every breath filled the lungs and replenished the heart and soul.

Brynn's shoes clicked on the pavement, a tiny but purposeful rhythm, until we reached her car. I watched as she unlocked it. She opened the door, but turned to me before she climbed in.

"Well, thanks again, Shea. I had a great night with the kids. And I had fun talking with you, too."

"So I'll see you back here again tomorrow?"

Looking up at me, she nodded. "Tomorrow."

"Good," I said. "Good."

Our eyes locked. Time slowed to a crawl. A charge in the air made the tiny hairs on my neck and arm stand straight up.

The moment was calling for something.

And I didn't know what to do.

But was the moment calling for something, *really?* Or was this just the perfect storm of coincidences?

A cute, young nanny. Great with kids. Perfect in every way for *my* kids.

The first woman I've enjoyed talking to in ages.

And of course, a bunch of teammates trying to convince me that I had a thing for her.

(Just thinking of them made their words of wisdom echoed through my head: *"Just make a move on her, Shea!" "Yeah, she'll go for you!"*)

She looked up at me, her eyes sparkling in the dark, still waiting to see what I'd do.

I looked at her rose red lips.

I wanted to taste them.

I wanted her mouth against mine.

I wanted her silky hair running through my fingers.

I wanted my rough, battered knuckles to glide across her soft, supple cheeks.

I wanted her slender body against mine.

So I inched closer to her.

But as I reached out for her—something stopped me.

The hell are you doing? Don't fuck this up! The kids need her more than you do!

I stopped myself at the last moment. Instead of cupping her face, I grabbed the car door instead.

An eternal pause ensued before I could manage to speak.

"Well, drive safe, Brynn."

"Um." She looked anxious, surprised. Her eyes darted and

flitted from side to side. Hurriedly, she lowered herself into her car. "Yeah. Thanks. Goodnight."

"Goodnight." I shut the door for her.

I waited and watched until she backed out of the driveway and sped off.

I made my way back inside, telling myself that I did the right thing.

But all I could think, deep down?

Well, you really blew that one, Shea.

11

BRYNN

Two Months Later

Chloe and I were sitting on the plush carpet of her bedroom while her favorite *Vampire Weekend* album playing over her stereo. Pickles was with us, too—he sat in Chloe's lap, loudly purring, while Chloe filled me in with the latest high school drama.

"But Sadie is super obsessed with Adam, and she thinks that just because she announced that she had a crush on him first, that no one else is allowed to flirt with him . . ."

Whenever Shea was in Boston and had custody, Pickles and I had to pack up our bags and head over to the Ellis house in Brookline. I wasn't sure how the eight-year-old cat would respond to all that moving and shuffling around—but the truth was, he loved all the attention that came with being a live-in-nanny's cat. He had four more laps to sit on, and an enormous house to explore with plenty of nooks and crannies for a feline to hide and sleep in.

". . . which, okay, fine. I won't flirt with Adam, because I don't even

know how to flirt in the first place! I don't know what to say, and I get really super awkward! . . ."

Chloe took a break from her story to appreciate Pickles's purr. "He's got such a loud motor! Don't you, Mr. Pickles? Yes you do!"

Pickles's chartreuse eyes rolled back in his head as he relished the scratching. He was so pleased with himself. Sometimes, I wondered if Pickles thought coming over to the Ellis household and acting cute was *his* job, too? He was really good at it.

Chloe continued her rant. *"But sometimes Adam talks to me, and then Sadie gets ultra mad at me. She won't even talk to me for days, because she says I'm flirting with him but I'm really not! . . ."*

I couldn't help but crack a smile when Chloe shared that very familiar teen drama with me. Did every teen girl go through that same experience, with that same exact type of friend? The jealous one who thought that merely telling her friends that she had a crush on a boy meant no one else was allowed to speak to him, lest they ruin their friendship and risk her eternal wrath?

All of Chloe's problems with friends and boys could be boiled down to one essential truth: teenagers have *terrible* communication skills, and highly volatile emotions.

Which was why it made me so happy that Chloe opened up to me, and so quickly, too. If nothing else, telling me about her problems was the first step in working through them. Now, I like to think that I can get her to stop and think about what is *really* bugging her, and how to define the problem in precise words.

I can't help but think how much I would've benefited from having someone to talk to when I was Chloe's age. Instead, I kept my problems buried deep inside—because to talk about my problems and fears would've made them *real*, I would've had to confront them.

Then again, a small part of me always wonders: what makes me so sure that I'm not doing the same thing now?

————

I guess I need to explain myself a little more.

Two months as the Ellis family nanny have flown by faster than I ever could've imagined. I've loved every second of it. 'Dream job' doesn't even begin to describe what I do. It has felt like it's more than a job. It feels like I've found a place where I truly *belong*. This family has been such a good fit for me, in fact, that when payday comes around, I feel almost guilty taking Shea's money. Like the financial transaction cheapens the authenticity of the bond I've forged with that family. And when Shea's out of town and the kids are with their mother, I've found myself feeling restless at my apartment, not knowing or remembering what it is I even like to *do* in my own free time.

My friends have noticed this shift. They think I've met someone I'm not telling them about. Technically, they're right—Shea made me sign a non-disclosure agreement when he hired me. All my friends know is that I'm a live-in nanny for someone important. The inside joke is that I'm sleeping with him. *Ha ha.*

Even though Shea made me sign a NDA, he was cool with me telling my family who I work for. And my brothers *cannot* believe it. Thing is, no matter how much they beg, I can't *ever* let them meet Shea—because they'd totally spill the beans on the whole 'childhood crush' thing.

Here's what has happened in two short months:

Chloe hasn't just opened up to me—she has started opening up to the world in general. You can see the change in her demeanor, the way she carries herself, the way she stopped hiding so much with hairstyles and clothes.

She still has an extremely short fuse with her dad—and I've

been working on helping them both out with that problem—but for a teen girl, that's not exactly some new or unheard-of phenomenon. It's a phase, and with a little patience, they'll both get through it in time.

Nick and Cam are still two rambunctious little squirrels. But only when they're together, I've learned. Split those boys apart, and they become so shy around me, they can barely manage to sputter a few words.

Here's something I've realized about them: they share a friendly, every-hour-of-every-day competitiveness. They're *always* challenging each other to some feat and trying to prove who is stronger or better. As off-putting as it can be sometimes —racing to see who can finish their dinner first, for example—it was easy to use that dynamic to get them into the weight room. All I had to do was show one of the twins how to bench press an unweighted bar, and *bam,* the other one had to do it, too.

That said, no, the twins have not exactly morphed into hulking bodybuilders just yet. Shea's right that they don't have much interest in the gym. Sure, I can talk them into doing a few lifts here and there—but they're still only ten years old. It's hard to get boys that young excited to have a regular lifting regimen. All I can do is offer to train them from time to time, and if they go for it, hey, great. But no arm twisting, like Shea said.

The twins *are* eating a lot more, though, and that fact has pleased Shea to no end. They've gained a little weight. Every pound helps, or so Shea has told me.

And then there was Shea. Who could forget Shea? The Boston Brawlers are just about ready to finish their season—and then they launch right into the playoff grind. The Brawlers have been winning, winning, and winning. The whole city has their hopes up that *this* is the year.

Shea has acknowledged again and again in his media interviews that he's playing the best hockey he's played in years.

Privately, he says he owes it all to *me*, because, for once, his household is actually running smoothly, and he can just focus on leading his team on the ice.

After having put up with so many weird remarks—like, 'nannying isn't a *real* job'—it feels really amazing to have Shea always telling me how much I do for him. And not *only* that, but telling me that my work is so important that it could affect the way a professional hockey team plays.

I mean, I'm not sure I really believe that myself, but it sure is flattering.

When Shea comes home from a game, I still sit with him at the table and we talk about our days. And it's always nice. When he's on the road, and I'm back at my apartment with Pickles, Shea still calls me just to ask about my day before he fills me in on the details of his. Sometimes, we'll lose track of time and just stay up late talking. He's not only been a great boss, but a great friend, too.

Friend. Keyword. Because beneath all that normalcy, there's a lingering awkwardness between us that just won't go away. And deep down, I know it's all my fault.

Because things have always been slightly tense ever since the night I made that mortifying mistake. When I even *begin* to think of that one mistake, dread immediately floods into my heart and I *have* to force myself to think of something else before the panic and horror consume my soul.

I'm talking, of course, about the very first night I worked for Shea—when I almost kissed him.

Gah!

Ack!

Just thinking about it makes me break into a cold sweat.

But could anyone really blame me? When Shea offered to walk me to my car that first night, I thought something was, well, just a little *strange.* Seriously, I was parked in the driveway. Did I *really* need his gentlemanly escort? Of course not.

So my heart started beating a little faster.

I got my hopes and dreams up, thinking the athlete was planning to make a move.

Yes, I convinced myself that *this* was how it all went down. This was how I got my fairy tale ending. The nanny who *somehow* ended up interviewing with her childhood crush, a famous hockey player, who was now struggling to juggle the demands of a pro career and single fatherhood. How perfect, right?

Uggg.

I fell for it. I fell for my own storybook narrative.

And so, when Shea walked me the twenty feet out to my car, I was sure it was for some *other* reason than the fact he was just a nice, stand-up kind of guy.

And while Shea was *actually* moving to politely close my door for me—*I* thought he was reaching out to kiss me.

So I shut my eyes and waited.

I even stood on my tip-toes to reach his lips.

But he wasn't trying to make a move on me, and the kiss never came. And when I opened my eyes again, Shea was holding the door, a look of regret on his face.

Oh.

Oh no.

I was so embarrassed. I came *so* close to calling Shea the next day and telling him that I wasn't a good fit for his family.

But something about those kids of his kept me from chickening out.

Thankfully, Shea has never brought that moment up. I guess it was just easier that we both pretend like it never happened.

———

Pickles craned his neck as Chloe scratched his favorite spot, right on the chin. Her rant about the Sadie and Adam love-triangle moved into teen self-deprecation.

"I'm so awkward ... my face is so weird looking ... I have all my *dad's* genes, ugh ... big nose, big eyes, big everything."

I laughed. "You're not weird looking at all, Chloe. You're very, very pretty. And this might not be what you want to hear, but your dad is a very handsome man, too."

Chloe squealed loudly. "I can't believe you just said my dad is *handsome!*"

"Chloe!" I whispered. "Quiet or he'll hear you!"

"So what if he hears us?"

"He could get the wrong idea. I wasn't being salacious about your father—I was trying to make a point. *He's* handsome, and you've inherited those good looks yourself."

Chloe rolled her eyes. "If I were a *boy,* handsome would be great. But there's a reason nobody ever calls a girl handsome, Brynn, and you know it."

"You're beautiful, Chloe. You just don't know it yet."

"Yeah, right." She sighed. "*You're* beautiful, Brynn. I wish I looked like you. I doubt you ever had to worry about being ugly when you were my age."

I laughed out loud. "Oh, God. You couldn't be more wrong."

"Pfft. I doubt it."

"You want me to prove it, then?" I asked, reaching for my cell phone.

"Sure."

"A few years back, my mom got on Facebook and uploaded all these old family photos." I loaded up Facebook and went to my mom's profile. "I immediately had to untag myself from all of them before anybody saw the evidence."

"Ha!" Chloe hovered nearby, eagerly awaiting the pictures.

I found the old album and started flipping through the

pictures of me in my awkward teen years. *Ugh,* just looking at those pictures transported my mind and body back in time. My brain released a chemical shower of those awful teenage hormones, and existential angst flooded my bloodstream.

"I thought I could handle this," I said, cringing as one awkward picture after another flew by the screen, "but maybe I'm not as tough as I thought."

"Oh my God!" Chloe giggled. "Your hair ...! What happened?"

"Told you," I muttered.

"Whoa. That shirt. *Whoa.*"

"Yup," I agreed.

I saw the next picture—wearing an athletic bra, flexing my biceps—and quickly tried to flick past it before Brynn could see.

"Whoa whoa whoa!" Brynn yelled. "Was that you? You have to go back!"

Sheepishly, I pulled the picture up again. I was nothing but skin, bones, and muscle striation. It hurt to look at that picture, in so many ways, but I hoped it might help Chloe to see it.

Chloe's jaw fell. "Holy *six-pack,* Brynn! You were ripped! And *so* skinny! What the hell?"

"Yep," I said.

"I knew you were a personal trainer, but I never knew you looked like *that.*" Chloe looked at me, then the cell phone version of me, trying to reconcile the two in her mind.

"I spent a lot of time jogging, and a lot of time in the gym," I muttered.

"Jeez. No kidding." She raised her brow at me. "You don't look anything like that at all anymore. It's like you're not even the same person."

Hearing that, the fifteen-year-old in me wanted to curl up into a ball and die. But the twenty-seven-year-old me knew that that was a *good* thing indeed.

"It's how I dealt with being unhappy with my body, Chloe."

"Getting super fit and shredded, you mean?"

I didn't want her to follow in my footsteps. "I *looked* fit, and I thought I was in great shape, too. But the truth was, I was the furthest thing from healthy. I wasn't eating enough and it caused me health problems."

"Whoa. Like what?"

"My hair and fingernails started falling out, for one. Then I started to have chest pain and heart palpitations."

"Oh my God." Her face crumpled with horror. "Scary. I can't even imagine."

"Yup. So don't be like me—learn to love yourself for who you are." I smiled at Chloe and reached for my phone. "This has been very educational for you, I hope."

"Wait, just a couple more!"

Chloe swiped her finger across my screen, looking at one picture and then the next—before a specific photo grabbed her attention. She stared at it, her head tilting with interest.

In the photograph, I was around her age, and I smiled for the camera in my bedroom. It wasn't a particularly embarrassing photo. I wasn't sure what she was looking for or what had caught her attention.

There was half-a-knock on the bedroom door before Shea pushed it open and stepped into his daughter's bedroom.

Chloe scrambled to shut my phone off and tossed it back to me.

12

SHEA

Chloe folded her arms and gave me a dirty scowl. "*Dad!* Once again, you didn't knock!"

I raised my arms. "What? Yes, I did. I told you, I always knock."

"Yeah—one whole *millisecond* before you burst right in here anyway! What if I wasn't dressed or something?"

"It's hard to 'burst' in when your door isn't even closed all the way, Chloe."

"It was closed *enough.*"

Living with a teenager was sort of like living with a tyrant. You weren't sure when or how they ever came into power, but now they had rules, and worse yet, their rules seemed to change on any given day. You had to pick your battles—and this one wasn't worth fighting.

"Alright, alright. Next time, after I knock, I'll try to give you more time to answer."

"*Thank you,*" Chloe said sarcastically.

The two of them were sitting on the carpet, with their backs against Chloe's bed. I loved that Chloe had opened up to Brynn so much—you could really look at her and see how much confidence Chloe had gained in two short months. Although I'll admit that sometimes, I wished my daughter would tell *me* whatever it was that she was always sharing with Brynn.

I stepped between the two girls and gestured for Chloe to scoot aside. "Make room for Dad."

"Da~ad!" Chloe grumbled as she begrudgingly scooted aside. Pickles leaped out of her lap and zipped right out of the room. "Oh, look, you scared Pickles off."

I lowered myself onto the floor. It was a snug, comfy fit between the two girls—which couldn't have repulsed Chloe more. Her body, no, her entire *existence* seemed to turn and lean away from me with disgust.

But Brynn didn't move an inch when our thighs touched.

I was breaking my own rules, and it never felt better.

See, that first night Brynn worked for us two months ago, I realized I needed to put a barrier in place. If I wanted to keep Brynn as a nanny, the last thing I could do was think that way about her, let alone actually touch her or try to kiss her. And seeing what a miracle worker she's been with my kids tells me that I was absolutely right.

I was sure whatever infatuation I had with Brynn would fade with time. But it hasn't. And now it's too late. My kids need her more than ever. All you have to do is watch them interact with her, and it's obvious.

Which is why it's so troubling to me that, over the past two months, I've found all sorts of reasons to get close to Brynn. Without being unprofessional, of course—or at least, that's what I tell myself. I just can't help it. I'll take a seat on the couch and find myself sitting a half-dozen inches or so closer to Brynn than I'd ever sit next to anyone else. When we're talking to each other, I'll find myself touching her—a graze on her arm, a brief rub on her shoulder, a tap on her knee.

God, what a thrill those small moments of physical touch

are. My heart starts beating fast and I wish I could touch her more—I know, I know. I'm a sad, lonely old man. You don't have to tell me.

A touch here, a touch there. That's *it*. I can't go any further than that. I know if I ever touched her, she'd leave us.

"So what are you two being so secretive about in here?" I asked the girls with a grin. "Are you talking about *boys*?"

"What are you even talking about, Dad?" Chloe countered.

"When I '*burst*' in here, you juggled your phone"—I pulled out my own phone and bobbled it from hand to hand like a hot potato—"before you stashed it back with Brynn."

"That's not *my* phone, it's Brynn's," Chloe said curtly. "And I was only giving it back to her."

Brynn laughed softly and explained. "I was showing Chloe some pictures from my teenage days."

My face lit up. "You were? Hey, I want to see."

But Brynn emphatically shook her head no. "Sorry, Shea, but I don't think so. Showing Chloe was embarrassing enough."

"You two never tell me anything," I griped, but with a grin.

The three of us sat, shoulder-to-shoulder, listening to Chloe's music.

"Well, this is nice, isn't it, girls? What's this music?"

Chloe rolled her eyes. "It's *Vampire Weekend*."

"Neat. What's that mean?"

"It's the name of the band."

"Yeah, but what *is* a vampire weekend?"

"I don't know! It's just the name they gave themselves!" Chloe huffed. "Is there a *reason* why you came in here, Dad?"

"Well, yeah. I wanted to say *bye* to my lovely daughter before I went to play my game." I kissed her on the top of her head.

"Uh-huh." Chloe stared at me skeptically. She could see right through me. She knew there was more.

I cleared my throat. "And, uh, I wanted to remind you that the players' gala is tonight, and I know you keep saying no—but this is your last chance to be my date!"

Her face scrunched up. "I told you when you first asked me —there's no way I'm going to that lame thing again. Besides, Mom is picking us up soon and we're spending the weekend with her."

"I can drop you off at your mom's house after the gala. It's a *tradition* for us, Chloe! And I thought it'd be a good way for us to spend some time togeth—"

"*Dad*! How many times do I have to tell you? I don't want to go to that thing! I'm too old for it! And it's so freaking weird that you want to bring your *daughter* to a formal ball that everyone else brings their wives to!"

A silence came over us. Even the music stopped playing as the album reached its end. I could see it in Chloe's face: she resented the fact that she had to use lethal force on me, but I hadn't left her a choice.

With a defeated sigh, I climbed to my feet. "Okay. I hear you. Loud and clear."

I made my way for the door.

"Dad ... wait ..." Chloe sounded apologetic.

I kept walking. "It's okay, sweetheart. No hard feelings."

"No—Dad—*wait*!"

I started to close the door behind me. "Really, Chloe, it's okay. I don't want you to feel like you have to go."

"Dad," Chloe blurted out, "you should take Brynn."

I froze in the doorway. I *would've* laughed at Chloe's idea, had Brynn shot the idea down immediately.

But she didn't.

"Take *Brynn?*" I repeated, my eyes searching Brynn's for some hint or clue how to feel about that idea.

Brynn's gaze never broke from mine. She looked just as startled as I did—and she was searching my face for an answer.

"Yeah!" Chloe nudged Brynn with her elbow. "You're free tonight, aren't you, Brynn? Since us kids are going to my mom's."

Brynn stammered for words. "Well—ah—yeah, I'd be free ... but—I couldn't butt in."

Chloe piped right up. "You wouldn't be butting in at all. The food is amazing, there's an open bar—not that they ever let me anywhere near it—and you get to meet all the Brawlers players and their wives. And everyone's dressed up all fancy and *blah blah blah*. Look, I won't lie; the gala *is* fun, but I want a break from going. You'd probably have a really good time, though."

Brynn looked at me for an answer. A hint of a blush had reddened her cheeks.

"*Would* you be my date, Brynn?" I asked quietly.

An infectious smile spread across her face before she answered in a hush. "Well ... sure. I'd love to go with you."

Chloe clapped excitedly. "Great! It's a date. And now I don't have to feel so bad about not going. It all works out in the end."

I tried to keep from smiling too big. "Okay. I've gotta get down to the rink. Have a good time at your mom's, Chloe. And Brynn, I'll pick you up after the game, so be ready to go."

"Bye, Dad!" Chloe sang.

"Bye, Shea," Brynn said quietly. "Good luck out there tonight."

"Thanks."

"Good evening, gentleman." I strutted into the locker room with a smile on my face. "Ready to kick some ass tonight, I hope."

The team greeted me with grunts and bellows:

"You bet, Captain!"

"Hey, Boomer!"

We'd been kicking a lot of ass lately, after all—and it was our last game before the playoffs began.

I took my place at my dressing stall and started to undress.

Lance sat next to me. "Hey there, big guy. So Chloe will be joining us at the gala tonight, right? Feels like it's been ages since I've seen her. Paige would love to meet her."

I frowned. "Unfortunately, no Chloe tonight."

"What? Chloe's a healthy scratch?" Lance gasped, his mouth hanging open. "But she's practically a Brawlers tradition at this point."

"Believe me, bud, I know it. I was as stunned as you are. Apparently, she's too cool for her old man's work parties. And now she thinks I'm weird and creepy for bringing her as my date all those years in the first place."

The boys broke into a belly laugh. *"Bwahahaha."*

"She's kinda right, you know," Quinton Brooks said.

"Oh, piss off, Brooksy."

Lance stepped in to defend me. "It's not weird. Chloe's just at that age where *everything* is weird and embarrassing. I remember when my sister went through that phase—and man, she was annoying as hell. I'm surprised this didn't come up last year, honestly." Lance clapped a sympathetic hand on my shoulder. "Well, shoot, I'm sorry, old man. That must've felt like a kick in the balls, eh?"

"Sure was."

"So you're going stag, then?" he asked.

"Er." I grunted and cleared my throat. "Well. Not exactly."

Everyone in that room, regardless of whether they were already engaged in another conversation or not, suddenly focused in on me and waited for my answer.

"Oh for God's sake," I muttered.

"*Not exactly?*" Lance repeated, a knowing smile creeping onto his lips. "Then who are you taking, Boomer?"

"I'm taking Brynn."

"Wait, that's your nanny, right?" Ilya asked.

"Yes."

While I waited for the laughter to die down, I tore off my shirt, balled it up, and threw it into my locker. I turned around to face the room with a finger held up in warning.

"Just so we're clear. She's *just* my nanny. If *any* of you guys give her a hard time, or make *any* nanny jokes, or say *anything* inappropriate to her—you're gonna have to answer to me later, and I'm telling you, I'm not gonna be happy."

Lance squeezed my shoulders. "Hey, relax there, Boomer. We'll be on our best behavior."

"That's reassuring."

"Besides." Lance leered at me. "I'm happy for you."

"Happy about *what?*"

"A little romance before the playoffs might be just what the doctor ordered. You know?"

"A distraction like that is the *last* thing I want before the play-offs begin," I said with a groan. "And by the way, that's the exact kind of sentiment I do not want you saying, or even *thinking,* at the gala. Brynn's only coming with me so I don't have to go alone. There's nothing romantic between us. We're just friends."

"A second ago, Brynn was just your nanny," Ilya remarked. "And now you're just friends? Boy, things are moving very fast!"

"*Bwahahaha.*"

Ilya's wisecracks continued. "But this is good news, boys. I think Boomer finally found his retirement project."

"Okay, and what's that?" I asked, walking right into his joke.

"Knock nanny up and have lots of babies, obviously," the Russian answered.

"Bwahahaha."

"I'm done having babies." I scoffed and pulled my shoulder pads on. "And we're done with this conversation, too. Let's talk hockey, boys, *hockey.*"

With that, the boys surrendered. *"Okay, okay ..."*

13

BRYNN

My heart was still fluttering when Shea shut the bedroom door and left me with Chloe.

A teenager just set me up on a date with my childhood crush.

What the hell?

What am I going to wear?

I stared into space and turned that thought over and over in my head, trying to make sense of it, until the gentle roar of Shea's Bentley left the driveway.

"You're welcome, by the way," Chloe said at last.

Slowly, my head swiveled to look at her. She was simply beaming. She looked so pleased with herself, you'd think she'd learned it from Pickles.

"Excuse me?" I asked.

"For setting you two up. Duh. That was *so* cute how you both got all tongue-tied and nervous, by the way. And here I thought *I* was bad at flirting—but watching my dad try to flirt with you was almost painful." She paused, horrified by a sudden revelation. "Oh *no*. I guess I got *that* from his genetics, too."

"Chloe ..." I began cautiously. "I hope you're not saying what I think you're saying."

"And what do you think I am saying, Brynn?" Chloe asked with a mischievous note.

I stared at her, not sure what to say. I tried another tack. "Look, I'm sure it'll be a fun dinner. But there wasn't, and there *won't* be, any flirting between me and your dad. We're going as friends. If you think there's anything more than that, you're mistaken." I paused to drive the point home. "I just don't want you to get your hopes up, okay?"

"Why, I appreciate your concern, Brynn," Chloe said, perfectly mimicking my detached and stately tone. "But P.S., you're a terrible liar."

"Excuse me?"

"You think I don't know?"

"Know what?" I asked, swallowing heavily.

"About you and my dad. I've never seen two people who need to bone more in my entire life."

"*Chloe!*" I said, aghast. "You shouldn't talk like that."

"Why not? It's true, isn't it? You two totally have a thing for each other. I've been suspecting it for a while, but now I have *proof.*"

I laughed nervously—dare I say, guiltily. "Proof? Because we're going to a meaningless party together? I'm sorry, Chloe, but that's simply not true."

"Uh-huh. Sure." The teenager tapped her chin while she swiped through a digital collection of music, hunting for a new album to play. "And I suppose you'd also say it's not true that, when you're hanging out with me, Dad always finds a reason to come in here and sit with us, too. And I suppose it's not true that he's always acting all handsy and touchy with you. Or that you two are always tip-toeing around together, giggling way too hard at each other's corny jokes. Did you think I wouldn't notice how my dad can't keep his eyes off you? He's never been like that with any of our other nannies, by the way. He barely even talked to the other nannies beyond making plans and stuff. But with *you*? Whenever Dad's home, if I need to find him for whatever reason, all I have to do is track you down—and voila, there he is, too."

Secretly, my insides were bursting with happiness to hear Chloe's suspicions. But on the outside, I had to pretend I didn't know what she was talking about, nor let it show any effect on me. So I bit my inner cheek to keep the ravenous smile from spreading.

"Oh, Chloe—"

"And *you,* when Dad touches you or sits right next to you, you don't even move away. You get this weird, *trying-so-hard-not-to-smile* look on your face. Yeah—like the one you're making right now!"

I didn't know what to say. A *teenage girl* had me figured out. I couldn't believe it.

"Heck, just a few minutes earlier, you said my dad was a *very handsome man.* Don't even try to deny it, Brynn, you think he's hot."

I huffed. "I said he's a *handsome man,* yes, but I didn't say he was hot."

"You didn't *say* it, no, but you think it." Chloe shrugged. "Don't get me wrong. I'm not mad that you like my dad, Brynn. Not at all."

"Chloe, I swear—it's just not like that."

"Would you stop lying to me?" The teenager rolled her eyes. "I tell you all about my life. And I tell you about the boys I like. I thought we could trust each other."

I laughed. "I'm not lying to you, Chloe."

"Okay then. You leave me no choice." She stuck out her hand and gestured for my phone. "Lemme see your phone."

"What? No. Why do you want my phone? What are you going to do, text your dad pretending to be me?"

"No! That'd be super weird and creepy and I would never do that, Brynn." She gestured for the phone again. "Give it."

"First, tell me why you want my phone."

"I *told* you, I have proof. And now I'm going to show it to you. So just lemme see it."

Cautiously, I pulled out my phone. I wouldn't hand it over. "You can do whatever you're going to do while I'm holding it," I said, "because I'm not letting go."

She rolled her eyes. "Fine, suit yourself."

I clutched my cell phone while Chloe tapped at the screen. She opened the Facebook app. The picture she'd been studying right before Shea entered the room was still on the screen.

"See?" she asked.

I looked at it. "See what? It's just an old picture of me in my bedroom."

But then Chloe pinched and zoomed in on the screen. Right over my shoulder.

And there it was. The detail that had captured Chloe's attention. Behind me, on my bedroom wall, was the poster of a young Shea Ellis, with flowing locks of hair beneath his helmet. The poster was covered in bright red lipstick smooches.

Oh my God.

A blazing heat flared in my cheeks.

"Chloe," I said, my throat as hot and dry as the desert.

"*Told* you I had proof," she said, grinning. "I almost didn't recognize him at first. But then I saw his name written in giant letters. He's so young-looking! How old was he in that picture?"

"I don't know," I answered huskily. "Twenty-three, I think."

"Which would make you how old in that picture?"

"Thirteen."

"And you had a crush on him, didn't you? Go on, the least you can do is admit it!"

She was right. The cat was out of the bag. There was no use pretending anymore—I'd only damage my own credibility.

"Yes," I answered quietly. "But it was just a childish, meaningless crush, Chloe. I didn't even recognize your dad when we first met. Promise me you won't tell him, okay? Or your brothers or your mom or *anyone* else."

"Of course I promise not to tell," she said, then she began squealing and dancing. "I love this, I love this, I love this. You have no idea how happy this makes me. What are you going to wear tonight? All the players wear suits and their wives get dressed up real nice, so you should definitely wear something fancy."

My heart pumped and hot, liquid shame churned through my body. This poor girl was getting her hopes up for something that could never be.

I shook my head. "No, Chloe, stop."

"Stop what?"

"That picture was a long time ago—your dad and I, we've *both* grown up a lot since that picture. Yes, I thought your dad was cute when I was young. And yes, he's still a handsome man. But I'm the nanny of his children now—" I trailed off. I didn't even know what to say anymore.

"Yeah, you're our nanny now, and you two can't stop flirting with each other! And now I find out you've always had a thing for him. It's almost like you two are *meant* to be together. Which is perfect, because we *all* like you so much—"

I clutched at my temples. "You don't understand what I'm trying to tell you."

"No, Brynn, *you* don't understand. I'm *so* happy right now that *I'm* the one who set you guys up on a date." She paused. "It almost makes up for what I did to Dad in the first place."

"Huh? What do you mean? What'd you do?"

A sullenness suddenly gripped Chloe. It was like she'd just

transformed into someone else, someone bleak and disturbed and unhappy.

"I just want to make up for it," Chloe said with a small nod. "That's all."

"Make up for *what?*"

There was the sound of a heavy car, fast and aggressive, pulling into the driveway, followed by a rapid burst of honks. I recognized that driver by now—it was Cynthia, Shea's ex-wife, and she was here to pick up the kids.

"Mom's here," Chloe said. "I have to go."

I helped Chloe and the twins pack up all their things and sent them off with their mom. From the living room window, I watched the car drive off and wondered what had gotten into Chloe.

What was that about?

And what have I gotten myself into?

14

SHEA

We ended the season on a good note, grabbing the 'W' in an overtime thriller. We left the ice in good spirits, and after our showers, we left the dressing room in our suits and ties.

"See you boys at the gala," I said.

I drove home and left the Bentley idling in the driveway. It was time to pick up my date. I stepped into a quiet house—the kids were at their mom's for the weekend.

Come to think of it, it was the first time Brynn and I were truly 'home alone' together.

"Brynn?" I called. "You ready?"

She answered not with words, but with the sound of her heels *clicking* and *clacking* on the hardwood hallway. I turned on my heels and, with a smile, waited to watch her entrance.

The second I laid my eyes on her, I felt my guts twist and turn.

Brynn strutted towards me, wearing a ruby red décolleté dress made of a fabric that flounced and swayed with her body, playfully exaggerating her elegant walk.

"Brynn," I whispered under my breath.

I'd never seen her in anything but her 'work' clothes—I'd certainly never seen her look like *this*. Her small but lovely breasts bounced with her step. The feminine swell of her stomach showed through the slinky fabric of her dress, begging for my eyes. A knot thickened in my throat as my eyes wandered down her long, toned legs.

She's stunning. More than I even realized.

She stopped in front of me. I couldn't help but stare into her glittering eyes. "Brynn. Wow. You look gorgeous."

"Oh, stop," she demurred, with a Sphinx's smile on her lips that was both lovely *and* haunting at the same time.

"Ready?" I asked her.

She nodded. I offered her my arm and walked her out to the Bentley, the engine quietly purring as it waited for us in the driveway. I went to the passenger side and opened the door for her.

"Oh Shea," she laughed softly as she climbed in. "You didn't have to do that."

"No, but I want to," I said as I gently shut the door.

I walked around the back of the car with a huge smile on my face. I was thinking about the time I'd tried to give Brynn a ride home in this car after our interview, and how she'd turned me down. Never in a million years did I think we'd be doing something like *this* together.

I climbed in on the driver side and stole a glimpse of Brynn's profile. She looked like a princess in that dress, with her hair up and a sparkling sapphire pendant hanging from her gold necklace.

I was sure I'd never seen a more beautiful girl in my life. But I had to shake my head and remind myself of something.

She's only going as your friend. Don't forget that fact, or you'll make this night weird.

"Thanks again for agreeing to go to this thing," I said as I put the car in gear and drove off. "I know it's probably not the way you want to spend your Friday night."

She smiled politely. "Oh, stop. I'm sure it'll be fun."

"Just a word of warning, though. My teammates are immature idiots. I say that lovingly. Just don't take anything they say seriously."

She chuckled quietly. "Noted."

The ride was quiet. The atmosphere was not *tense*, but not quite comfortable, either. We came to a red light and the silence was deafening.

I looked at her. "Hey, is everything okay?"

She gave me a pained smile. "Uh-huh. Everything's fine."

My eyes focused on the road ahead.

What isn't she telling me …?

———

I handed the keys over to the valet, and Brynn and I walked up the red carpet and into the convention center. Members of the media stood outside the convention center, snapping pictures of us as we walked up the carpet.

"I thought this was a private event for your team?" Brynn whispered to me as the bright white camera flashes exploded around us.

"It *is* private," I answered. "But the whole organization is invited to these. Everyone who works for the Brawlers' parent company, not just the athletes. Members of the media show up, too."

"I see."

We stepped into the cozy, cocoon-like atmosphere of the convention center. A hundred different lively conversations were softened by the static sound of rushing water, thanks to an enormous bowl fountain in the middle of the venue. Columns and arches supported a second-level mezzanine, where one could get a better view of the domed and ornately-detailed ceiling. The polished marble floors sparkled, reflecting the warm lights.

Wide-eyed, Brynn took in all the sights and sounds. "Oh wow. It's so beautiful here."

"It's supposed to resemble a fifteenth-century Italian courtyard," I said.

She giggled. "How specific. I had no idea you were a cultured man."

"Don't get your hopes up; I'm no historian. I've just read the inscription on the plaque every year I've come to this thing." I saw some familiar faces milling around by the fountain. "Hey, you ready to meet the jerks I have to spend all my time with?"

"Sure."

Brynn took my arm and I escorted her to the fountain.

"Guys, I want you to meet Brynn," I said. "That's Lance and his wife, Paige."

Brynn shook their hands.

"That's Radar and his wife, Ella. Ella is Lance's younger sister."

Brynn shook their hands, too.

"That's Ilya and his girlfriend, tennis star Natalya Anasenko."

"How do you do," Natalya said in her husky Russian accent.

"An athlete couple! How neat!" Brynn repeated as she shook Natalya and Ilya's hands.

"In Russia, Natalya bigger star than me!" Ilya exclaimed. "Believe it or not!"

Our teammates laughed and slapped at Ilya's back. *"You're a nobody in Russia, comrade!"*

The intros continued. "That's Stoner, that's Brooksy, and somewhere around here are their ladies . . ."

Well, you get the idea. Brynn had approximately twenty-five hockey player names to remember, and then the names of their significant others—and that was just the hockey-side of things. But if she felt overwhelmed or out of place here, she didn't show it. She moved gracefully and elegantly, not just physically, but socially, too.

Thankfully, none of my teammates said anything weird right off the bat. But I didn't like the way the guys had a habit of looking at Brynn and then looking at me. It felt so obvious—like they were trying to see if there really *was* something between us.

"So Brynn," Lance began at last. "I hear you're quite the miracle worker with kids. Boomer's been talking about you a lot."

Brynn looked at me. "Boomer ...?"

"Yeah, that's my newest nickname," I muttered.

"I figured that, but why Boomer?"

Radar, with his arm draped around Ella's shoulder, laughed. "Someone called him Boomer because he's retiring at the end of the year and it stuck."

Brynn's head tilted at me with confusion. "But Shea's not a Boomer. He's Generation X. Right, Shea?"

"Yeah, that's right. That's what *I* keep telling them, but they won't listen," I said.

The boys laughed.

"Yeah, she sounds like Boomer's girl, alright," Brooksy said.

I glared at Brooksy, shooting daggers at him with my eyes. *Don't even.*

Everyone else had glasses in hand—bottles of beer, glasses of wine, flutes of champagne, tumblers of liquor. I hated the idea of leaving her alone with *these* guys for any length of time ... but it'd be rude not to offer Brynn something to drink.

"Can I get you a drink, Brynn?" I asked reluctantly. "Beer, wine, champagne? Something harder?"

"A glass of red wine would be wonderful."

"You got it." I turned to the boys and threatened them with a face that said it all: *whatever you're thinking about doing, don't.*

15

BRYNN

Shea looked *so* dashing and distinguished in a suit. Walking into that convention center on his arm, I should've felt like I was a fairy tale princess on top of the world—but instead, a sickening feeling lingered in my stomach.

I thought I could manage to hide that fact from Shea—that something was bothering me—but I could tell on the drive over that he knew something was wrong.

It was *obvious.*

I felt awful about it. I had to let him know what Chloe had said—but I figured I'd wait until the event was over and done with. I wanted him to be able to enjoy himself. I didn't want to ruin his night.

Once there, Shea led me to the fountain and introduced me to his teammates. They were goofy, and I couldn't help but feel like I was being *watched* by them. Not in a bad way. More like— they were sizing me up. As if they were trying to gauge what my intentions were with Shea.

Or am I just projecting ...?

When Shea went off to get me a glass of wine, Ella and Paige pulled me into a small circle while their husbands joked around with their teammates.

"So what do you think?" Paige asked, her arms encircling the whole of the place. She had just a touch of a southern accent. "Wild, isn't it?"

"This place is *incredible,*" I said.

"Isn't it?" Ella asked, eyeing a massive Roman column. "I am geeking out *so* hard over this place. Talk about going all in on an idea, eh?"

I remembered what Shea had told me about Ella. "Ella, you're the interior decorator, right?"

"Sure am," Ella said.

Shea had also told me that Ella was Lance's little sister. They hadn't always gotten along—but now that Ella was married to Radar, who was Lance's best friend, things between the siblings were a lot easier.

I looked around the breath-taking venue, and at all the strapping athletes and their gorgeous wives. Everyone was dressed so fancy and looked so important.

"I have to admit, I feel like I don't belong here," I said with a nervous chuckle. "Everyone looks so fancy and amazing."

"Oh, stop it, Brynn! You look beautiful and you absolutely belong here," Ella said.

"Ella's right, you're gorgeous," Paige said as she laid a sympathetic hand on my arm. "But *pst.* I know exactly what you mean. I feel the same way. Probably more than you do, in fact."

I remembered what Shea had told me about Lance's whirlwind romance with Paige. Two years ago, Paige and Lance had a one-night stand, but she ended up pregnant and giving birth to a baby girl. But Paige *never even knew* who Lance really was. Luckily, they ended up finding each other earlier this season and were now married and raising their baby daughter, Irie, together at last.

"Yeah, it still feels like a dream," Paige reflected as she glanced at her husband, who was regaling his buddies with a story that had them roaring with laughter. She gave me a big, genuine smile. "What can you say? Life has a funny way of working out sometimes!"

"So what's it like, nannying for Shea?" Ella asked.

"Oh, it's been a dream job. I'll be honest, I've never nannied for kids as old as Shea's, but they're all so much fun. I've *also* never done the whole live-in-nanny thing before, but really, it's surprisingly nice. When Shea's on the road and his kids are with their mom, I stay at my apartment. You'd *think* I'd be relieved to go back to my own life, but honestly? Being back in my empty apartment? Those are the times when I feel lonely, like something's missing."

"Aw!" Paige mewled. "That's so sweet."

"Yeah, sounds like you've really meshed right in with the family," Ella agreed. "Speaking of Shea's kids, why'd Chloe bail tonight?"

I smiled. "You know how teen girls are."

"Oh yeah," Paige channeled her inner teen and rolled her eyes. "I *never* would've gone with my dad to something like this."

"Yup. No chance I'd go to this with *my* dad," Ella agreed. She swirled the wine in her glass before she took a gulp. "Although I am a little sad that Shea and Chloe's six-year reign is coming to an end."

I raised an eyebrow. "What reign?"

"Shea didn't tell you? At the end of the night, everyone votes on a couple and crowns them the *Brawler King and Queen.* It's pretty cringe-worthy, but I think that's half the appeal. If you know anything about hockey players, lemme tell ya, these guys seriously get off on giving each other a hard time. I'm pretty sure that's why the gala exists in the first place, in fact. But the money they raise *is* for charity, so at least there's a good cause behind the joke. Anyway, Shea's won the award every single year since his divorce, when he started bringing Chloe instead of his wife."

I winced. "Shea didn't tell me that, no." *And neither did Chloe.*

"Although I have a funny feeling that, with *you* at his side, Shea's going to take the title home again!"

I held up my hands. "Whoa, whoa. We're not a couple. I'm just his nanny, and I only came because Chloe canceled."

"I know, I know." Ella finished off the rest of her wine and wiggled her eyebrows at me. "But with how good you are with his kids? And how much Shea talks about you? Let's just say that plenty of people here are pulling for you two."

Oh, that's just great, I thought to myself. *First Chloe, now the entire Boston Brawlers hockey team are expecting something to happen?*

Paige discreetly bumped her hip against Ella's and quietly reprimanded her. "*Ella!*"

"Sorry," Ella giggled. "That's the wine speaking. It really hit me all of a sudden! Empty stomach, that's why! I'm probably saying more than I should, mm?"

"Just a touch," Paige agreed with a polite smile.

But Ella's wine had more to say.

"You know, Shea's teammates like to joke around and give him a hard time—they joke about his age, call him Boomer, and all that. But the truth is, you won't find a *single* player in that room that they respect more than Shea. He's been with Boston since day one of his career, and he's helped all those boys through so much—on the ice, off the ice, you name it. He helped Radar get his head straight when we met. He shaped Lance into the player he is today. But when it comes to Shea's own life?" Ella let out a contemplative sigh. "His teammates, they all want him to find someone and be happy. Especially now that he's about to retire. Wouldn't it be nice for Shea to retire, and find new love, and maybe start a new fam—"

"Okay, Ella, that's *definitely* enough!" Paige laughed uncomfortably. On the sly, Paige gestured for Lance to come over to help out.

Ella shook her head. "Gosh, after what Shea's ex-wife did to him ...? I mean, are you *kidding* me? He's such a sweet guy! Who could *do* that?"

Lance rushed over, grabbed his sister by the shoulders, and tried to haul her away. "Oh, sis! Wasted on one glass of wine again, are we? You're such a lightweight, Honey Badger. Some things never change, eh?"

Ella whimpered. "Yeah, but only because I didn't eat anything!"

"Come on then, let's get you something to nosh on," Lance said as he swept his sister away.

I turned to Paige. "Did he just call her *Honey Badger*?"

"Yeah. Long story. It's a brother-sister thing."

"But what was Ella talking about just then—about Shea's ex-wife? All Shea has told me about her was that she was his 'biggest fan' and that she lied to him. What exactly did she do ...?"

Paige shook her head somberly. "Sounds like you know more than me. If you really wanted to know, you'd have to ask Shea."

16

———

SHEA

I hurried back from the bar as fast as I could without spilling Brynn's glass of wine.

That took forever!

In my head, I could already hear all the idiotic things my teammates were saying to Brynn. All the bawdy jokes, the questions about whether we were 'banging' or not, the crude pickup lines from the single guys.

God only knows what terrible shit those guys could say to an innocent girl like Brynn.

I found her standing with Paige, and sure enough, she looked shell-shocked. I passed her the glass of wine.

"Here you go. Sorry it took so long. You should've seen the line to the bar."

"T-thank you," she said, her eyes nervously darting from side to side to avoid mine. She immediately took a long sip of the Merlot.

"Okay, tell me who said it," I grumbled.

"What?" Brynn stammered.

"One of my teammates said something stupid to you, didn't they?"

"No—actually—I was talking with Ella."

"*Ella?*" I asked with a gasp. Sweet and honest Ella said something rude to Brynn? I never would've expected that in a million years. "What did Ella say?"

"She, uh." Brynn's gaze dropped to her feet. "She just told me about the *Brawler King and Queen* award. I—I had no idea that you and Chloe had such a great streak going. It's so sad that it's coming to an end."

I laughed. "That? Oh, trust me, it's not a big deal. Honestly, I'm glad someone *else* is going to win it this year. There's so many great couples here. Lance and Paige. Radar and Ella. Ilya and Natalya. Someone else deserves to wear the crown and do the dance for once."

"There's a crown?" Brynn asked, and she took another heavy gulp of her wine. "*And* a dance?"

"Yeah, and I know what you're thinking: that this whole thing sounds really corny in this high-school-prom kind of way, right?"

She bobbed her head. "Yeah … sure does …"

"But it's for a good cause, because the Brawlers owner, Jim James, makes a ten thousand dollar donation to the winner's charity of choice. Last year, Chloe wanted to pick the charity, and she—"

I stopped talking when I saw Brynn tilt her glass back and let the rest of her wine rain down her throat.

"Oh. Wow. I guess you need another," I said, my eyes instinctively going in the direction of the mile-long bar line.

"I'll wait in line this time," Brynn said as she and Paige rushed off together.

I watched Brynn and Paige scurry off, wondering, *what the hell was that about?*

Ilya, Brooksy, and Stoner materialized at my side. They clapped me on the shoulders and shook me around.

"Boo~oomer," Brooksy said with a whistle. "You said she was attractive but you never told us that she's a *beaut*. Wow. So when are you going to make your move? Tonight, right?"

"Would you guys cut it out with that?" I groaned. "I'm not making any moves. It's not like that."

No matter how much I wished it could be.

"Yeah, sure. You should see the way you look at each other," Ilya said. The goalie clasped his hands together, batted his eyelids, and gave me these obnoxious doe-eyes. "*Oh, Shea!*"

I gave him a shove.

Frankly, I didn't even know what all the fuss with these guys and Brynn was about. The truth was, I barely even saw her through the night. It seemed like wherever I was, she was somewhere else. I was happy that she was making friends with the Brawlers wives and girlfriends, but I started to feel a little left out. A little abandoned by my date.

And when I *did* find her, we never talked for long. It was like she couldn't even look me in the eye. Then one of her girlfriends would grab her and they'd race off somewhere else, always with a wine glass in hand.

I started to feel like she was avoiding me or something.

And okay, whatever, she wasn't *really* my date. So it's not like she was obligated to spend the night with me. In fact, technically speaking, I couldn't even be mad if she hit it off with one of the single guys. Hell, they could even take her home, and I'd be way out of line if I made a scene over it.

Although the thought does make me irrationally angry ...

When the time came for dinner, we took our seats. While Brynn and I sat at a table together, there wasn't much talking between any of us at the table—because this was the part of the night when the Brawlers owner and various bigwigs passed around a microphone to give their big end of the season and playoff pep rally speech.

And then our GM, Mr. Tremblay, took another turn with the mic. "The votes have been counted, and I have written here, on this very piece of paper, the names of this year's *Brawler King and Queen.*"

The crowd cheered and jeered. I caught eyes with the couple *I* voted for—Lance and Paige—to let them know that I thought they had this thing in the bag. I mean, it's not every day that a couple has a story like theirs and still ends up happy and together.

But then I noticed Brynn staring at me. She had something she wanted to say to me.

Over the sound of the drumroll on the PA, I mouthed the word, *What?*

She mouthed back, *It's us.*

I waved my hand at her. *That's ridiculous.*

But her gaze never strayed, and her knowing smile never wavered as Mr. Tremblay unfolded the piece of paper and finally read the names.

"For the seventh year in a row, it's your Captain! Congratulations to Shea Ellis and his date, Brynn Conley! Come on up here, you two!"

The audience roared.

And I laughed. I laughed, because what else could you really do?

As I stood, I clapped my howling teammates on the back and whispered in their ears, "Very funny, Ilya." "Hilarious, Brooksy." "You had something to do with this too, Radar?" "You know I voted for you, right Lance? You only robbed your lady of the crown."

Brynn took my arm and walked with me to receive our crowns.

She tugged on my arm and whispered in my ear, "I told you so."

"How'd you know?" I whispered back.

"I had a funny feeling."

"I'm sorry. I think this is my teammates' idea of a joke. I hope you're not embarrassed."

"Just a bit."

The owner and Mr. Tremblay placed the weighty crown on my head and a glimmering tiara on Brynn's. "And now, music please, as the King and Queen lead us with the ceremonial first dance."

With several feet separating us, Brynn and I looked at each other for what felt like an eternity. Making the moment seem like it lasted even longer was the fact that the music hadn't started.

The two of us did the only thing we could do—we laughed. The audience could sense our hesitation, and they all laughed, too.

And then, finally, the slow song started to play.

I stepped forward and asked for her hand. "Dance?"

She took my hand. "Yes."

I held her waist with my other hand. The two of us began to glide to the music while the crowd watched.

"So, Brynn, on a scale of one to ten Mortified Chloes, where do you rank right now?" I asked her quietly.

She gave a gentle laugh. "Hm ... I'd say I'm at a solid two."

"Two. Hey. That's not so bad. I'll take that."

We moved as one. I have to say, I liked it. I liked it all—the warmth of her delicate hand clasped in mine; her eyes locked on mine, and twinkling in the low light. It was nice enough that I could *almost* forget about my jackass teammates' smiling mugs out in the audience. (Although I shot them a dirty stare anytime I happened to catch their eyes.)

"So are you having flashbacks to your high school prom right about now?" I asked her.

"No. I wouldn't have any prom to flashback to."

"Huh?"

"I never went to the prom. Or *any* of my high school dances, actually."

My eyes widened. "None of them? No one ever asked *you* to a dance?"

"Believe it or not. I was sort of a mess back then."

"I don't believe it. The boys were probably completely in love with you, but too shy to ask you out."

"Well, I won't stop you from believing that." Her smile strained. "But if someone *had* asked me to go, I probably would've said no, because at that age, I thought all this *pomp and circumstance* bullshit was super contrived and lame."

"Ah-ha." I grinned. "See—that right there—explains why the boys were too afraid to ask you to the dance. Plus, it makes me understand why Chloe likes you so much."

She winced. "Yeah ..."

"Something wrong?"

"No," she said, but I could tell she wasn't being honest.

I didn't want to call her out on it. So we danced, and didn't speak, until the pressure grew too strong inside me. I had to say something.

"Brynn, are you upset with me?"

"No," she said, pressing her head against my chest—and I wondered if it was so I couldn't read her face. "Not at all."

"Really? Are you sure? I feel like I've done or said something to bother you. All night you've been acting strange, and I can't figure out what it is."

"Oh, Shea." She lifted her head from my chest to give me a puppy dog pout. "You haven't done anything wrong. But yes, there is something serious on my mind."

I swallowed. "And what's that?"

17

BRYNN

The tall hockey player had one giant hand clutched at my waist. His other hand, so big and warm, firmly held mine aloft. The lights were dim, the music romantic, and the crowd fawning as we slow danced our way into their adoring hearts.

All night, I'd run away from what I had to tell Shea. But I couldn't keep lying to him—I was a bad liar when sober, and *twice* as bad when I had enough wine in me—and he knew something was wrong.

More than anything, I hated the fact that I had to be the one to ruin this moment.

"I'm worried about Chloe," I said at last.

Shea launched into *Dad Mode.* "What about Chloe? Is she in trouble?"

"No, she's not in trouble."

"Then what is it?"

God, how do I even begin to explain this?

"Shea ..." I buried my face in his chest once more. I loved his smell—was it his cologne, or his natural scent? It was so manly, so peppery, so clean. I could breathe that and *only* that for the rest of my life, and I'd die happy. "After you left earlier today, Chloe said some worrying things."

"Like what?" Shea asked in a startled panic.

I felt bad. I was scaring him over something that wasn't very serious at all. Obviously, there was nothing between Shea and I, so what did we have to worry about?

"Don't be alarmed," I said soothingly. "For all I know, it could be nothing. But she alluded to wanting to make up for something she did to you once?"

Shea's brow furrowed. "I don't follow."

"This is sort of embarrassing to say, but she seems to think that she 'set us up' on this date—and that this somehow might make up for something she did to you once."

Shea frowned. "Oh, Chloe ... my poor girl."

"Does that mean anything to you? She wouldn't tell me what it meant."

"She feels guilt over the divorce. That's all." But the heavy look on his face told me there was a lot more to the story than that. "I had no idea she blamed herself."

"They say it can be awfully hard on kids," I said.

He paused. "Did she say anything else?"

"A little. I don't know how much I should tell you. I think she has this idea in her head that we could end up together."

"Ha." Shea belted out a laugh, like a single bubble from his belly. And then a few more emerged. "Ha, ha ha. Oh, Chloe. Oh, no."

I hated the fact that he laughed. And I hated even more how his grip on my waist loosened. I wondered if he'd consciously done that or not? I didn't want him to let go of me. I wanted him to sink his claws into my waist and really *grab* me, claim me, own me.

Even though it can't ever happen.

"We have to be careful how we act around her, or she'll get the wrong idea," he said.

I felt like he was driving the stake right through the heart of my own teenage fantasy. But that was fine and healthy, right? Better than continuing on in denial.

"Yeah. I know. It's sad, isn't it?" I agreed.

"Very sad. I should've seen it coming," Shea said, shaking his head regretfully. "It's only because she looks up to you so much, Brynn. I can't believe she'd think something like that about us. It's ridiculous, really."

Okay—I could get behind no longer living in denial. But something about Shea's denial made me feel defiant, bitter, and unwanted. I didn't know what I'd *expected* him to say. Of course he didn't want me. And even on the incredible off-chance that he did want me, he couldn't outright say it was true! But still, it hurt to hear him say that the idea was *ridiculous*.

"You're probably right," I said. But the combination of being hurt and tipsy put me in a feisty mood. "I don't know *why* she thinks we're always tip-toeing around the house, flirting with each other, for example."

"She—she said that?"

"Oh, yeah. That, and a lot worse."

Shea gritted his teeth. "Do I even want to know?"

"I don't know. *Do* you?"

Uncertain, Shea gulped. "Yes?"

"She said that she thinks you're always finding excuses to sit next to me. That you're really handsy and touchy with me. That you never behaved with the other nannies like you behave with me. I don't know—what do you think? Crazy, right?"

Shea didn't say a word. His expression grew stony and serious.

"Then, she said—" I covered my mouth and giggled. "She

said she's never seen two people who needed to *'bone'* more in her entire life."

"*Chloe!*" he muttered under his breath.

"I'm sorry. I didn't tell you earlier because I wanted you to enjoy your night and not worry. I guess that's why you noticed I was acting strange."

"It's okay," he said softly. "Thanks for telling me."

"Yeah. Sure. Figured I had to. I'd hate for Chloe to think something so outrageous could be true."

There was a lull. I glanced out at the audience—all those people, smiling and watching us, totally oblivious to what we were talking about. If only they had any idea!

"But Brynn ..." Shea trailed off, his eyes heavy.

Before he could say what he wanted to say, the song faded out, and the audience stood and clapped for us. A man in a suit ran up and thrust a microphone into Shea's hand.

He stared at it, unsure what to do.

"Speech!" the crowd chanted. "Speech, speech, speech!"

Reluctantly, Shea pulled the mic to his mouth and began to speak.

"Wow. I don't know what to say. You really voted for *me* again, huh? And all this time I thought you guys were voting for my daughter, Chloe." He paused to let the laughter die down. "Thanks to everyone for coming out tonight." Shea turned to me. "Thanks to Brynn—who did doubly-duty as my kids' nanny by day, and my lovely date by night—for agreeing to come with me."

At Shea's mention of my name, a rowdy, male segment of the crowd—with deep and booming voices—went wild. "*Wooooooo!*" "*Brynn!*" "*Awww, yeah!*"

Ah. Shea's teammates, of course.

Shea continued on the mic. "And thanks to Brawlers owner, Jim James, for throwing tonight's gala and giving such a generous gift to charity. Tonight, I'm asking Mr. James to donate that money to *Hockey Fights Cancer,* and I'll be matching his donation."

The audience went *oooh* and applauded.

"Thanks again, everybody. Enjoy the rest of your night—now get up here and dance, so I can stop making a fool out of myself." Shea almost passed off the mic before he remembered one last thing to say. "One last thing. This is for my teammates out there. Remember, boys, don't drink too much; we've got an early flight to Tampa in the morning."

The Brawlers in the audience laughed and booed, and then the music started again. The women pulled their reluctant men onto the dance floor, and soon Shea and I were surrounded.

Without the pressure of all those eyes watching us and us alone, Shea and I moved closer together. My arms went around his neck. His colossal hands went to my sides. His irises smoldered with a cocky glint, and his eyes occasionally darted down to steal a glance at my cleavage.

"During our dance, you were about to say something," I shouted at him, over the music.

He smiled coyly. "Was I?"

"Yeah, what was it?"

"I don't remember," he said.

He was lying, but what could I do about it? I just liked being close to him.

I let it go and we danced. And as we moved, we pulled each other closer into the blistering heat that lingered between our bodies. Shea's thumbs and fingers dug and clenched at my waist. His touch was subtle, but I liked it—I wondered if he thought I wouldn't notice? It was a comforting pressure. I wanted his king-sized hands running over every inch of my body ... even if I knew there were a thousand good reasons why it should never happen.

We danced the night away, until it was way too late, and we were way too drunk to think about getting in his car and driving home.

After we said our goodbyes to Shea's teammates and my new girl friends, Shea called a cab.

We slid into the leather back seat of our car, the two of us giggling and laughing like two drunken buffoons. Shea gave the cabbie his address, and the driver stepped on the gas. The lights of Boston in the early morning streaked past in long trails of red and amber.

"Thanks again for coming, Brynn," Shea said. "I hope you had a good time."

He set his palm at my knee. His touch was electric. My legs opened the smallest amount, an inaudible sigh escaping my lungs.

"That was so fun, Shea," I said. I laid my head against his shoulder, so firm and strong.

"Yeah. Wasn't it?" Shea freed his burly arm, wrapped it around my body, and pulled me snugly against him. He was so big and warm.

"I can't believe we had to do that slow dance in front of everybody," I said, giggling. I set my hand on his abdomen. Through his dress shirt, I could feel the hard, sexy ridges of his washboard abs. I tasted the texture with the tips of my fingers.

He chuckled. "We made a good couple though, don't you think?" His hand traveled down my side and grazed over my ass. "*Queen?*"

I knocked his sneaky paw away. "Shea!"

He smirked. "What?"

"You know what." I patted my palm against his prickly

cheek. He was clean-shaven when we left for the gala, but now his cheek was already coarse with stubble. "What would Chloe say if she saw us like this?"

Shea's hand went to my face, too. Softly, his fingers stroked my cheek, and his eyes burned into mine.

"Honestly?" he whispered in my ear. The deep rasp of his gritty, sexy growl warmed my ear lobe and sent a chill down my spine. "Chloe's right."

My nerves tingled, but I didn't say a word.

"I want you, Brynn. I want you *bad*."

"Shea ...!" I panted. "I don't know what to say."

"Don't say anything."

And just like that, the hockey player made his move.

His lips met mine, and the sucking and smacking of wet kisses replaced our silly backseat banter. I melted in his mouth —his lips so warm, his taste so right, his kisses so perfect. Two months of pent-up lust, denial and frustration flowed through our mouths. Shea's tongue searched for mine, and without hesitation, I gave him mine. Our tongues touched, slithered, and wove together.

Shea's desire grew and he kissed me with an ever-rising urgency. I yielded to him, slowly retreating under his immense weight, until my back was pressed into the seat and Shea was on top of me.

"You're so beautiful, Brynn," he snarled in my ear.

The athlete dragged his massive hands up and down my stomach, torturing my nerves with the tips of his fingers. He had a touch as light and soft as a feather. With hushed whimpers and soft moans, I implored him to put his hands all *over* my body. I opened for him like a flower.

His hands traveled higher, higher, higher—until I was certain he'd grab my breasts. But Shea was an artful and deliberate tease. And as we kissed, his hands cruelly fell just short of my breasts. My nipples, straining against the silk of my dress, ached for his touch.

It was my turn to whisper in *his* ear.

"I want your hands *all* over me."

Those were the magic words.

Shea growled like an animal and cupped my tits with his titan-sized hands. He squeezed my boobs, jiggled them in his palm, pinched and tugged at my nipples. I writhed and moaned, kissing the hockey player deeper and harder, kissing him like I'd never kissed *anyone* in my life.

We'd forgotten where we were. I'd slid further and further under Shea's weight, and he pressed his hips against mine. My eyes widened when I felt it at last—the bulge between his legs, huge and long and hard. I wanted it. I *needed* it. I wrapped my legs around his trunk and pulled him deeper into me, rubbing his rock-hard manhood against my crotch.

That's when I realized the car wasn't moving, and the driver awkwardly cleared his throat.

"Ahem. Excuse me, sir, but we have arrived at your destination."

18

———

BRYNN

We bolted upright and separated like we'd just been caught.

Shea plucked a hundred-dollar bill from his wallet and gave it to the driver. Then he gave the driver a second one "to keep this confidential."

The driver nodded. "Of course, sir. Thank you very much."

Shea and I climbed out, and the car sped off.

Shea put his arm around me. We didn't say a word as we walked to the front door. He fished his keys from his pocket, opened the door, and let me step in first.

I watched as Shea closed and locked the door behind him. I wasn't sure what was supposed to happen next. I wondered if, being back in his own house, a moment of clarity might grip him—and keep him from making what could end up being a *huge* mistake?

It wasn't *just* that I was the kid's nanny. *I* lived here too, after all—he shared his house with me. We could still stop ourselves here and blame alcohol for our steamy little moment in cab. But if we couldn't stop ourselves from going too far, who *knew* how badly we might regret this night in the future?

Hell, *I* was starting to have second thoughts. But before I could do or say anything, Shea pressed himself into my rear.

"Couldn't keep my eyes off you all night," he said. As we stood in the middle of the living room, he wrapped his huge arms around my front.

He planted his lips on my neck and sucked. I wilted under his touch.

"Mm," he panted. "You taste so good, Brynn."

From behind, he rubbed his hard bulge against me. Sensing his desire, the spot between my thighs grew damp and throbbed. If he kept teasing me like this, I knew I wouldn't be able to hold him back for long—so if clear heads were going to prevail, they needed to *now*.

"Shea ..." I gulped, my knees buckling.

"Yes, Brynn?" Shea teased as he slowly tugged the zipper at the back of my dress.

My voice was a quivering whisper. "Do you think ... maybe ... this could end up being a bad idea?"

He chuckled, and puffs of his breath tickled my sensitive neck.

"You said you wanted my hands *all* over you," he said. "And *that* sounds like a pretty good idea to me."

Then there was a *swish* as the silk garment fell to my feet. I stood nearly naked in front of my former childhood crush, and current boss, wearing only heels and a thong.

He turned me around to face him. I covered my breasts in my hands. Shea's eyes traveled up and down my body, drinking me in.

"Wow," he grumbled.

Without hesitation, he scooped me into his arms as if I weighed nothing. My heels fell to the floor and our hot, juicy lips came together once again as Shea carried me to the sofa.

There's no turning back now.

The captain tossed me into the sofa's cushions. I dared to keep my breasts buried in my arms, but Shea wouldn't have it.

"*Mine*," he roared possessively.

Overpowering me easily, Shea pried my hands from my tits and sucked at my nipples so hard I yelped out in pain—though a part of me loved his rough treatment of me, and loved it even more when he didn't let up.

His large hands ran up and down every inch of my bare skin. He pawed at me greedily, grabbing and pulling at my flesh, always wanting more, taking more.

"You're so damn beautiful," he growled once more. "I've wanted you for so long."

His hand went between my legs and slid up my thighs. His fingers stroked against the crotch of my panties. We both knew it then—I was sinfully wet.

"You soaked your panties," Shea muttered huskily. "Fuck, that's hot."

The hockey player grabbed hold of my thong and yanked it down my legs. Without looking, he tossed it carelessly over his shoulder.

Shea grabbed my bottom and pulled me to the edge of the sofa. He knelt before me and parted my legs. I was so open, so exposed for him.

"Shea," I moaned.

"Oh, wow." He hungrily eyed my bareness and licked his lips. "You've got such a cute pussy, Brynn."

Spreading me wide, Shea began to lick. Softly, gently, he used only the tip of his tongue to delicately trace my folds.

"Yes, yes," I whispered, encouraging him to give me more.

His tongue flattened. Starting at my entry, Shea painted long, broad brushstrokes up my pussy—always reaching higher, higher, higher for my clit ... yet always falling *just* short, leaving me gasping for air and mewling in agony.

"Please," I whimpered. "Please, Shea!"

"Please *what?*" he teased, a sparkle in his eye.

"Give me your mouth ...!"

He smiled.

Instead of his mouth, he gave me his finger.

I moaned, deep and guttural, as he stuck his thick finger past my folds and burrowed into my tightness.

"Oh my God," I cried hoarsely, my inner muscles gripping at his finger uncontrollably.

And only *then* did Shea give me his mouth. The tip of his tongue found my clit, and he flicked my swollen and sensitive nub. With his finger buried in my hole, Shea French kissed my pussy, sloppily slurping at my wetness.

"Shea!" I howled, running my fingers over the sharp texture of his short hair.

With his mouth on my pussy, a cute smile tugged at Shea's lips—he really *loved* seeing me like this. And then harder, faster, his tongue lapped at my clit, while his fat finger cork-screwed in and out of my opening, hammering my g-spot again and again until—

I wailed, choking on air, "You're gonna make me come!"

He didn't let up. His wet muscle thrashed and batted my clit, bringing me right up to the edge. He finger-fucked me harder, faster, dirtier—until the bright, shining ecstasy erupted from my core. My limbs trembled and flailed, and I belted out screams of bliss.

"Yes!"

When I managed to open my eyes again, the athlete was still crouched between my legs. He held his fingers up to his face, studying the juices that trickled and ran down his thick finger

—*my* juices.

And then he wrapped his lips around his finger and sucked the cream right off.

A wildfire swept through my belly. It was such a naughty, filthy act to witness—and yet an undeniable turn on. I'd never had a lover worship my body like Shea ... and now I *truly* felt like a Queen. *His* Queen.

"Shea," I gasped, my stomach still twisting into knots. "I never knew you were so dirty."

"Only for you. I *love* your taste, Brynn."

His wild, hungry eyes shined in the darkened living room as he drank me up. He looked like a man who couldn't wait to wreck me, a man who *needed* to be balls-deep inside me. As far as I was concerned, he could have me anyway he wanted me. I sat up and unbuckled his belt and whipped it from his trousers.

Shea motioned for the upstairs. "Should we go to the bedroom first?" he asked as I pulled at his zipper.

"No," I said. "I want you to fuck me, right here, on the couch."

He growled with thick, male desire. "*Damn*, Brynn."

"Like that idea?" I sang. "Is it dirty enough for you?"

"I *love* it."

I yanked and tugged at his trousers to peel them off his tree-trunk thighs. With his trousers off, his cock rose, tenting his boxers comically high. I giggled and swiped his boxers to the ground—and then gasped.

Shea was *hung*.

His big dick sprang out before me, bouncing and swaying in the air with a mouth-watering heft. The masculine scent of his warm, salty flesh flooded my nostrils and hijacked my brain.

I wanted him, needed him, buried deep inside me. I didn't want him to waste any time. Shea could sense it. He pushed me onto my back and spread my legs over his shoulders. He glided his cock along my sopping wet folds, teasing me, wanting me to beg for it.

"Fuck me, Shea," I whispered between my moans of anticipation. "Please, I want you inside me."

With a groan, Shea set his tip at my entry.

Ever so slowly, Shea began to sink his weight into me.

"Yes, yes, yes," I moaned, encouraging him to go faster, deeper.

The very tip of his manhood parted my folds and began to stretch me wider—when, suddenly, the large living room windows behind us were bathed in a blinding white light.

We froze in terror.

Gravel crunched beneath a set of quickly moving tires. The hum of a car engine neared as it pulled into the driveway.

I recognized the specific sound of that car, of course.

Shea's ex-wife.

Shea jumped off me and crawled over the sofa to peek through the window blinds.

"Fuck, that's Cynthia's car," he snarled. "What the hell is she doing here right now?"

He jumped off the couch and stepped into his boxers. I was almost too stunned to move—until I heard the sound of a car door opening and then slamming shut.

Eyes wide, I leaped off the couch, scooped my dress and heels off the floor, and *ran* for my bedroom upstairs.

19

———

SHEA

We're so fucked, I thought, my heart pounding in my chest as I heard the door slam shut. We had only a few short seconds to get dressed.

Brynn slipped off the couch, snatched up her dress and heels, and ran butt-naked for the upstairs.

Cute butt, I thought to myself as I hopped around the room, trying to pull my trousers up. Yeah, I know—bad timing—but I couldn't help but appreciate it.

Chloe and her mom screamed and yelled at each other in the driveway. It might bring some ex-husbands a certain pleasure to see their daughter arguing with their mother, but I hate to see it. That said, this time? Their disagreement, whatever it was about, bought me precious seconds.

Hurrying, I hid my shoes under the couch. I flipped and fluffed the cushions, making things look nice and neat and generally trying to hide any evidence that Dad was about to fuck the nanny on the living room couch.

Chloe banged on the door.

I reached for the deadbolt. Before I unlocked it, I turned around and took one last survey of the room—only to see

Brynn's discarded thong lying in a crumpled little ball in the middle of the floor.

"*Shit*," I hissed. I ran over, picked it up and stuffed the item into my pocket.

Then I unlocked the door. Chloe stormed in and shoved right past me. She'd obviously been crying.

"Chloe!" I yelled after her. "Hey, what happened?"

"I *can't* talk to you about this, Dad!" she sobbed. She raced upstairs, heavy feet stomping all the way to her bedroom.

Cynthia's car was still idling in the driveway. She wasn't going anywhere.

I sighed.

I'd gone from being *this close* to having what would've been the hottest sex of my life ... to needing to have a chat with the angry ex-wife instead. Trust me, there was no need for a cold shower.

I stepped outside. The second Cynthia saw me, her window lowered, and I saw the ol' familiar scowl that always managed to lay my heart out on ice.

"What's going on here, Cynthia?"

"That daughter of yours is a *wreck*," she said. It never failed to amuse me how Chloe became my daughter when things between them went poorly.

"Just tell me what happened."

"She has a *toxic* tongue. Every word out of her mouth is pure poison—it's like she's hell-bent on punishing me for every mistake I've ever made! I'm sorry, I'm not perfect, but I won't accept that kind of abuse from a teenage girl! We've been arguing for hours—I can't even get any sleep in my own house!" She tutted. "Chloe sure loves staying with *you*, though—so here you go! You can take her!"

I sighed. Somehow, I doubted I was getting an unbiased account. "Cynthia, I know it can be hard with Chloe—"

"Oh, I'm *sure* you do," she said with a healthy roll of her eyes. "You were always *sooo* helpful with raising Chloe. Oh, what a fantastic help you were—spending months on the road, or when you actually *were* in Boston, going out for beers every night with your hockey '*boys*.' And now you just pass the parenting duties off to your hot-to-trot nanny, am I right?"

I shook my head. I was never a perfect parent—and neither was *she*, for that matter—but I'd changed a lot since our divorce. Not that I cared to debate all this old shit with her. Frankly, I thought all these arguments were supposed to come to an end once we got the hell out of each other's lives.

Oh, and I wasn't even going to go anywhere *near* that hot-to-trot nanny remark.

"Cynthia, my point is, I know it's hard, but you *have* to let me know before you just show up with Chloe. I can't take her now."

"I tried to let you know. I called you a hundred times but you never answered."

I reached into my pocket for my phone. I pulled it out, but something else came with it—Brynn's racy thong, still soaked with her juices. Eyes wide, I stuffed her underwear back into my pocket. Cynthia didn't say anything—so she must've missed it, because she *definitely* wouldn't let that go without some sort of smart comment.

Close one.

I checked my phone. Cynthia hadn't called a *hundred* times, no, but she had tried to call me plenty over the past hour. I hadn't noticed.

I frowned. "Sorry. Guess I didn't hear it."

"Mm," Cynthia said skeptically.

"Anyway, that doesn't change our problem. It's your weekend to have the kids, Cynthia. The playoffs are about to start and I have to leave for Tampa first thing tomorrow morning."

"So have your nanny take care of her. That's what you pay

her for, isn't it?" She huffed. "Or hm, do you pay her for something else, I wonder?"

My eyes narrowed. "I don't like what you're implying. I think you better go now, Cynthia."

"Did you have a good time at the gala?"

Does she have some kind of problem with Brynn?

"Yeah. Sure," I answered curtly. "Bye now, Cynthia."

"Bye, Shea. Oh, wait, one last thing before I go?"

I groaned. "What is it?"

"Those ridiculous slut panties you're carrying around in your pocket—do those belong to her? Your new number one fan?"

Fuck.

I grimaced. "... I don't know what you're talking about."

She cackled as she put her car into gear. "Oh, Shea. You were always *such* a bad liar."

"And you were the best."

She laughed bitterly. "Ha. Good one." Scorned, Cynthia's window immediately began to roll up. But she left the window cracked open an inch to spew one last remark. "It'd be nice to leave your kids a healthy inheritance, don't you think? Try not to let a gold digger make off with all your cash."

She threw the car into reverse and sped off into the night.

Number one fan?

Gold digger?

The hell is she even talking about?

20

SHEA

I felt bad leaving Shea downstairs to deal with whatever was about to happen, but then again, at least he had *some* clothes on. I was totally nude when I went bounding upstairs. I was certain that Cynthia was going to bust through the front door, maybe with all three kids in tow, and catch me running away as naked as the day I was born.

But hey, I made it.

I slammed the bedroom door shut and jumped into bed, pulled the covers over my bare body and pretended I was out like a rock. A second later, I heard the front door open, and an upset Chloe came barging through the living room.

That was also the precise moment I remembered that my panties were still down there.

Shit!

It was too late. Chloe ran upstairs, and I heard her foot-steps coming down the hall. She stopped at my door and knocked.

I didn't answer. She cracked the door open anyway and poked her head in.

"Brynn?" she called out quietly.

My heart thumped in my chest. I didn't say a word—because I was, *ahem*, very asleep.

"Brynn?"

I ignored her again. But she neared and started rocking my shoulders. "Hey, Brynn, are you awake?"

Argh. She's not going anywhere until I answer.

"Mm?" I groaned, pretending like she'd just woken me. "Chloe?"

"Sorry to wake you," she sniffled.

"It's okay. What's wrong?"

"I think I did something bad ..." she said as she sat on the edge of the bed.

Afraid she might discover that I was nude under the covers, I clutched the comforter as tight as I could and sealed it against my body.

"What happened?" I asked with a sleepy, gravelly voice.

"I told my mom."

"About what?"

"You and my dad."

Okay. Fuck. Why?

"What about us?"

She hung her head in shame. "Everything we talked about earlier, basically."

"Why'd you do that, Chloe?"

"Because she wouldn't leave me alone until I did. I even showed her the picture of you in your bedroom. With my dad's poster on the wall and everything."

I gnashed my teeth, but I didn't say a word.

"I'm so sorry, Brynn."

"It's okay."

"I hope you don't hate me now."

"Of course I don't hate you, Chloe."

"I think my mom is going to tell my dad."

"That's okay. I'll talk to your dad about it, Chloe. Don't you worry. You better get some rest now, okay?"

"Okay. I'll let you sleep." She stopped at the door, a glimmer of hope in her voice. "Did you have fun at the gala, Brynn?"

"It was a very fun night, Chloe. Thank you for asking."

Maybe a little too much fun ...

21

SHEA

I trudged upstairs, walked past Brynn's room, and stopped outside Chloe's.

The door was open a half-dozen inches, but I knocked and waited anyway.

"Come in," Chloe sniffled at last.

I entered. "How'd I do that time? I knocked and then I waited. See, you *can* teach an old dad new tricks."

She laughed, but it was a mad-laugh—mad that I had the gall to make her laugh when she was clearly upset. "Dad, c'mon. I'm not in a good mood."

She was on her bed, curled up in a ball under the sheets. I sat on the mattress next to her. "So hey, what happened tonight?"

She hesitated, the only sound her sniffling.

"I can't tell you, Dad," she said at last.

"Why not?"

"Because I promised I wouldn't."

"Promised who? Your mom?"

"God, no, not her."

"Nick? Cam? Who else could it be?"

"Stop trying to guess. Even if you get it right, I'm not going to tell you."

"Okay." I gave a shrug. "Your mom said you two were fighting all night. She said she couldn't get any sleep. What were you arguing about?"

"*She* couldn't get any sleep because she wouldn't leave *me* alone. I just wanted to be left alone, but she kept wanting to argue and dig, dig, dig for information."

"Dig for what information?"

"I can't tell you!"

I lowered my voice. "Chloe, was your fight with your mom about Brynn?"

She hesitated before she answered. "No."

Almost convincing, but given Cynthia's strange comments and what Brynn told me earlier, I didn't quite believe my daughter.

Chloe could sense that I didn't believe her, and she went into damage control mode.

"Okay, *yes*, sort of. Mom was picking fights with me ever since she asked me why I wasn't going to the gala with you this year."

"And what did you tell her?"

"I told her the truth! That I didn't want to go because I'm too old for it and I think it's lame! But then she asked me who you were taking instead, and I said I didn't know, that you were prob- ably going by yourself, but she could *tell* I was lying ... so she followed me around all night, badgering me non-stop, until I finally told her—not because I wanted to tell her, but because I just wanted to get her off my back."

"And?"

"It didn't work! It just made her go *more* crazy! She started asking all these questions about you and Brynn, and ..." Chloe bit her tongue. "And I don't know. She went even more nuts from there."

I rubbed my forehead. "Ugh."

"How was the gala, anyway?" Chloe asked with a sudden optimism in her weary voice. "Did you two have fun together?"

The red-hot sensation of Brynn's plump, pink lips against mine flashed through my memory, and I looked away guiltily.

"We did," I said with a husky knot in my throat.

"Good," she sniffled. "I really like Brynn."

My shoulders sagged under all that guilt. "I know you do, Chloe. But Brynn and I went to the gala just as friends, understand?"

"Of *course*, Dad. What, did you think that I thought you guys were going as *lovers?* I'm not stupid. Why would you even say something like that?"

I stared at her. *Should I let this go?* If it weren't for Cynthia's comments, I probably would have let it go. But clearly, Chloe told her mom something, and I thought I needed to know.

I tried a different approach, though.

"Chloe, you know that you had *nothing* to do with the divorce, right?"

"Yeah. Sure, I know that." She tutted, but behind her eyes, I could see that she was only placating me and giving me the answer I wanted.

"Chloe, really. It wasn't your fault. You didn't put your mom in that situation—she put *you* in that situation. You only did what you thought was right. Which is *very* admirable. You're an amazing girl with an honest soul. You're not to blame for our divorce, and I just want you to know that you don't have anything at all to make up for—"

But Chloe's expression hardened with anger. "Wait, did Brynn say something to you?"

I took a deep breath. "Earlier, at the gala, Brynn might have told me that you said a few things that had her a little worried."

"And what did Brynn tell you?"

"She was just worried that you might get the wrong idea about us." I squeezed Chloe's shoulder. "I know how much you like Brynn, Chloe. But I don't want you to get the wrong idea. She's our nanny, that's all. I hope that she stays with us for a very long time to come—but Brynn and I aren't anything more than that."

My stomach flipped and flopped around in my gut—it was my body's way of telling me that I'd just told a bad lie and it hated me for being dishonest. It was the reason Cynthia knew I was such a bad liar; she could see it happening to me in real time. Thing is, this time, the reaction took me by surprise—I guess I wasn't even *aware* that I was being dishonest.

But of course Brynn wasn't just the nanny.

Not anymore. Not after tonight. She couldn't be. Even if we managed to have a healthy working relationship from this day forward, she'd always be the nanny that I fooled around with one night and very nearly slept with.

But I couldn't tell Chloe any of that—besides being a completely inappropriate thing to tell your teenage daughter, the truth would only mess with her head.

Chloe stewed with her arms folded. "I can't believe she *told* you that. It's like I can't trust *anyone* anymore. Jesus, I can't believe you people!"

"Chloe, sweetie, she's only watching out for you. She has your best interests at heart. I know it doesn't feel like it now, but you'll see that when you're older."

She grunted with disgust. "Wow. Yeah. Gee, thanks. Once again, I'll have to be older to understand. As if I'm not already 'old' and 'mature' enough to see through everyone's bullshit. It's seriously annoying."

Angry teen rant #1,337, I figured.

But then a devilish smirk appeared on Chloe's lips. "Since Brynn was being *so* honest with you, did she happen to tell you about her poster?"

"Huh? What poster?"

"Ha. She didn't. I knew it ... that just figures."

"What are you talking about, Chloe?"

She grabbed her iPad and tapped away at the screen. A few seconds later, she thrust the screen into my face.

What the hell?

It was a picture of a young Brynn. Pasted on the wall behind her was a poster of me in my rookie year. The damn thing was covered with lipstick kisses.

I was both flattered and creeped out all at once. Most of all, I wondered why Brynn had never mentioned this before.

And then Cynthia's remarks began to make sense.

Number one fan. Gold digger.

"So you showed this to your mom?" I asked.

"I didn't *want* to, but like I said, she wouldn't leave me alone until I told her more and more about Brynn! And once I showed her this she freaked the hell out and said I *had* to tell you, and that's why she drove me back here."

"Unbelievable," I muttered. "I'm sorry you had to go through all that with your mom. Chloe, what would you think about going to therapy?"

"Therapy! What! *No,*" she blurted out. "That's a waste of time and money, and besides, I'm *not* crazy."

"I know you're not crazy. But you've been stuck in the middle of something ugly for a long time, and it's not right to expect you to deal with it all on your own. Don't you think it'd be nice to have someone to talk to abou—"

"*No.* I can talk to my friends when I want to tell people about my crazy-ass family. I don't need therapy. If you make me go, I won't say a word to them. I'll just sit in silence the whole time and waste your money. So don't even *think* about sending me there."

I frowned. I knew my daughter well enough to know that I wasn't about to change her mind tonight.

"I just want you to think about it, okay?"

She made a harrumph.

"I'll leave you alone. You should get some sleep, alright sweetie? It's late and you've had a tough night. Thanks for telling me everything."

Regret filled Chloe's eyes. "You're not going to fire Brynn now, are you?"

"No. Chloe, I'm not going to fire her. Goodnight, sweetheart."

"Goodnight, Dad."

I left Chloe's room, shut the door, and went to Brynn's room.

I stood outside. I didn't know what to do, what to think. My hand went to my pocket. Brynn's thong brought a pained smile to my face. I squeezed her panties into a tight ball in my fist and sighed.

What am I supposed to do now?

22

BRYNN

There was a knock at the door. I knew it was Shea. I'd heard him go into Chloe's room only minutes before.

"Come in," I said.

The door opened and Shea's statuesque figure loomed in the doorway. Quietly, he entered and shut the door behind him. With a tired sigh, he walked near and lowered himself onto the bed. I'd kill to have him climb under the sheets and be with me —*not* because I wanted to finish where we left off, but only because I wanted his strong arms wrapped around me. I wanted his breath on my ear, I needed his gentle reassurances that everything would be alright, everything between us could work out ...

But he faced away from me instead.

I sat up, wrapped my arms around him, my bare breasts pressed against his back.

I spoke his name forlornly. "Shea."

"Hm?" He sounded so disinterested.

Gently, I kissed at the nape of his neck. I clutched and kneaded at his powerful pecs. I'd do anything to be the object of his desire and affection again. But he leaned away from me and pried my hands from his chest. He reached into his pocket for something. He dangled my thong from the tip of his finger, as if it disgusted him.

"Here," he said. "You left this downstairs."

He didn't want me. He couldn't have made that any more clear.

"Just throw it somewhere," I muttered.

"Where?"

"Throw it in the trash. I don't care."

I collapsed to the bed, crawled under the sheets and curled away from him.

"I'm sorry," I said.

"For what?" he asked.

"Cynthia or Chloe showed you, I imagine."

"Showed me what?"

I could tell that he knew—he just wanted me to come clean. I turned around to face him.

"The picture of me. With your poster. Right?"

He didn't answer, but his silence all but confirmed that he knew.

"Well, yes, it's true. I had a crush on you when I was young."

He didn't say a word.

"You want the whole story? Fine, here it is: I thought my older brothers were so cool, and all I wanted to do was hang out with and be accepted by them. They loved hockey so, naturally, I had to love hockey, too. And who started getting all this media attention at the same time I started watching? A handsome young rookie. You were a hero before you'd even set foot on the ice. And unlike the other Brawlers, you weren't missing teeth, your nose didn't zig-zag in ten different directions, you didn't look like somebody's weird mullet-wearing uncle. No, you were such a pretty-boy with your long locks of hair—but on the ice, you were dangerous. And you were so fun-loving and well-spoken in your interviews. You were a gorgeous bad boy that everyone respected. Shea, for a teenage girl with raging hormones, you were like *catnip*. Can you blame me?"

Shea stayed silent.

"I didn't *want* to like you. If anything, my crush on you made me even more girly and pathetic in my brothers' eyes. They teased me endlessly once they saw my stupid, kiss-covered poster of you. So there. Now you know. It was a childish crush, and I never would've imagined that it could possibly come up when I worked for you."

Still, he didn't talk.

"Aren't you going to say something?" I asked.

He let out a deep breath. "Did you *know* who I was when you first applied for the nanny job?"

"No! Of course not. How could I have known that? Your ad had so few details in it, I wasn't even sure if it was *real* or some type of scam. I even made sure I brought pepper spray to that interview!"

"So when did you realize it was me?"

"When that fan asked you for the autograph. And not a second sooner, I swear."

"Really. You had a poster of me, yet you didn't recognize me as soon as I walked into that cafe?"

"No offense, but you're not the twenty-something rookie I crushed on all those years ago. You're a *man* now. The flowing locks are gone and you're all salt-and-pepper now. And it's not like I followed your entire career or anything. Once I stopped trying to impress my brothers, I moved on, from hockey and from that silly crush. Trust me, I had a lot of crushes on men I'll never, ever meet. This—us meeting—was just a freak coincidence, okay?"

"So why didn't you say something?"

"Was I really supposed to disclose during our interview?

That I had an embarrassing teenage crush on you once upon a time?"

"It just seems like it should've come up at *some* point. All this time, I thought you didn't care who I was."

I scoffed. "I *don't* care who you are."

"Really? So everything that happened tonight had nothing to do with your crush?"

I took a deep breath. "I guess I can't honestly say no. Of course it's a little exciting, to think that things were meant to be this way—still, I know that's just a fantasy. But do you know what's *far* sexier than a professional hockey player? A man with a heart of gold, who is a loving, caring father to his children."

Shea grumbled, almost dismissively.

"So, yeah," I mumbled, "I guess I'm admitting that I *still* have a crush on you. This time, it's just for different reasons."

"Brynn ..."

"Do you want me to leave?" I asked. "I'll leave, if that's what you want. I wouldn't blame you. I haven't been professional about any of this at all."

He put his hand on my arm. "No. I need you."

"As your nanny," I said.

Shea grimaced. "Yes."

I nodded. "Right. Of course."

"Cynthia dropped Chloe off here for the weekend. They had an awful fight. Would you be able to stay with her while I'm in Tampa? Or did you have personal plans?"

Personal plans. The idea was nearly absurd—I barely had a life outside the Ellis family anymore. And yet, here we were, making a drunken mess of it.

"I can stay," I said quietly.

"Just a heads up. I had a chat with Chloe about everything we talked about at the gala. So, er, there's a good chance she'll be pissed at you."

"I'll survive."

"Brynn."

"Yeah?"

He pinched the bridge of his nose. "Look, I'm attracted to you, okay? And I have been since the beginning, or I wouldn't have tried to kiss you on your very first night—yeah, I admitted it, so we can both stop pretending like it never happened. Things have been *so* screwy and tense ever since that night, and it's all my fault. I don't blame you for feeling that tension."

Ah-ha. He did want to kiss me. I wasn't imagining it!

"So I'm sorry for grilling you," he said. "I just ... I got scared when I saw that picture. I thought I was being conned or set up or something."

"Conned? Why would you think that?"

He winced. "I have my reasons. It's personal."

I knew he was talking about his ex-wife, but he clearly didn't want to talk about her.

"Fair enough," I said quietly. "I guess I can't blame you for feeling that way."

"Yeah." He lowered his voice. "I mean, holy *shit,* Brynn. We almost fucked without protection."

I nodded shamefully. "Yeah ... I know it doesn't mean anything now, but I swear I'm normally not like that ..."

"Me neither. But what if I'd gotten you pregnant? What the hell would we do then?"

Oh, you have no idea how happy I'd be if I could get pregnant, I thought—but I bit my tongue for *obvious* reasons.

"We just have to remember that things are complicated. And it's not just about us, it's about my kids, too. Just look at the trouble Chloe's going through because of the gala." He paused. "Brynn, I think what I'm trying to say is, it'd be better if we kept things strictly professional between us."

"Agreed," I said, my heart withering.

"Besides, I don't need the distraction. I need to be focused on hockey. This is my last chance at the Cup. I need to be focused."

"I know."

"And I'm old, Brynn. My body aches. You need to find someone your age, someone young. Someone who is excited about starting a family with a woman who'd make a *great* mom. Don't waste your time with an old fogey like me. I don't want any more kids, and even if I did, I couldn't keep up with them."

Right. About that …

I stayed quiet, though. I'd said enough already. I didn't need to tell Shea anymore embarrassing details from my life.

"Well, anyway. I had fun tonight, all things considered," he said.

I scowled at him. *Really?*

"Er. Maybe not the right thing to say? I don't know. I'm bad at this." Shea shrugged. A pregnant pause came and went. "Goodnight, I guess."

I waited for him to leave, but he didn't. Instead he sat on the edge of the bed, staring at me—as if he we were waiting for something.

"Goodnight," I said.

But still he didn't leave. A smirk creased his mouth. He looked as if he didn't believe me, as if he were calling my bluff. Did he expect me to beg him to finish what he started, or something? Did he think I wouldn't let him go until he gave me that *one* good fucking that he'd gotten me all worked up for before we could call it quits?

I hoped not. Because I wasn't that type of girl, and if he thought I was, he was sorely mistaken.

With eyes of lust, the athlete confidently moved forward, cupped my face and tried to kiss me.

I leaned away and gave him a shove.

"*Shea*," I reprimanded him. "No. Do not."

"Sorry," he gulped. "Shit. Sorry. I don't know what got into me just there."

"Just go."

He stood and made for the door with his tail between his legs. He stopped in the doorway. "Goodnight, Brynn," he said apologetically.

"Goodnight. Good luck with the playoffs."

"Yeah. Thanks."

I rolled onto my side and stared at the wall.

What a mess we've gotten ourselves into now.

23

___

SHEA

On a normal day, Brynn wakes up before anyone else and starts breakfast. Today, she slept in and took the morning off. I couldn't blame her. I let her sleep in.

A hangover clouded my mind like a morning fog. I wasn't sure if it was from the alcohol or last night's revelations. Regardless, I stumbled around the kitchen and whipped up a breakfast for Chloe and me: eggs, bacon, toast and oatmeal. She didn't feel like talking *or* eating—she stared at her food and pushed it around her plate without interest.

"Not as good as when Brynn makes it, huh?"

"Nope," she said, purposefully popping the *p*.

"Hey, be good for her while I'm gone, okay?"

"Yeah. Sure. Whatever."

"Please, Chloe. She was kind enough to agree to stay here to take care of you. She has her own friends and life outside of us, you know."

"I get it, Dad. I'll thank her."

"Okay."

By the time I'd showered, packed my bags, and needed to

head out the door, Brynn still wasn't up. I hugged Chloe and told her to say bye to Brynn for me instead.

I *would've* woken Brynn so I could say goodbye to her in person—if I wasn't feeling like a complete jackass over the fact that I'd tried to kiss her *again*. Right after I tried to tell her we needed to keep things strictly professional, too.

That's *twice* now I've blown a kiss with Brynn.

Hopefully the Brawlers can manage to do a little better in our series against Tampa.

———

The Boston Brawlers must've been a sorry sight at 10:00 AM on the team plane. Coach was the last member of the team to board, and he didn't like what he saw.

"For Chrissakes," he grumbled as he slowly patrolled the aisles, wafting his hand in front of his nose. "Stinks like rum and puke in here. Great way to kick off the playoffs, gentlemen. Nothing says Stanley Cup contenders like a plane filled with groaning drunks. Boston Boozehounds, that's what they oughtta call us."

Coach saw me and his face crumpled with disappointment. "You too, Ellis?! I expect it from them, but *you*?"

"Sorry, Coach. Guess I got a little carried away with the festivities last night myself ..."

He threw himself into his seat with a groan. "I really gotta get Mr. James to move that damn gala until *after* the playoffs. What's the point of throwing a rager right before the most important stretch of our season? Makes no damn sense to me. Year after year, we shoot ourselves in the foot with that idiotic party."

Even though Coach had a right to be mad, the good news was that today was still an off-day. We flew to Tampa three days before the playoffs actually began: the first day was for travel and rest, the second and third days were for practice. We didn't play Game 1 until the fourth day, so we had plenty of time to recuperate.

But I wasn't dumb enough to try to speak up and make Coach feel better about his *plane full of drunks.* He was right to be pissed.

The plane taxied down the runway, fired its engines, and with a lurch, rushed forward.

The plane tilted back and became airborne. A few rows behind me, one of my teammates went *uuurp.*

"Oh, great," Coach said. "That's just great."

Tampa, FL.

We arrived at our hotel in the afternoon. The normal non-stop banter of the Boston Brawlers was completely missing as we dragged our wheeled suitcases down the long hall to our bedrooms.

My room came up first. I broke off from the group, swiped my key card, and staggered into the room. I shut the window curtains to blot out the bright Florida sun, climbed into bed, and tried to pass out.

But something wouldn't let me.

My damn balls. They'd ached all day.

Last night, I'd gotten so worked up with Brynn. But obviously, life had other plans for us. And since I never got my release, well, the pipes were feeling awfully backed up, and things were feeling sore and tender.

There was only one thing to do.

I reached into my pocket and pulled out the little black ball of fabric. *Brynn's thong.* I'd tried to give it back to her, but she didn't take it. She told me she didn't care what I did with it. I didn't know why I stealthily snuck it back into my pocket—and I *really* didn't know why I took it with me on the flight to Tampa. It seemed like the right thing to do, in some sort of depraved way. I guess I didn't want to let her go. I guess it was a memento? A really fucking twisted one.

But all flight long, I sure liked thinking about the naughty little secret in my pocket.

Jesus, I thought with a self-deprecating snicker—the irony wasn't lost on me, of course. I remembered all the shit I gave Radar last season for the panty collection he kept before he met Ella.

All this time, I thought I was better than those guys. I thought I had my shit figured out. But clearly, I'm no better. I just haven't met a girl that made me want to do dumb things in a long, long time.

I laid her thong across my abs. Just looking at that black lace lying atop my chiseled muscle made last night come rushing back. I could still taste the juicy heat of her lips against mine. I could feel the small weight of her tits, bouncing and jiggling in my palm. I could hear her screams of orgasm as I licked and sucked at her sweet, sweltering pussy.

Damn.

I slipped my pants and boxers off. My cock eagerly inched up my navel as if it were reaching for Brynn's thong.

I closed my eyes and started to tug.

Brynn. She was all I could see, all I could hear, all I could taste.

It didn't take long.

"Ungghh!" I groaned.

I opened my eyes and looked down. Brynn's thong was drizzled with thick white lines. Cum was painted in streaks up and down my abs and chest.

A guilty lump swelled in my throat. *Damn. I'm sick. What the hell got into me?*

I pulled out my cell phone and took a picture. Yeah, the scene was kinda hot, but it was incriminating as hell to snap that picture. I didn't know why I was so compelled to take the picture, except a feeling that I ought to document my crimes. Maybe so next time I got all high and mighty about my teammates' transgressions, I could look at it and remind myself the kind of guy I was, too.

After I cleaned up and the shame went away, I called Chloe to let her know I made it in safe. She didn't answer.

I called Brynn next. My heart raced while the phone rang, but she didn't answer, either.

Huh. Great. Guess I'm getting the silent treatment from both girls.

24

BRYNN

When I woke, Shea was still home and busily moving about the house. But after last night's events, I was too ashamed and embarrassed to see or talk to him. I waited until I heard his Bentley leave the driveway before I emerged from my bedroom.

I found Chloe at the kitchen table, poking around on her iPad with buds plugged into her ears.

"Morning, Chloe."

She didn't answer. I tapped her shoulder and she pulled the headphones out.

"What?" she asked with that infamous teen attitude.

Shea was right. She was mad.

"I said, good morning."

"Oh. Okay. Morning."

"How are you doing?" I asked.

"Pretty crummy. I slept like crap since I was up so late crying."

I frowned and set my hand on her shoulder. "Chloe, I'm so sorry to hear that—"

"I bet," she said as she shoved the earbuds back into her ears.

"Hey, wait, do you want any breakfast? I'm about to cook."

"Dad already cooked breakfast since you weren't up. There should be a plate in there for you."

"Okay."

In the fridge, there was a plate covered with plastic wrap. A note was stuck to the top of it.

"Brynn, Sorry for leaving without saying bye. I didn't want to wake you. Thanks again for staying with Chloe. Hope you enjoy breakfast—but be warned, I'm not a good cook like you are! Shea."

I wondered if this false pretense that everything was fine and dandy was our new normal. Were we supposed to just forget about the things we'd done last night? It was impossible, of course—if either one of us thought that things would ever be normal again, we were in for a rude awakening.

I crumpled the note with the plastic wrap and tossed them both in the trash. I sat across from Chloe and ate my breakfast in silence while she tapped away at her iPad in her own little world. She wouldn't even look up at me. I knew she was mad, but I wasn't going to grovel for forgiveness. When she was ready to talk, we could talk.

I'd finished my meal and was about to leave the table when Chloe caught my eyes and smirked.

"When I asked how the gala went, you didn't tell me about *this.*" She spun her iPad around to show me the screen. Someone on Twitter had shared a photo of Shea and I, gala king and queen, during our slow dance.

I forced a smile. "That's because it's not really a big deal."

"Huh." Chloe examined the picture closer herself. "You sure? You look pretty happy. So does Dad. And you guys are dancing pretty close for being 'just friends.' "

"Chloe ..." I groaned. I didn't know what to say. I *really* didn't want to go through this again—especially now that Chloe's suspicions had come true. I couldn't act oblivious anymore.

"What?" Chloe asked. "What's wrong, Brynn? Are you going to run off and tell my dad that I'm getting my hopes up again?"

I smiled and bobbed my head. "Ah-ha. Okay. There it is. Let's talk this through, Chloe."

She stamped her foot under the table. "I can't believe you told him all that! Do you know what he wants to do now? Send me to *therapy*. All because you told him that I thought you guys were flirting with each other." She pointed at her iPad screen again, with the damning picture of Shea and I staring into each other's eyes. "When you *clearly* have a thing for each other. So, that's cool. Send me to the loony bin because *you're* the ones living in denial. Thanks a lot, guys. I really appreciate it."

Chloe could be so dramatic sometimes, it was hard not to laugh—but that only incensed her more.

"Why are you laughing?!" she yelled.

"Because therapy isn't a *loony bin,* Chloe. Lots of perfectly normal people go to therapy. Talking to a trained professional about your problems *can* help, whether you've got big problems or tiny ones. Look, I went to therapy for years, so I know first-hand how much it can help."

Her anger was displaced by a sudden curiosity. "You did? What'd you have to go to therapy for?"

"My divorce, for one. Also for my body image issues, and the damage I did to my health because of it. And it helped me a lot."

"Oh. So in other words, *you* want to send me to therapy, too."

"I've never given it any thought, Chloe. I understand it could be a scary thought for you, but I really don't think therapy could hurt. It can only help to have someone to talk to about what's on your mind."

"So wait, is it good or bad to talk to people? I can't keep it straight anymore. Because I talked to *you*, didn't I? I told you that I thought you and my dad have a thing for each other. And then I got in trouble, because you told my dad. Which is super messed up, because all I'm doing is telling the *truth,* and *you* two are the ones who can't stop lying, either to me or yourselves."

I took a deep breath, turning her words over in my head. *Hate to say it, but she kinda has a point. What's worse, I can't even tell her that she's right.*

"First of all, Chloe, you're not in trouble. Second, I told your dad because I was worried. Your dad and I, we *can't* be together—"

"Why not?" she interjected before I could finish my thought.

"Because," I sputtered. "I'm just your nanny."

"But if you and my dad liked each other, you could stop being my nanny and maybe be my step-mom or something."

My heart shattered. I reached over the table and held her hand. "Chloe, that's very sweet of you, but you're getting too invested in this idea of your dad and I being something we're not. That's why I was worried, and that's why I told your dad. Maybe he's right. Maybe it *would* be a good idea for you to talk to someone about this."

"Great. I knew it. You *do* want to send me to therapy." She rolled her eyes. "All I want is for everyone to be happy. I guess that's what makes me so fucked up in the head, huh?"

I squeezed her hand. "Can I ask you something?"

"Might as well. Everyone wants me to talk about all my problems, right?"

"Yesterday, you said something about how, if your dad and I got together, it'd make up for something you did to him."

Chloe gulped loudly and nodded. "Yeh."

"What did you mean by that?"

"The divorce," she murmured.

"What about the divorce?"

"It was all my fault."

I shook my head. "I don't know much about your mom and dad's relationship, but I seriously doubt that."

"It's true. You know how I know?"

I shook my head. "No. Tell me."

"It's kind of a long story."

"I don't have anywhere else to be."

"Okay. So, one of Dad's teammates—his name was Ben Parker, but everyone called him Buddy—had a daughter, Carly. She's the same age as me. We were six when we first met. We also went to the same school, so she became my first real best friend."

"Okay ..."

"Now, Carly's parents were split up, and they shared custody of her. So, at games, Carly and her nanny would sit with me and my mom, and we'd watch our dads play hockey. It was great, 'cause I always got to see Carly—since our dads were teammates, they obviously got along and had a lot to talk about. Carly and Buddy would come over for dinner at our house, or we'd be at their house, almost every other night."

"Uh-huh."

"But one year, Buddy had some bad injury problems and he missed most of the season. So he wasn't traveling with the team for months. So, while my dad was out on the road, Mom would take me and the twins over to the Parkers' house and we'd all watch the game. My mom and Buddy really got along, too. Carly and I would play together, and the twins would tag along with us—and Mom and Buddy would hang out with each other."

I was starting to see where this was going.

"I never thought anything about it. Okay, I might have thought it was a little strange, because Carly and I would be playing together, and then my mom and Buddy just sort of disappeared together, and we were left all alone and had to watch over the twins. Which yeah, was sort of weird, because normally adults were always somewhere nearby to make sure we didn't get into any trouble or whatever. But we were only six or seven; what did we know? You never think that your parents could be up to anything bad."

"Oh, Chloe."

"But then, one day at school, I saw Carly and she was so excited she couldn't stop jumping up and down. She told me that *my* mom liked *her* dad, and that meant we were going to be sisters someday soon."

My jaw dropped.

"And I might not have totally understood what that meant, but on some level, I *knew* it wasn't right. I liked Carly a lot—but I didn't want her to be my sister, because *what about my dad?* Where was he going to go? I didn't want Buddy to be my dad—I wanted *Dad* to be Dad!"

"So ... what happened?"

"As soon as I got home from school, I told Dad what Carly told me. And then the fights started. They yelled and screamed at each other for days. It was awful. And then Mom moved out of the house, Dad hired our first nanny, and that was it. They got a divorce."

"Oh, Chloe. So did your mom and Buddy date after that?"

She tutted. "No. After I told Dad, Dad must've told the team, because Buddy suddenly got traded to Calgary. So my parents got divorced and, on top of it, my best friend moved away. And my mom was pissed at me because I 'betrayed her trust.' She still brings it up today, how she can't trust me."

I stood, walked around the table, wrapped my arms around Chloe and squeezed her for what must have been minutes without knowing what to say.

"I'm so sorry, Chloe," I said at last. "I totally understand why you'd feel guilty, but that is *not* your fault. It sounds like your mom and dad had serious problems. Once those problems reached *you*, their relationship hit a breaking point."

"But I never wanted to break them up." Her voice wavered. "I wanted them to stay together!"

I hugged her tighter. "You're a sweet girl, Chloe. You did the right thing. There was nothing else you could do. It's not your fault."

"Yeh ..." She wiped her tears away and looked at me. "Did my dad talk to you about that photo?"

"Yes, last night."

She frowned. "I'm so sorry I told him. I don't know what came over me. I thought he knew, and he was telling me everything that *you* told him, and—"

I put her head against my chest and soothed her. "It's okay, Chloe. I'm not mad. It's better to have the truth out there."

"What did he say when you told him?"

"He wondered why I hadn't told him earlier."

"And what did you say?"

"That I didn't think it mattered. Because I'm not here as a thirteen-year-old girl with a stupid crush on a hockey player. I'm here to do my job—to be a nanny."

She deflated in my arms. "Yeh ..."

I kissed her on top of her head. "I know you want your dad to be happy, Chloe. He'll find someone someday. He'll have a lot of time to date around once he's retired. And that's coming up real soon, too."

"But I don't *want* him to date around. I want him to date y—"

"Shh. I know. But it just can't be like that, Chloe."

———

Our emotional bloodletting seemed to take a tremendous weight off of Chloe's shoulders. After our talk, she took a shower and got dressed. Her friends came over, including her crush,

Adam, and the group went to the mall together. It was nice to see her smile again, and talk and laugh with her friends.

I wished I could say our talk revivified my spirits as well—but I felt worn down instead. It was exhausting to lie. To pretend with a straight face that Shea and I *didn't* have a thing for each other. To act as though I was merely his employee and nothing more, and nothing ever made me so happy than that.

Whereas Chloe could tell the truth and feel a million pounds lighter, I had to lie for her sake. Because telling her the truth would only screw with her head. So instead, I had to screw with my own head. But maybe that was the burden of being an adult.

Sigh.

Rather than sit around an empty mansion moping about how confusing my life was, I put myself to work.

That's what I'm here for after all, right?

I went from room to room, gathering up all the laundry, and threw it in the wash.

Hours passed as I folded the Ellis family clothes, deep in thought.

Cynthia sounds like a real bitch.

She should be groveling for Chloe's forgiveness—not suggesting that Chloe somehow *betrayed* her for telling her dad the truth. It was no wonder that Chloe still had issues over it. Her mother was holding her as an emotional hostage over their divorce.

Shea's right; Chloe probably should be in therapy.

She was obviously dealing with a lot. A lot more than any fourteen-year-old girl should have to deal with. Once Chloe got over the fear of being in therapy, it'd turn out to be a really good thing for her.

Chloe wants us to be together—and just getting a mere whiff of me and Shea's mutual attraction made all her old wounds resurface.

I could only imagine how much worse it'd be for her if she knew the truth—that she was right and, in fact, her dad and I had already fooled around.

Hell, she nearly caught us last night.

At what point are we gaslighting this poor girl and making her problems worse?

Unless, of course, Shea and I manage to keep it strictly professional.

Like he wants.

I finished folding the laundry and returned the sorted, organized stacks to everyone's bedrooms.

But when I got to putting *my* clothes away last, I realized something was missing.

My thong from last night.

I looked all over my bedroom for it—under the bed, in the trash, lost somewhere in the bed sheets, *anywhere* Shea could've thrown it.

But I just couldn't find it. And I had a funny feeling it wasn't exactly missing.

Really, Shea?

I sat on my bed and shook my head with a sigh.

Who do we think we're fooling?

This isn't going to work out.

25

SHEA

The next day.

Last night, Ilya and Brooksy managed to lure the entire team out to dinner—and afterward, to the bar.

"A hair of the dog that bit ya, that's all," Brooksy told us.

I had to admit—a beer sounded decent. But while I kept it limited to a beer, some of the other guys on the team got carried away. And Coach caught wind of our activities when a few guys staggered back to the hotel wasted, worse yet, after curfew.

Coach, of course, wasn't pleased.

During the next day's practice, Coach exacted his revenge on the *Boston Boozehounds* with a grueling, hours-long practice. Drills, drills, drills, until our stomachs were weak and flighty. Line rushes until our legs were weak and trembling. Scrimmage until lunch came and went and no one had any gas left in the tank.

"Hustle. Hustle! Harder, damn it!" Coach barked at us, never satisfied with our effort.

I started to wonder if Coach was *ever* going to put an end to this madness, or if his plan was to skate us to death.

"You're looking awfully pale today, Brooksy! What's the

matter, gentlemen? I thought a little 'hair of the dog' was supposed to do us wonders? I thought we were supposed to be feeling great today?"

After hours of torture, the moment finally came when Coach had seen enough, and he blew his whistle and told us to hit the showers. We practically crawled off the ice to the dressing room.

Coach strutted into the room last. He paced around the room, staring us down, letting us marinate in the physical pain before he delivered his final sermon. No one dared meet his angry gaze; it'd be like trying to stare down a pit bull. Instead, we sat in terse silence and studied the floor as we struggled to peel the sweat-drenched pads off our bodies.

"If you're going to hurt the day after," Coach finally snarled at the team, "I want you to hurt because of *hockey*. Not because you're out late drinking."

Everyone nodded, the lesson learned.

"Time to get serious, boys. Curfew's at six tonight."

"Six!" Brooks protested.

Coach whipped around to face him. "You got a problem with that, Brooksy? You wanna sit Game 1?"

"No," Brooks weakly grumbled in surrender.

"Didn't think so."

Back at the hotel hours later, I tried reaching the girls again. Brynn didn't answer her phone. Chloe didn't answer either, but she did send a quick follow-up text message.

"Hi Dad, what's up? I'm with friends, I can't talk right now."

"You can text but you can't talk?"

"I guess I can talk if you really need to, but we're just about to sit down and eat dinner with Nicole's family."

"I just want to make sure everything's going good with you and Brynn."

"Everything's fine, thanks Dad, love you."

I grumbled.

I tried calling Brynn one last time before I called it a night.

This time, she answered. "Hello?"

I couldn't believe it had only been a day since I heard her voice. Having her in my ear again made my heart skip a beat and brought a smile to my face.

"Brynn," I said.

"Hi, Shea. You sound surprised."

"I am. I haven't been able to get a hold of you all day yesterday or today." I paused. "Started to wonder if you were mad at me."

"Sorry. I'm not mad. I've just been busy."

"That's okay. How's everything with you and Chloe?"

"It's going well. We worked things out over breakfast yesterday, so everything's fine now. Today, she did photography in the park with Nicole. As for me, same ol', nothin' new. How are you?"

"Beat," I said with a yawn. "Coach is furious with us because a few of the guys broke curfew last night and came back wasted. He really rode us hard today during practice."

"Oh," she said, with a distinct lack of interest in her voice.

"But I guess I won't bore you with my war stories," I said, a touch defensively.

"Oh, okay," she said without much concern.

I frowned. I didn't want her to be cold towards me. I wanted things to be normal. You know, normal, where we'd talk to each other about our days, and our conversations were always fun and playful ... *and maybe a little flirtatious, too?*

"Is something wrong, Brynn?" I blurted out.

She went silent for a moment or two. "We can't keep doing this."

"Doing what?" I chuckled. "I just called you to get an update, that's all."

"And I gave it to you. But you want something more from me —friendship, companionship, someone to tell your day to. And I don't blame you for wanting that, but I can't be that person for you, Shea. I'm just your nanny, and we're supposed to be strictly professional, remember?"

"Oh. Okay," I said dryly. "Yeah, if that's how you want it."

She didn't reply.

I thought I'd hold her feet to the fire and see if that was what she *really* wanted. "In that case," I began in my very own cold and sterile voice, "thanks again for watching Chloe, and I'll see you in a few days when I get back from Tampa."

"Wait. Shea."

I smiled smugly, victoriously. I *knew* she'd change her mind once she saw I could be stern and serious, too. "Yes?"

"Do you remember where you put my thong? I've been looking all over for it, but I can't find it."

Oof. That wasn't what I was expecting.

"Have you looked under the bed?" I asked as I stood and slowly made my way to the bathroom.

"Yes, I've looked everywhere for it. I can't find it. It's not a big deal, I just don't want it laying around the house somewhere."

Guiltily, I opened the bathroom door and spied the lacy intimates. After I'd nutted on her thong, I'd washed it in the sink and hung it on the towel rack to dry.

"Weird," I said, lying through my teeth. "I don't remember where I put it."

"Okay. Just thought I'd ask. If you do remember, let me know."

"Will do."

I hung up my phone, grabbed the TV remote, and started flipping through a thousand dumb channels on the big screen TV, feeling like the world's biggest liar.

If that was how Brynn wanted things—then fine.

It's not how she wants it, genius. It's how you *told her you want it.*

I sighed.

I was only days away from the playoffs—the *last* playoffs I'd ever play in, my one last shot at the Cup—and I wasn't feeling it at all.

This sucks.

26

BRYNN

I *can hear it in his voice. He's lying.*

That was the first thing that crossed my mind when I asked Shea if he knew where my thong was, and he stammered and told me to check under the bed.

The second thing that crossed my mind was, *Ew! If he's lying, what could he possibly have done with my panties?*

I probably didn't even *want* to know the answer to that question. Men sure are weird, disgusting animals sometimes.

Shea's guilty status was further confirmed over the following days, when he didn't even bother to call in and check on me. I figured it was also my punishment for refusing to stay up chatting on the phone with him for hours, giggling at all his stories, like we were a high school couple.

Fine. Act like a childish dick, Shea. You're only proving my point.

At least he still called Chloe every night to stay in touch. If he hadn't done that, I would've been forced to *drastically* rethink my opinion of him as a generally good guy.

Chloe and I had a fine few days to ourselves with none of the boys around. She got to spend plenty of time with her friends on the weekend. And when it was just us, I took her out to the city and we pampered ourselves with some girly things—we went shopping for new clothes, got our nails done, had a fancy brunch, and went to the movies, too.

For the first playoff game, we made a big bowl of popcorn and goofed around in the den. We didn't pay too much attention to the game, but every time we *did* look at the TV, things seemed to go from bad to worse for Boston.

As the broadcast announcers put it, the Brawlers were getting 'stomped.'

"Oh wow," Chloe said, looking up at the TV. "Tampa scored again since the last time I looked."

"Yikes. Six to one."

The camera zoomed in on a surly Shea, who angrily shoved a Tampa player to the ice and looked for someone to fight with. The ref blew his whistle, grabbed Shea by the arm, and skated him over to the penalty box.

"Yikes. Dad doesn't look very happy."

"No, he certainly doesn't."

———

Hours after Game 1, late at night, my phone rang. It was Shea. I shut my bedroom door and answered.

"Hi."

"Brynn," he said, sounding somewhat strained. "How are things at the house?"

"Everything's going fine. Chloe and I had the game on TV earlier."

"Awful," he said. "I don't want to talk about the game."

It wasn't unusual for Shea to be impatient after a bad loss— but now he seemed even more testy, because the team had blown an important game.

"Okay. Is there something you do want to talk about?" I asked.

"Yeah."

"And what's that?"

"I don't like the way things are between us right now," he said, sounding a little incensed.

I guess he had to get that off his chest after the Brawlers' embarrassing loss.

Still, I didn't know what to say. "Oh ... okay?"

"See? That, right there. Stop it. You're being short with me and it's fucking my head up."

I guess that makes three of us.

I sighed. "We've talked about this, Shea."

"You're doing it to punish me."

I chuffed. "No, actually, I'm not. And I resent you saying that, honestly."

"Then why are you doing it?"

"To protect your daughter."

"What does Chloe have to do with this?"

"The other night, she told me about Buddy and Carly Parker."

"Oh." I could hear Shea recoil over the phone. "She told you about the affair, then?"

"Yes. And she told me that she was the first person to find out about it."

"Eh." Shea grumbled. "Yes and no."

"Wait—are you saying that you knew your wife was having an affair?"

"Why do you care? I thought you didn't want to be my phone pal."

I rolled my eyes. I was starting to see where Chloe had gotten some of her flair for the dramatic.

"Stop it. You can either tell me or not, but don't act like a vengeful dick."

Shea huffed. "I just don't know why you'd care."

"I care because whatever happened obviously affected you and Chloe both. And I'm just trying to understand."

Shea had no response. His end went silent.

I spoke into the void. "Hello? You there?"

"I didn't know about her thing with Buddy until Chloe told me," he said at last. "But it wasn't her first affair, so it didn't exactly come as a surprise."

"I'm sorry," I said. "Why'd you stay with her?"

"Because Chloe was just born. And we'd just gotten married. Everything happened so fast—we met, she got pregnant, we had a shotgun marriage, then Chloe was born, and then my teammate came clean to me."

"Wait, you mean she cheated on you with *another* teammate? Before Buddy?"

"Yup. When I met Cynthia, she told me she was my biggest fan. Thing she never told me was that she was a big fan of all my other teammates, too."

"Wow. I don't know what to say—that's just awful."

"Cynthia begged me to stay. She said it'd never happen again. And she swore she only cheated because she was lonely with how much time I spent on the road—but that didn't really explain why she'd cheat on me with my D partner. It's not like he was around any more than I was, after all."

"What a bitch. I think I hate her."

"I wasn't exactly a perfect husband myself. I wasn't around as much as I should've been. Even when the team was in Boston, I'd rather hang out and party with the boys. It's why I always pushed Lance and Radar so hard to grow up the past couple years. It's why I want them to be good men, good husbands, good fathers."

"Does Chloe know there was another affair?"

"No."

"Maybe she *should*. It might make her feel a lot less guilty."

"No way." He thought it over, then sighed. "I don't know. Maybe you're right. I always worried it could cause more problems, though."

"For who?"

"Chloe and her mom." He lowered his sad voice. "Or the twins."

"Why the twins?"

Shea threw up a wall. "Doesn't matter. Why do you keep asking me all these questions, anyway? Haven't I told you enough?"

"Don't act like that, Shea. I want to talk to you, okay? But I can't right now. I can't do it without conflicting feelings getting in the way. I'm so confused. On one hand, I like you. On the other hand, I love working for you, I love your kids, I love the way I fit in so perfectly in this household and feel so needed and respected. I love everything about being here."

"And we love having you," he said, vulnerably.

"And you know what makes that even worse? I feel the same way. Because that just makes me like you more. Which is a problem," I said, lowering my voice to a whisper, "because Chloe can *sense* that. For two months, I did a pretty damn good job of lying to myself about it. But now, things are different, because we've fooled around. We can't continue on in blissful ignorance anymore. And I'm telling you, Chloe can tell that we're lying to her. And you know what? She's right to be mad. I'd be mad about it, too. I'm starting to feel like we're gaslighting her."

Shea let out a long, tired sigh. "I know. It's fucked up. There's no easy way out."

"There *is* an easy way out, actually," I said.

"What's that?"

"I want to quit, Shea."

His end went silent again.

"What?" he finally blurted out. "You're not serious, are you?"

"I'll start interviewing my replacement immediately. I can't do this anymore. With the tension between us, and Chloe's guilt, and the fact that we've fooled around? It's too much to continue on, Shea. Things are too complicated, too fragile, too weird."

"Brynn. No. C'mon. I'll give you a raise. How much am I paying you right now? Two grand a week? Make it three."

"You don't get it. It's not about money."

"C'mon, Brynn. What's it going to take? Four grand?"

I huffed. "Go ahead. Keep throwing more money at me. You're only making me *more* mad and certain that leaving is the right thing."

"But Brynn, I don't want another nanny. You said it yourself, you fit in with us so perfectly. You can't go. I want you—"

"Yeah, you want me. But do you want me as your nanny or something else? I can't be both. I can't do my job if this *thing* is always lingering between us. And I can't keep having this same conversation, either." I sighed. "I'm hanging up now, Shea. Goodbye."

"Wait—Brynn! Wait!"

I hung up and powered my phone off.

27

SHEA

Game 1 was bad.

Before Game 2, the Brawlers held this big dressing room pep rally about how our play in Game 1 was unacceptable, how we all had to step up and be better, how we had to look around the room and hold each other accountable. Above everything else, we had to come out tonight determined to make a statement: that Game 1 was a fluke and we were still capable of winning this series.

I gave a pre-game speech of my own about how this roster needed to be better from top to bottom. During my speech, I wondered if my teammates could tell that my head wasn't in hockey at all—it was pondering the Brynn-sized hole that was left in my heart.

What am I gonna do without her?

I can't just let her go. But she won't stay. She turned down four grand a week.

Hell, she won't even answer her phone!

Whatever the cause, the Brawlers came out flat in Game 2. We failed to score a single goal. When the final horn sounded, we left the ice staring at our skates. We were too embarrassed to look up and see 7-0 on the scoreboard. Too ashamed to acknowledge Tampa's ecstatic fans, who taunted at us as we left the ice, yelling, "*Sweep! Sweep!*"

Tampa's fans had every reason to believe that they wouldn't lose a single game and sweep this series, after all. And we sure looked like a team that knew it'd never climb out of the hole it just dug itself.

"Pitiful," Coach said as he entered the dressing room. "Dumb. Lousy effort. Every last one of you. What's our excuse tonight, boys? We're down 2-0 in the series now. Lose two more and we're out. Each and every one of you needs to take a deep, long look at yourselves and realize that this isn't acceptable. Wake the fuck up, boys, before it's too late."

Coach headed for the door but stopped in front of me. "Is this really how you want your career to end, Ellis? This how you planned to go out? Not on top, but with a pathetic whimper?"

"No," I answered, but even I could tell that there was no strength, no meaning, no *spirit* in my voice.

"Then you better find your balls—wherever the hell you put 'em—and lead your team again, Ellis. They need you." He poked his finger into my sternum. "*Lead.*"

Coach addressed the room. "Don't be late for the flight."

Then he was gone.

The room was silent as we stripped off our gear. Everyone stewed in misery, all mired in our own personal hells.

Lead? I wondered.

How was I supposed to lead these men when my own life was a wreck?

This *was* how my career was going to end: not with a victory lap, but with a pathetic whimper.

There wasn't a peep in the showers—no jokes, no laughs, no

singing. We all had the sense that this series was already over before it'd even begun.

No one dared to talk as we dressed, either. We boarded our bus and headed off to the airport for our midnight flight back to Boston.

But something funny started to happen.

In the airport, while we waited to board our plane, I started thinking about what to do—and I started to have a glimmer of hope. And the more I thought about that glimmer of hope, the more certain it seemed, and the wider I started smiling.

I boarded the plane smiling from ear to ear, while my sullen teammates stared at me like I had a second head sprouting from my shoulder.

"The hell are you so happy about, Boomer?" Brooksy grumbled. "Can't you look like your dog just died, like everyone else?"

"Boomer's thinking about the nanny again," Ilya joked, but without much gusto, and without the usual laugh track backing him up.

"Ilya's right, actually," I said. "I am thinking about the nanny."

I waited for the outraged hoots and hollers, but still they didn't come.

"Ah, cheer up, you miserable bastards," I said, addressing the team at the front of the plane. "So we dropped the first two games. Yeah, we fucked up, we already know that. Time to stop beating ourselves up over it. The truth is, now we got 'em right where we want 'em."

"Leading us 2-0 in the series is right where we want them?" Brooks asked cynically.

"They think it's already over, so their guard is going to be down, boys. All we have to do is surprise them, and we'll have them on their heels. And we know we can play better hockey than we have these past two games. Listen, I've got a plan, alright? We're going to win our two games at home, Brynn's going to stay, and everything's going to be fine."

Over the idle hum of jet engines, I heard my teammates confused murmurings.

"Anyone know what he's talking about?"

28

BRYNN

Hours after the Brawlers were massacred in Game 2, I got a message from Shea.

"Plane just landed in Boston. On my way home now. What are you up to?"

"Watching a movie in the den with Chloe."

"Have you told her that you're leaving yet?"

"No."

"Perfect. See you two soon."

I stared at that last message and wondered, was he plotting something?

"Who are you texting?" Chloe asked.

"Nobody," I lied, stuffing my phone away.

Chloe gave me a look. "Really, Brynn? *Nobody?* Even though I can hear your phone receiving text messages?"

I chuckled. "Okay, yes, it's your dad. He told me he's on his way home."

"See? Honesty. It's not that hard."

"I just didn't want to get your hopes up."

"Did you ever stop to think that acting *strange* is what got my hopes up in the first place?"

"Oh, you." I smiled and patted Chloe on the head.

You're too smart for your own good, child.

With the news that I would be leaving the family soon, I felt like I was carrying around a ticking time bomb. I knew it'd be a sad scene, and I figured it'd be easier to tell Chloe if Shea was there to help. Plus, I wasn't sure *when* I was leaving—either immediately after I found a suitable replacement, or once the playoffs were over. I didn't want Shea to have to worry about a new nanny when he was playing the most important games of his career.

As long as Shea could *promise* to keep things as normal and professional as possible between us—and that meant no weird phone calls or texts, definitely no touching or kissing, etc.—then I'd stick around until the playoffs were over.

But if he couldn't keep good on that promise? I'd be out the door as soon as possible.

Not much later, there was a sudden mechanical groaning as the garage door began to open its maw.

"There's your father," I said to Chloe.

She gritted her teeth. "Think I should run upstairs and go to bed before I see him?"

"Chloe! Why would you do that? You haven't seen him for days."

The purr of the athlete's Bentley grew louder as he pulled into the garage.

"Because the Brawlers *blew* during those two games in Tampa. And you know how he gets when they lose an important game. I bet he's in a real shit mood."

I frowned. "You're right."

We heard the sound of his car door open and slam shut.

"See?" Chloe jumped off the couch, ready to sprint for her bedroom. "I'm outta here. Tell him I went to bed."

But I grabbed her arm and pulled her back onto the couch.

"Wait, Chloe. You really should say hi to your father."

"Fiiiine."

The door opened, and the tall hockey player stepped in. But when I saw his smile—and what he tried (and failed) to hide behind his back—I found myself wishing I'd let Chloe run off after all.

———

"*Dad!*" Chloe squealed, beaming with delight. "Who are those for?!"

"Hi girls!" Shea said, an enormous bouquet of red roses clearly visible, no matter how much he tried to keep them hidden behind his wide frame.

I folded my arms and gave Shea the death stare. *Yes, Shea, who are those for? Because I know they're not for me. Those are for* anyone *but me.*

Sure, they were beautiful, but ... c'mon. After everything? Really? Was his plan *seriously* to make an even bigger and more confusing show about our—er—whatever it was?

Shea neared, his eyes on me.

No no no no.

He held the bouquet out to me. "They're for Brynn, of course."

"*Yessssss!*" Chloe hissed and pumped her fist.

"Shea," I said, straining. "You shouldn't have."

Like, really shouldn't have, ever.

Chloe continued her victory dance. "That's so sweet, Dad! Good job! Good going!"

Giving Shea the stink eye, I begrudgingly took the bouquet from his hand. *See how worked up you've made your daughter? Was this really supposed to impress me?*

"Well, they are gorgeous," I muttered as I immediately slid

off the couch and began the search for a vase large enough to hold all four or five dozen roses.

Meanwhile, Shea sat on the couch next to his daughter. "How was your week, sweetheart? I missed you."

She leaned her head on his shoulder. "I missed you too, Dad. My week was good. I'm sorry your games didn't go so well."

I kept an eye and an ear trained on those two while I arranged the roses in a vase.

"Hey, it's okay. It's not over just yet. What's that sage piece of advice I'm always telling you?"

Chloe quoted him with a disaffected teen groan. "'*Play to the whistle.*'"

"That's right." He bopped her on the shoulder. "Hey, it's pretty late, kiddo. Why don't you run upstairs and get ready for bed?"

"Okay." Chloe jumped off the couch and ran upstairs, but not before giving me a giant, exaggerated wink.

Ugh.

When it was just the two of us alone in the den, I quietly reprimanded him. "Are you *insane?*"

He smiled. "Maybe."

"It's not funny! Why are you smiling? Did you think roses would change my mind about quitting?" I pointed angrily at the bouquet on the table. "Did you even stop to think how badly those damn things would screw with your daughter's head?"

"Don't worry. I'm going to talk to her in a few minutes."

"And tell her *what,* exactly?"

"I'm going to tell her the truth, which is what she deserves to know."

I slapped my forehead. "And what exactly *is* the truth, in this case? At this point, I can't keep track of what we're telling her anymore. Or each other, for that matter."

"Hey, take it easy."

He neared and tried to grab my hand, but I snatched it away.

"I'm only going to tell her that she was right—that I did have a secret crush on you all along. That she noticed it even before you did. Which is all true, by the way."

"*Risky,*" I said, a stern finger in his face. "Very risky to tell her something like that. You'll only get her hopes up."

Shea began to pace back and forth. "Unfortunately, because of my unprofessional crush on you, you can't continue to be our nanny anymore."

"She'll be crushed when you tell her that," I said, shaking my head.

"She'll be crushed when you tell her you're leaving regardless. At least this way, Chloe understands there's a *reason* behind you leaving, rather than being told that she's too young to understand why it didn't work out with a nanny who is otherwise a perfect fit. She already suspects we're pulling the wool over her eyes—she'll just hate us both when we break her heart and expect her to believe even more lies. This way, if anyone has to be the bad guy over you leaving, it'll be dumb ol' Dad with his hopeless, but totally understandable, crush."

I grumbled. He had a point. "Okay, what else? Or is that the extent of your big master plan?"

"There is more, actually." He lowered his voice. "I'm going to let Chloe in on a little secret: that I brought you those roses because I'm going to ask you out on a *real* date."

"*Shea!*" I protested. "*No!*"

"—but don't get your hopes up too much, 'Chloe,' because I have no idea how Brynn feels about going out on a date with me in the first place."

"*Obviously,* she'll think that I'm going to leap at the chance for a date with you, because of that stupid picture of me standing in front of your kiss-covered poster."

Shea broke into a cocky grin. "Well, yeah, I was kinda banking on that same thing, too."

I tutted. I wanted to stay mad at him, but he was slowly starting to win me over. "Do you really think that's going to work? And not just create an even bigger drama bomb for us both?"

"I don't see any other way out of this, Brynn. Do you? It's the closest thing to the truth that I can tell her. And yes, after hearing that she's still feeling mixed up about the divorce, of course I'm worried about her getting her hopes up for us—and that's why I'm *also* going to tell her that regardless of what happens between you and me, I really want her to start therapy."

I bobbed my head. "I think that's a really good idea."

"*Lastly,* I'm only telling her all of this because I think she's grown up and mature enough to handle it, and so I need her to promise that she won't tell the twins about Dad and Brynn. Or her mom, for that matter, because that'd only cause her trouble."

I mulled it over, trying to find a flaw in his plan. It wasn't perfect, no, but then again, nothing about this situation was perfect. Whichever path we took, things were going to get a little messy.

After thinking it through, I wasn't crazy about the idea, but I couldn't come up with any hard objections, either.

"I don't know what to say. If you think that this is the right thing to do, I won't stop you."

"It's the best I've got, Brynn. Look, the truth is, we fucked things up the other night. Bad. But now the cat's out of the bag, and we can't keep denying it to each other. Or to Chloe."

Hesitantly, I nodded. "Yeah."

"Sometimes, I wonder if maybe I should've kissed you that first night after all. Maybe then, we would've realized right away that we had something—and we could've tried dating instead?"

He shrugged. "Who knows, though. Maybe that kiss would've scared you off entirely and we'd have never seen you again."

I giggled. "Your face *was* kind of gnarly looking, with the stitches and the dried blood. You'd gotten into a fight that night, remember?"

He laughed. "Ah-ha. You would've pushed me away. I was right to wait, then."

"No," I said, surrendering to a smile. "I wanted to kiss you anyway. You really blew it."

"Figures," he groaned. "But that's why I want a clean start with you." He neared and took my hand. "Brynn, since your very first day, it's like you stepped into this house and filled a hole in *everyone's* heart. A hole that none of us even knew we had."

That was so sweet, I frowned.

"But now that you've filled it, I realize how much you mean to me, and I can't just let you go. You're so much more than a nanny, Brynn. And now I realize that I was a fuckin' idiot to think that I could keep you around as a nanny. A smart, sexy, hilarious nanny with a great butt that I've been secretly checking out since the very beginning—"

The captain put his massive hands on my waist and turned me to the side so he could steal a glance at my rear.

"*Shea!*" I wiggled away from him and gave him a harmless smack to the cheek.

"And I *also* realized, that's because of my own screwed-up brain. Because if you're *just* my nanny, you can't break my heart. I can keep you … forever … as long as I pay you so much money, you can't quit." He shook his head. "But that's not true, either. I'm sorry, Brynn."

He put his arms around my back and pulled me near. I ran my hands along his thick, muscled forearms.

"Think I'm fucked up in the head?" he asked, inching closer.

"Honestly?" I giggled. "Sorta."

Shea leaned in for a kiss, but I stopped him.

I shook my head. "No."

"Why not?"

"Technically, you haven't asked me out on a date first."

"Right." He broke away from me. "I better go talk to Chloe before she falls asleep."

"I'll be waiting here," I said, burying my nose in the silky roses.

And then, once I've told you my piece, we'll see if you still truly want to date me ...

29

SHEA

After I had the talk with Chloe and tucked her into bed, I went downstairs and found Brynn still waiting at the table.

"That's that," I said, dusting off my hands.

"How'd it go?"

"Good, I think." I held up my car keys and jangled them. "Want to take a quick ride with me to the store? Chloe said she's out of tampons. And apparently, every time I buy tampons, I come back with the kind she hates."

"She ran out?" Brynn's eyes filled with doubt. "I could've sworn I bought her a box just the other day."

"Maybe *you* bought the wrong kind, too?"

"No, I actually know what she likes." A look of concern spread across her face. "But do you really think it's okay to leave her home alone this late at night?"

"Yeah, that's what I was worried about, too. But she got all huffy and reminded me that we had *just* gotten done talking about how she's more mature now, and that her friends' parents all leave them home alone for days at a time, etc., etc. Oh, and if she doesn't have tampons before school tomorrow, she'll freak out all day and it'll all be my fault."

Brynn gave a laugh. "Sounds like her, alright. Sure, let's go."

We climbed into the Bentley, buckled up, and backed out of the driveway.

"So tell me how the talk went," Brynn said.

"It went fine. She felt—hm—I guess the word is *vindicated.*"

She patted my shoulder. "Oh, look at you. Hockey player with a vocab. Hot."

"Ha ha. Anyway. She got all excited at first, saying 'I knew it,' and 'I *told* Brynn, but she wouldn't believe it,' blah blah. I made it seem like you truly had no idea all along."

"Thanks," she said. "But how'd it go when you told her that you were *firing* me?"

"I'd say she was shocked and confused at first. But once I explained it to her, she seemed to understand. She ended up saying that it wasn't fair to expect you to be a nanny *and* a love interest at the same time. She even used the phrase, 'conflict of interest.' "

Brynn's eyes lit up, and she teasingly backhanded my pec. "Well, well! Ya hear that, Shea?"

"Ha," I grumbled, growing warm under the collar. "Yeah, she's a little faster on the uptake than her old man."

She smiled at me and gave my shoulder a squeeze. "I'm just teasing you."

"I know. I deserve it."

"How'd she react to being told you wanted her in therapy?"

"She wasn't wild about that, no. But after it was all said and done, she reluctantly agreed to give it a try. She said it might help with the problems she's been having with her mom."

"Very good. Very, very good." She patted my thigh. "Sounds like you did good."

We pulled up to a stop sign on Boylston. The car's turn

signal went *tik-tok-tik-tok* as I searched for a seam in the traffic. When a Bentley-sized pocket emerged, I stomped on the accelerator, and the car quietly growled as we charged up to speed without ever breaking a sweat.

Brynn stretched, running her hands over the taut leather of her seat, and gave a tiny but satisfied moan. "Have I ever told you how much I love this car?"

I chuckled. "No, actually, you haven't."

"Well, I do." Her hands glided over the pristine dash. "I feel so ridiculously fancy in this thing. Is it wrong to say a car feels *sexy?* It sounds wrong, but that's how it makes me feel."

"That's not wrong at all." I glanced at her, admiring her form. "But if you ask me, *you* make it look sexy."

She choked back a groan. "Oh, stop it, cheese ball."

"I'm serious—you do. And I always knew you'd like it, which was why I tried to give you a ride home in it after our interview."

She let loose with laughter. "I knew it. I *knew* it."

"You did?"

"Yes!"

I grinned. "What'd you think?"

"That you had some serious Dad-level game."

"Dad-level game?" I repeated. "What's that? Is that good or bad?"

She stifled an amused laugh. "Honestly? It's not quite either."

"I don't get it ..."

"Your attempts at flirting are sort of hopelessly lost, but also very cute and sort of endearing."

I grumbled. "Great."

Now I was *really* growing hot under the collar. I shifted in my seat, thinking to myself, *I never should've admitted that. She thinks I'm a klutz.*

She rubbed my shoulder. "Don't clam up on me now. Really, I think you're sweet."

"A sweet guy with hopeless Dad-game," I muttered.

"Yeah, but you stepped your Dad-game up big time when it mattered," she said with a sudden flirtatious note in her voice.

"Hm?" I glanced at her. Her eyes were small slits, sparkling and wild.

"In the cab, after the gala? Remember?"

I smiled. "Of course I remember."

"The way you put your big hands all over me? The way you just went for it and kissed me?" The cab grew silent, the air between us tense and charged. "God, just thinking about it makes me ... well ... you know."

Brynn crossed her legs and gave the quietest moan under her breath. Her sounds were irresistible to me—all I could think about was being between her legs. My cock began to thicken and inch down my thigh.

But we'd reached our destination, and I pulled into the parking lot.

"Aaaand, here we are." I killed the engine. "Target."

Brynn burst out laughing. "And *that,* Shea, is the ultimate in Dad-game."

I leaned over the center console and stole her full lips for a deep, but brief, kiss. I wanted to leave her wanting.

"I *am* pretty hopeless, aren't I?" I joked as I pulled away.

But she pulled me back in. "Don't go yet. Just one more kiss."

30

BRYNN

As we walked through the parking lot, Shea's hand reached for mine. It struck me as a move so natural, I wasn't sure he even knew he'd done it. I wasn't sure if it was *too early* to hold hands—my head was still *spinning* from the night's developments.

But I didn't point it out to him. I let go of my worries and gave him my hand. At least for tonight, I could stop wondering about what we were, or what the implications of this night were … and just let myself enjoy the moment with Shea instead.

Together, we walked into the store, hand-in-hand. The glossy vinyl floors reflected the blinding brightness of the overhead fluorescent lights. This late at night, there was an almost surreal, dream-like quality to our outing. Or maybe it was just the fact that here I was, in a random Boston Target, holding Shea Ellis's hand. I kept catching myself taking peeks at him, as if I didn't quite believe this were really *real*.

Instead of making a beeline straight to the feminine hygiene aisle—or the 'pink aisle,' as Shea called it—we wandered through the rest of the store's aisles instead. We stopped every few feet, pulling products from the shelves for a quick laugh, or to gab about home needs or gift ideas or the perfect piece of furniture. We could've talked for hours about whatever we came across and whatever came to mind. Every little thing in that store offered an opening to talk, to learn about each other, to lean closer together, to admire his radiant white smile and smell his manly scent and squeeze his hand and flirt.

It was sweet, it was light, it was fun. I could've spent hours there with him. But in the end, we finally found ourselves standing in the *pink aisle.*

"Okay, let's have a test," I said. "Tell me which one you think Chloe wants."

"Well. Hm. Let's see." Shea tapped his foot as he examined the wall of tampons. "The generic one. Super absorbent, right?"

"You make all that money, and you'd buy your daughter store brand?" I slapped at his shoulder. "I really hope you're kidding, Shea Ellis."

He laughed. "I am. But seriously, I don't have a clue which brand she prefers."

"Here. This is the brand she likes." I grabbed the box from the shelf—even though I *knew* Chloe didn't really need it—and handed it to him. "Forty in a box, light flow, unscented, applicator."

"How do you remember all that?" Shea asked as he tossed the box into his basket.

"It's not that much to remember at all," I said. "Though I will admit, I used the same tampon back when I used to—" I cut myself off before I accidentally said too much.

Shea raised an eyebrow. "Back when you used to ...?"

"I meant, back when I was her age," I croaked.

If Shea knew something was up, he didn't show it.

"You ready?" he asked.

"Yup."

We made our way to the registers.

In the checkout line, Shea kept me pressed against his side. I noticed a couple shoppers ahead of us kept turning around and staring at us. I wondered, did they recognize Shea? Did they think I was his girlfriend? Or were we merely a hopelessly attached couple, for whom a midnight run to Target was still a saccharine-sweet adventure, the sight of which nauseated the grizzled masses?

I guessed I'd never know. Unlike our interview at the cafe, no one ever approached Shea for an autograph.

Shea paid, and we made it back to his car.

"Well, thanks, Shea," I said as we buckled up. "That was one of the most fun and sweetest dates I've ever been on."

He looked at me like I was nuts. "I don't know what kind of dates *you're* used to, but that wasn't a date, Brynn. You really thought I was taking you out to Target and calling it a date? I mean, sure, I've got bad Dad-game, *ha ha,* I get it. But I don't think I'm *that* bad."

"No? You and Chloe didn't arrange this?"

He started to laugh. "No."

I didn't buy it. "Really, Shea. Good work. I applaud you and Chloe both for putting your heads together and finding a way to get us out of the house together. But I *know* I'm not crazy. I bought her a box of tampons this past Friday. I remember it clearly."

"You did?" Shea asked, his smile fading.

The wheels began to turn in both our heads at once.

"*Chloe,*" we muttered at the same time.

Shea turned the key and drove us home.

31

BRYNN

The only light left on in the house was the chandelier that hung above the dinner table, casting a romantic light on the vase of roses. Next to it, Chloe had set out a bottle of wine with two glasses. Romantic jazz played, a whisper over the speakers. Next to the wine stood a folded note. Shea hurried over, unfolded the note and began to read.

"What's it say?" I asked.

Shea read aloud. *"Hi Dad. Sorry to leave on such short notice. I made up with Mom and she came to pick me up. But I'll be back tomorrow with Nick and Cam. P.S. Don't worry, I won't tell anyone about our secret! I hope you and Brynn have a fun night to yourselves."*

"She played us," I laughed as I set the unneeded box of tampons to the table. "I don't even know what to say."

"Outfoxed by a fourteen-year-old." Shea turned to me. "Well ... should we have a glass of wine?"

"We're certainly supposed to."

He poured two glasses of wine and the two of us sat on the couch. I sipped my wine and laughed.

"What? What is it?" Shea asked.

Truth be told, it was the whole scene: the ease and convenience at which we found ourselves home alone, the sudden closeness as I curled up next to the athlete on the couch, the mood-setting music, the smoky wine ... it was almost too much.

"Are you *sure* you didn't plan this?" I asked.

"I swear, Brynn."

"So she did it all on her own," I mused, taking another sip of wine. "That daughter of yours? She's a smart one."

"Believe me, I know it. That's half the reason I've had problems with her. Too smart for her own good."

"I'm so glad she's willing to give therapy a try," I said. "That makes me feel a lot better."

"Yeah." Shea nodded. "She said that you were in therapy for years, and you recommended it."

"Oh. Yep. That's true." I downed the rest of my wine.

Should I tell him now?

Shea refilled my glass. "You're so steady, Brynn. I never would've imagined it."

"I guess therapy helped, then."

He smiled. "Good. I hope it helps Chloe."

Nervously, I fidgeted with my hands. I felt it building up inside me—it wanted to come out. Now was the time—before I'd allow myself to get my hopes up about Shea, I had to let him know. I had to give him the talk.

"Shea ..."

"Yeah?"

Here goes.

"Remember when I told you that the boys in high school never asked me to a dance because I was a mess?"

"Yeah."

"I had body image issues."

He gave a sympathetic frown. "I'm sorry to hear it. A lot of young girls suffer with that, don't they?"

"Yeah, but mine took a slightly different path. I feel like I should show you what I showed Chloe."

"You can show me whatever you're comfortable showing me."

I pulled out my phone and showed him the pictures from my mom's Facebook.

"Oh, Brynn, you poor thing," he said, a hand over his heart. "You were so thin."

"And yet I thought I was *so* healthy," I said, flipping through the pictures. "I worked out every day. Jogging, cardio, weights. Literally every day for years."

"That's why you became a personal trainer?"

"Yeah. I already spent hours at the gym, so why not make it my job?"

"So what happened?"

"I started having health problems when I was twenty. I started feeling weak all the time—my body was so tired, it didn't *want* to work out, it wanted a break. But I *couldn't* take a rest because I had to work out every day. In a weird way, I thought I was tired because I was at the peak of physical fitness, and staying there was hard work. So I forced myself to soldier on. Until funny things started to happen, like, my hair falling out."

He put his massive arm around me and squeezed me. "Oh, Brynn."

"And then I started having heart palpitations, which made me so scared to move or do anything that would get my heart rate going. I thought I was constantly on the verge of a heart attack."

"Damn," he murmured. "Was this happening while you were still married?"

"Yup. My husband, Michael, thought I was ridiculous. And even more ridiculous for not going to the doctor—but I didn't need the doctor because I was in such *great shape,* wink wink."

"Is that why you two got divorced?"

"Well, there's more to it than that ..." I trailed off.

I took a deep breath.

Just tell him.

"I got worse. It was hard to get out of bed. Some days I didn't. I started losing clients. Finally, Michael managed to talk me into going to the doctor. One of the things I told the doctor, that I hadn't told Michael, was that I'd stopped having my period. After a bunch of tests, I was told that I likely had hypothalamic amenorrhea."

Shea tilted his head at me. "You have what now?"

"That was my reaction, too. Basically, it's a condition where menstruation temporarily stops. What had I accomplished with all my working out and dieting? I'd starved and stressed my body to the point that it halted my reproductive system. I've been infertile ever since."

Shea's mouth fell open. "Oh, Brynn. I'm so sorry." He didn't know what else to say. Neither did I. "But you said it's temporary, right?"

"The doctors say that I *might* be able to have kids someday, but no one really knows. Usually, if you get your body back in order, menstruation begins again within a few months. I had to learn to eat and not hate my body. To be okay with having fat on my body. To not want to spend hours on the treadmill to jog it all off."

"Well, you seem like you're doing great," Shea said, his soft eyes locked on mine. "Not only are you a great person, but you have a lovely body, Brynn. Really. You're so feminine and womanly and beautiful."

I smiled at him. "Thank you. That means a lot, because I don't always feel that way." My smile faded. "Especially because I've always been led by this promise of a light at the end of the tunnel—that someday I could get my period again. But with every day that passes, and it doesn't happen, it's like that light gets dimmer and dimmer."

"Have you been following up with your doctor?"

"Oh, sure, but they just don't know enough about my condition. On one hand, my period could return tomorrow. On the other end, it might never happen. No one can really say."

"Damn."

"Michael didn't even wait to see if I could get my period back. He left shortly after I got my diagnosis. He was so pissed that I'd destroyed my body and ruined our chance at having children together. I begged him to stay, that in the *worst-case* scenario we could adopt a baby, but he wouldn't have it. He yelled that he would never '*raise another man's seed.*'"

"What an idiot." An ember of rage kindled in Shea's eyes. "I guarantee you, he regrets leaving a girl like you."

I chuckled. "Thanks. That's kind of you. But honestly, I doubt it. Michael married another girl pretty quickly after our divorce." I paused. "She's already given him three kids."

My gaze dropped to the floor, but Shea lifted my chin.

"I doubt she's *half* as amazing or beautiful as you are."

I wrapped my hand around his muscled forearm. "Shea, you're sweet. But I'm a completely different girl than the one I was with Michael. I told you, I was a mess. I bet he still thinks from time to time what a bullet he dodged by dumping me. Honestly? I can't even blame him."

"Then he's an even bigger idiot," Shea snarled. "An immature boy."

I laughed. "Why do you say that?"

"Because he doesn't even know the quality of the woman he

left behind. The ability to have a baby isn't the only thing a woman is good for, Brynn."

I nodded, but the lump in my throat grew so swollen, it ached.

"You're not perfect—but so what? Who is? You've learned from your mistakes, and they've molded you into an incredible person. And now you're helping mold *my* kids into incredible people, too. The difference between who Chloe was two months ago, and the confident, *slightly* more patient girl she's starting to become?" Shea paused to reconsidered. "Besides the hijinks she pulled tonight, that is."

I laughed.

"Or how about the twins? They're actually doing their homework now. Their grades are up. They're eating more and starting to put on a little weight. Small things, sure, but I was struggling with those small things before you came along. And I owe it all to you, Brynn. You've taken your life's lessons and used them to help other people out. I mean, damn, isn't that the most important thing anyone can do on this Earth? Hell, what have *I* done in my life? I'm just a big dumb hockey player who gets treated like some kind of larger-than-life hero, but all I do is play a *game* for a living. That's it. I haven't done anything compared to you."

A tear silently rolled down my cheek. "That's sweet, but no, you've done a lot. You've been a role model for kids. You've helped your teammates grow and become men. You even made a thirteen-year-old girl smooch a poster ...!"

We both laughed, and when the laughter died down, Shea gently stroked the tears from my cheek with his thick finger. He cupped my cheek and I closed my eyes and waited. We'd bared our hearts and souls to each other, and now our mouths met in a soft, tender, almost somber embrace—and sure enough, I could taste the salt of my tears on his lips. I'd never been so moved, so touched by a kiss in my life.

But there was still more to say.

I pulled away. "But wait."

"Hm?"

"There's a *reason* I told you all that, Shea."

"What is it?"

"Because I *will* have a child of my own someday. If my period doesn't return, I plan to adopt. Being a parent is a big thing for me now—it's why I became a nanny. The funny thing is, I wasn't baby crazy at all—all I cared about was working out—until I was told I was infertile. Now, the thought of not having kids just kills me on the inside."

"Makes total sense, Brynn."

"Every time I date a guy, I have to give them this speech—because I don't know what the future holds. And I know, it's awkward to bring this up so early, but after Michael, I *need* to be certain that I'm not wasting any more of my time. So if I know a guy doesn't want kids, or simply isn't willing to adopt if we have to go that route, then ... the writing is on the wall for us."

I stared at him, studied his reaction, made sure he understood *totally* what I was telling him.

Shea chuckled, slightly uncomfortably. "Well ... uh ... I honestly thought I was done having kids."

I frowned. "I know. I remember you saying that."

"But if you're saying what I think you're saying ... and everything between us works out ..."

Shea let out a deep breath. Slowly, he began to nod.

"I'd do it, Brynn."

I laughed in disbelief. "Really?"

"Yeah. It obviously means a lot to you. And you'd obviously be a great mother, too. It seems wrong to rob the world of a great mom."

"You wouldn't even mind adoption?"

He shrugged. "No. Why?"

I squinted at him. It felt too good to be true. "Huh. This seems almost too easy."

He grinned sneakily, like he knew something I didn't. "You don't believe me?"

"You should've *seen* all the reactions of the guys I've had this talk with. Never, not once, has a single guy been so cool and accepting of it. Usually, they straight up refuse to even *think* about kids, period. If they manage to get past that hurdle, they draw a line in the sand at adoption."

Shea was unfazed. "These are younger guys, I'm guessing?"

"Well, yeah, usually around my age or so."

"Then maybe I've got a little more self-awareness and life experience than they do, Brynn."

"Yeah ... but you're a famous athlete ..."

He scoffed. "So? Anyway, hockey players truly aren't that famous. Once we retire, we're pretty much forgotten."

"Aw. So sad. I'll always remember you, Shea Ellis." I patted the hockey player's stubbly cheek. "But my point is, you're famous, you're rich, you can have practically any girl you want. Why would you ever go for a woman who has to adopt? Why would you spend your resources raising another man's seed, when you've *literally* got the genetics of a professional athlete to pass on?"

With a laugh, he shook his head. "You still don't get it? I told you, a woman is so much more than a baby factory."

"You *say* that ..."

"Yet you don't believe me?"

"I'm sorry, it's just hard to believe, given what other guys have said to me."

"Younger, dumber guys, you mean."

"Well, sure."

"I'm not them, Brynn."

"I know ... *but.*"

Shea suddenly stood from the couch and offered me his hand. "Okay then. Come with me."

"Where are you taking me?"

"I want to show you something."

I put my hand in his, and he hoisted me to my feet.

What's this about ...?

32

SHEA

"What's this about?" Brynn asked again and again as I led her to the living room.

We stopped in front of the family photographs.

"I wanted to show you these," I said.

"I've looked at them dozens of times already," she said, laughing as if I'd lost my mind. "You really think I wouldn't have noticed the family pictures after two months of living here?"

"I want you to look at this one."

I pointed out a specific picture of me with the kids. It was after the annual Boston Brawlers Family Day Skate. In the photo, I knelt on one knee, and the kids—donning Dad's name and number and wearing their ice skates—were huddled around me. I had eight-year-old Chloe on my left side, and the four-year-old twins on the other side.

"Okay. I'm looking. What am I supposed to see when I look at this picture, exactly?" Brynn asked.

"Hopefully nothing," I said calmly.

"Okay ..." She laughed, confused. "I don't *think* I see anything. Um, do I? I don't know what I'm supposed to see or not see, Shea!"

I grinned. "The other night, you mentioned that Chloe might feel less guilty about the divorce if she knew that Cynthia had other affairs. And I told you, I didn't want to do that, because it could cause problems between her and Cynthia."

"But you *also* said something about the twins," Brynn said, and she examined the photo closer.

I nodded. "This picture pains me to look at, Brynn, but it's also the most important picture I have."

"Why?"

"First of all, this was the first Brawlers Family Day Skate since the divorce. It was three months to the day, to be exact."

"That must've been tough," Brynn said.

"I put on a good smile for the kids, but yeah, I was in a pretty bad state."

"Was Buddy Parker there that day?"

"No. When I learned about Cynthia's affair, I went to management, and Buddy was traded less than twenty-four hours later. Good thing, because I told the Brawlers brass that I might kill the guy with my own two hands if I ever had to see him in our locker room again. Never felt so betrayed in my life. Not just by my wife but by one of my best friends? Ugh."

"Did your teammates know?"

"I didn't tell anybody. But there were rumors. Especially after the trade. I suspect some guys knew all along." I shrugged. "I had to forget it and move on, though."

"I'm sorry. I don't know what to say. That must've been really tough."

I pointed at the picture. "The second reason this picture is so important to me is because that was the same day I got the paternity test results for my children."

"Wait." Brynn slowly turned to me. "Shea ... are you saying what I think you're saying?"

"Chloe's mine," I said. "Nick and Cam, on the other hand?" I forced a smile through the pain. "But seeing those boys wearing my jersey, smiling so big, so happy to be on the ice with their Daddy that day? I couldn't take that away from them, Brynn. Not then. Not ever. I swore I'd do my best to forget it and raise those boys as my own."

Her hand covered her mouth. "So they still don't know?"

"Nope."

"Does Cynthia know?"

"See, that's another thing. I didn't *want* to tell her, because like I said, as far as I'm concerned, those boys are mine. On the other hand, there might be some guy out there with no idea that he has twins. And maybe the twins would someday want to know their real father? It doesn't seem right to keep the truth from everyone."

Brynn hooked her arm through mine. "You're such a good man."

"So one day I talked to Cynthia, and I *hinted* at the possibility that maybe, just maybe there could be a chance that the twins weren't mine—and boy, that set her off. She accused me of trying to get a lower child support payment, and she'd see me in court, blah blah blah. Whatever. Not worth the hassle to me. I figure, deep down, she very well might know. And maybe she has a guilty conscience about it. Does she even know who their real dad is? I know about two affairs, but how many were there *truly*? Who knows. I do know the twins aren't Buddy's, because the twins were born before Buddy and I were teammates."

"I am *so* sorry." Brynn threw her body against mine, wrapped her arms tightly around my back, and buried her face in my chest. "I can't even imagine."

"Honestly, I almost wish I never took that damn test. Hell, I took it out of spite; I never imagined it'd actually uncover something. It's like the doctors took something from me. And ever since, I've only wanted to forget what I learned."

"I know exactly how you feel," she said. "But to those boys, there's not a doubt in their mind. *You* are their dad. They look up to you so much."

"I know."

"Do you think you'll ever tell them?"

"Maybe when they're adults. If I were in their shoes, I'd want to know. As much as it might hurt."

"Oh, Shea."

"Just promise me that you won't ever treat them differently now that you know, Brynn."

"Of course I promise."

We held each other, gently rocking from side to side, our lives bound by a sweet misery.

"Thank you for telling me that," she said at last.

"So yeah," I said, "I've got a little experience with adoption, in a way. Hopefully that means I'm still in the running for a date with you. A real date, that is; not Target."

She laughed through gritted teeth, and tears began to well in her eyes and spill down her cheeks. "You're still in. But I'd be happy to go to Target with you any day."

I wiped her tears away. "Aw, Brynn. Don't cry."

She choked back tears. "You're a great man. A great father. Better than anyone knows."

I kissed her on the head. "Thanks. It's hard to hear that but I appreciate it."

She stood on her tip-toes and put her arms around my neck. I grabbed two handfuls of her ass and we leaned into each other. Our lips melted together with a juicy, fiery heat. We pulled ourselves into each other, tighter, closer. Her small hands grabbed and squeezed at my hard muscle; my hands pawed and groped at her soft curves.

We wanted each other.

I didn't wait around. I threw her over my shoulder and made for the stairs.

"Where are you taking me?" she squealed.

"To my bedroom."

———

With Brynn over my shoulder, I bounded upstairs. I hadn't been able to stop thinking about it—our night after the gala, the tightness of her on my finger, the sweet tang of her on the tip of my tongue, the smells and sounds of her arousal.

I wanted it all.

Again.

Exactly as I had her before.

But this time, I'd have her all the way.

"I can't wait to go down on you again," I snarled as I carried her down the hall.

"Shea!" she giggled.

I pushed my bedroom door open and threw Brynn into the bed. But before I could tear her out of her clothes, she sat up in a hurry.

"Wait," she said, shooting a finger into my face.

"What?"

"My thong. I asked you where you put my thong, and you lied to me. I could hear it in your voice."

"You ... you could?" I asked gravely.

"Yes."

Damn.

"So what'd you do with it?"

I groaned. This was the part of the night where I blew it with Brynn, *again,* all on account of being a giant perv. Silently, I cursed Radar's name for ever putting the idea of panties in my head in the first place.

"You really want to know?"

"Yes!"

"That night, I put your underwear back in my pocket."

She folded her arms. "And what did you *do* with it after that? And where is it now?"

I went over to my suitcase, unzipped the side pocket, and pulled out her clean and neatly folded thong. I gave it to her. "Here."

She inspected it skeptically. "You took my panties with you ...? To Tampa?"

"Yes."

"For God's sake, why would you do that?"

"I guess I couldn't let it go. I couldn't stop thinking about what we'd done. I liked carrying your thong around in my pocket. It kept me thinking about you all day."

"Is that *all* you did with them?" she asked, grinning. "And don't lie to me. I'll know."

I shook my head. "No, that's not all."

"Tell me, then!"

I sighed and pulled out my phone. Without letting her see, I scrolled to the bottom of the photo gallery until I found the picture—her black thong, balled up and resting on my abs, and dripping with rivulets of cum. I stared at the photo, my heart pounding, afraid to turn the screen around to show her what I'd done.

"What is it?" she asked.

"It's bad. Real bad," I said. "I don't know if I can actually show you."

"Show me." She gestured for the phone. "I showed you *my* embarrassing photos."

She had a point. "Fine."

I turned the phone around. Her jaw dropped and her eyes, wide with shock, feasted on the sinful photo.

"Shea!" she screamed. "You came all over my panties?" A twisted pleasure pulled the corners of her mouth up into a gleeful smile. "You are *so* dirty!"

"I know. I swear, I've never done anything like that before." I shook my head in shame. "All I could think about that next day was you. How bad I wanted you. How close I came to having you. And then I was all alone in my hotel room and—well, you can see what happened. I couldn't help myself."

"That is so … *so* wrong," she panted. "Why did you take the picture?"

"I can't even say. I knew it was wrong to do. I felt guilty just looking at it. But at the same time? I thought it was really, really hot."

Her eyes darkened. "You're right. It is really, really hot."

Wha'?

Without another word, Brynn reached for my waist and unclasped my belt in a hurry. She yanked at my trousers and boxers until she had them both between my ankles.

"I want to suck your dick so bad."

Her dainty hands wrapped around my thickening flesh. She tugged at my throbbing cock until it was as solid as steel in her fist.

"Damn," I grunted, my mind still reeling. "That's good."

"You like it, don't you?"

I nodded.

"I bet," she said with a grin. "But just wait."

Brynn slid off the bed and knelt between my legs. Slowly pumping my cock in her fist, she stuck out her tongue and licked my length, from base to head, over and over again. Her eyes never left mine as she dragged her tongue up and down my manhood.

"Fuck, you're good at that," I growled.

She turned and squeezed my balls in her tiny fist, kneading

my nuts until pleasure bordered on pain. When I thought I couldn't take it anymore, she wrapped her lips around my balls and sucked, hard—until every last nerve in my body was on pins and needles.

A dewy bead emerged from the tip of my glans, leaving a shiny trail as it trickled down my shaft. Pre-cum—she had me excited. My cock pulsed and jumped in the air, begging for her mouth.

"You're leaking," Brynn said. She licked it right up, whispering under her breath, "mmm, I love your taste. You better have more in there for me."

"Brynn," I groaned, "you're perfect."

She locked her lips around my glans and pushed.

"Oh ... My ... God," I bellowed as she buried me in the blistering wetness of her throat.

She moaned as she swiveled back up my length, treating me to the tightness of her cheeks.

"Holy fuck, Brynn."

She pulled my manhood out of her lips with a suction-breaking *pop*. Glistening tendrils of her saliva dripped to the floor. She didn't give me much time to catch my breath—instead, she wrapped her lips around my manhood again and pushed, swallowing my inches down with a sexy purr.

Pleasured grunts and weakened groans filled the air as she worked me faster, harder, sloppier.

"You're so good at sucking cock," I gasped breathlessly.

A pressure was building in my balls and quickly rising up my shaft. *Am I going to come already?* I tried to bear down and fight my climax off—but it wasn't any use. Once Brynn peeked up, I could see it in her eye—she could sense my closeness.

Her hand joined her mouth, and the two moved together in perfect harmony, stroking and sucking me from base to tip until my whole body trembled, quaking with rising ecstasy—

"I'm coming!" I roared at last, pulsing, throbbing.

Brynn's smiling eyes never strayed from mine as I spilled my seed in her mouth.

When it was done, she jumped into my arms and kissed me, and the two of us fell to the bed together.

She's amazing.

33

BRYNN

I *knew* Shea had done something with my thong ... but actually *seeing* evidence? Seeing, with my very own eyes, the giant load that the hockey captain had splattered all over my intimates?

Okay, as I said before—men sure could be weird animals sometimes. And what Shea did was *definitely* strange. It was so primal and shockingly animalistic—it was as if he were marking his territory or something.

And obviously, I'm *not* his territory.

Yet I couldn't deny how it made me feel—so sexy, so powerful. *I'd* done that to him. My panties had turned him into a sex-crazed animal who was compelled to commit this unspeakable act. And he *knew* it was wrong, which was why he took a picture of it.

Call me crazy, but it was one of the sexiest things a guy had ever done for me.

Okay, the sight of his cum-drizzled six-pack sure increased the sexiness, too.

I wanted him in my mouth so bad.

I didn't just want to blow him, though—I wanted to blow his mind.

I gave Shea everything I had. I worshiped his every inch, letting his sounds of pleasure guide me. Slower, deeper, faster—Shea's gritty, raspy groans told me exactly how he wanted it.

He was an easy man to please. And it wasn't long before his sounds grew louder and more urgent, and his cock swelled impossibly firm in my mouth, and I knew what was coming.

The first shot of his cum, warm and velvety and rich like cream, hit the roof of my throat. I swallowed his salty-sweetness, accepting him, *all* of him, into my body.

———

My head, resting on Shea's great chest, rose and fell with his breath. Panting for air, Shea was still in shock over the blowjob he'd just received. Between breaths, he blurted out his surprise:

"Oh my God, Brynn."

"That was incredible."

"And you swallowed, too. Whoa."

I could still taste him in the lining of my cheeks. I sucked and licked at my cheeks, indulging in my salty reward.

"I'm glad you enjoyed it," I said.

We laid in his bed together, basking in bliss.

Eventually, Shea caught his breath. He rolled onto his side and kissed me, long, deep, and hot. With a whimper, I kissed him back. Our tongues touched and twisted together, and it wasn't long before a pressure began to poke against my thighs. Shea's thick cock slithered between my thighs.

"Brynn," he growled hungrily. "I want you."

"I know," I said, clamping my thighs shut on his manhood. "But we need to be careful."

"About what?" he asked.

The tips of my fingers traced the coarse outline of his jaw. "You. Me. The kids. Everything."

"So ... you want to take things slow?"

"Is that okay?" I asked in a moment of vulnerability. "At least until we get this whole nanny situation sorted out. I don't want to be sneaking around the house, sleeping with you behind the kids' backs. That's just asking for more trouble."

He nodded. "You're right. That's a bad idea. We'll wait."

I grabbed the back of his head and mashed my mouth into his.

"Thank you for understanding."

"Of course." He kissed me again. "So no sleeping together until you move out. Is that right?"

With his thick finger, he drew half-circles on my belly. I was keenly aware that, with each circle, his hands moved suspiciously lower—and my insides began to long for him, aching and throbbing in agony. As far as my pussy was concerned, I wanted him *now*.

But I had to stay strong.

"Th-that's right," I croaked.

"That's going to be tough," Shea said playfully. "But we can still do other things, right? Because, hey, you just sucked me off. It's only fair for me to pay you back."

His giant hand crept past my navel and burrowed under the waistband of my jeans.

"I sucked you off, yeah—but that only means we're *even*," I said.

But my body betrayed me. I dug my heels into the mattress and thrust my hips into the air, trying to force the captain's hand closer to my mound.

Shea pulled away in the nick of time. Abandoned, I let out a disappointed wail.

"Are you sure we're even?" Shea teased. "Because I'd really love to go down on you right now. And you seem like you want it, too."

I squeezed my eyes shut and mewled. His touch was *so* good—and his tongue was even better. Of course I wanted him—I was dripping wet just from sucking his cock! But ... shouldn't we be responsible? Shouldn't we try to stay out of trouble? Shouldn't we think of the kids, or something?

On the other hand, all I had to do was crack my eyelids open and see before me this muscled athlete kneeling next to me, built like a Greek God, with a thick dick standing high in the air, and a troublesome little smile on his face as he practically *begged* to eat me out. How could I ever resist?

"Ugh, yes," I whispered. "I want your mouth."

"I thought so," Shea chuckled as he grabbed hold of the waist button on my jeans. With a sudden release of pressure, the button popped free, and I let out an embarrassing loud moan. He tore my panties off, and then my top and bra, and our naked bodies and our mouths came together again.

He grabbed at my bare sides, clawed at the flesh of my belly, sucked at my hardened nipples. His manhood, throbbing and erect, rested against my folds as we kissed.

I couldn't take it anymore. I didn't even want his tongue anymore—I wanted *him.*

I set the tip of him at my entry and dared him to push into my wetness.

"Fuck me," I whispered.

His eyes went wide. "But ... you just said ..."

"I said, *fuck me*," I repeated, my tone demanding and needy.

Shea didn't have to be told again. With one hand, he joined my wrists and held my arms above my head. With the other hand, he grabbed my side and pinned my body to the mattress.

Slowly, he let his hips fall forward. His tip parted my folds and he sank his thickness into me.

"Oh my God, Shea," I gasped, choking back the pain—I wasn't used to his size.

Our mouths locked, muffling my whimpers. Shea took it slow and eased into me: gently, inch by inch, he opened me, until I was stretched properly for him—and his chiseled, sweat-glistened hips rested against my pelvis at last.

I could feel his cock, long and hot and hard, throbbing with his pulse in my walls. I whispered in his ear. "You feel *so* good buried inside me."

The captain pulled out slowly, quietly grunting as I gripped him as tight as I could, before slowly pushing his girth back in.

"Yes," I gasped. "Harder."

He withdrew and pushed in again, but only a touch harder.

"I said, *harder.*"

Shea's pelvis began to swing like a pendulum, and with each thrust, his hips stapled mine into the bed with a hefty, fleshy *clap.* But still, I knew he was holding back—and I wanted *all* of him. The big man had to be convinced that he wouldn't break me. I couldn't blame him—because in a way, that was exactly what I wanted. I wanted the hockey player to wreck me, make a mess of me, *own* me—just like he had with those dirty panties.

"I said, *harder!* Deeper!" I screamed at him, digging my nails into his round ass. "What are you waiting for? I want you to *fu*—"

Shea cut me off with a battle roar. He grabbed my ankles and spread my legs wide and began to truly lay into me, began to truly *fuck* me. Wildly, he entered me from every angle, like a bull tossing its horns, his dick ramming against the sides of my walls. Once buried in me, he swiveled inside me, stretching me wider and grinding against my insides like a mortar and pestle.

"Yes!" I screamed as the captain used me like we both

wanted, his big dick ruthlessly thrusting in and out my tightness.

He pounded his weight into me as if he were hammering a stake into the Earth. Each mattress-shaking blow brought me closer to a toe-curling climax.

"Harder!" I yelled over the quickening noise of the headboard slamming against the wall, *bam bam bam*.

Shea's eyes were fierce—he was determined to please me. Sweat streamed down his hairy chest and chiseled abdomen. My body was covered in sweat, too—though I wasn't sure if it was his or mine.

"Faster, harder!" I demanded. "I'm so close!"

Shea tried to give me what I needed, but soon he began to slow. He shook his head, disappointed in himself, and the steely determination in the athlete's eyes began to fade.

"I can't, babe," he whispered in my ear, his voice sweet like honey yet coarse like sand. "You're gripping me so tight. If I go any harder, I'll come."

"So?" I whispered in his ear. "*Do it*. Come inside me, Shea."

He liked hearing that. His eyes rolled back and he threw his head to the sky and he growled and *finally,* Shea gave *all* of himself to me. Faster, harder, deeper—the captain's big dick turned as hard as granite inside me as he fucked me with everything he had left.

My limbs quaked and I screamed, "I'm going to come!"

Shea's heavy body crashed into mine again and again. I couldn't take it anymore—the pleasure boiled over and my senses plunged into pure ecstasy.

"I'm coming!" I shrieked.

Shea let out a manly roar and his frenzied pace ground to a halt. Deep inside me, Shea's cock pulsed with his release, coating my insides with his seed. I clenched his thickness as tight as I could, never wanting to let go.

"Yes," I moaned, our mingling juices trickling down my ass cheeks.

Shea was spent. He collapsed on top of me, and I wrapped my arms around his barrel of a chest. We were a sweaty, breathless heap of flesh.

34

SHEA

With the late-morning sun stabbing through the bedroom window curtains, I woke in bed, still naked. My muscles were heavy and tired. My skin was sticky, coated with a layer of dried sweat and sex fluids.

Not that I minded—the tired, grungy haze was a delicious reminder of a long, *long* night. After months of tension, we couldn't just screw *once* and then roll over and fall asleep, could we? Instead, our rough-and-tumble romp was only an appetizer to a night filled with amazing sex. From sweet and soulful love-making, to downright dirty on all-fours on the bedroom floor, we finally did everything we'd been secretly wanting to do to each other all along—and everything in between.

Once we saw the first light of day cracking the horizon, we *finally* managed to keep our hands and mouths off each other long enough to fall asleep.

Brynn laid on her side, facing away from me. She was still sleeping, and still naked, too. I wrapped my arm around her and pulled her into me.

"Mm," she moaned as I woke her. "Morning, Shea."

I nibbled on her earlobe. "Morning, beautiful."

"Do you have hockey practice today?" she asked sleepily.

I had to stop and think—I couldn't remember. Truth was, hockey was the furthest thing on my mind. And while we were in the playoffs, too? Strange. Maybe I really was ready to retire. I guess it hadn't hit me until that moment. But I didn't feel old for once—the opposite, actually. Young and fresh and ready to move on.

"No," I answered, remembering at last. "Coach gave us the day off to rest up."

"Oh, good," she said with a breath of relief. "Because if you're as tired as I am … it wouldn't have been much fun."

I kissed the nape of her neck. "You sleep in. I'll make breakfast."

She started to kick her legs to toss the bedsheets away. "But that's my job—"

I pulled the sheets back up her body and tucked her in nice and tight. "Not anymore."

"Why? Because you're firing me?" she asked, always a tease.

"If that's what it takes to keep you," I said with a grin. "Then yes. You're fired."

"Oh, good," she sang, snuggling up with the bedsheets.

———

I woke Brynn an hour later with a breakfast-in-bed tray: scrambled eggs, sausage links, bagel with cream cheese, a fruit and cheese plate, and coffee. For a lousy cook, it was the biggest feast I could whip up.

Brynn loved it. She shook off the sleep and cooed with delight, and the two of us ate in bed, trying to figure out the future: the short *and* the long-term.

"I guess we shouldn't tell anyone about this, should we?" Brynn asked.

I thought it over. "Definitely shouldn't tell the kids. Probably shouldn't tell anybody else, either, or else word could get around."

Brynn nodded. "Secret it is, then."

"Cynthia is bringing the kids over after school," I said. "So, if you really want to take off, I guess before then would be the time to do it?"

She shook her head. "Even though you fired me," she began playfully, "I'm obviously not going to leave until we find a suitable nanny to replace me. The playoffs are too important to you."

"Hey, thanks. I appreciate that."

Brynn held up a finger. "Of course, *I* will be in charge of choosing the candidates and setting up the interviews, which means I get final approval over who gets hired."

"What? You do?" I laughed. "Since when?"

"Now that I know you have a thing for nannies? I've got to defend my territory. And if you think I'm going to set you up with some young, bright-eyed nanny, just *waiting* for the chance to steal you away from me ... well, you're wrong!"

"A thing for nannies?!" I laughed. I had a thing for *her*, not for nannies.

"Well? How would I know? Maybe you do! After all, Chloe said all the other nannies you'd hired before me were older ladies."

"Huh. Maybe you're right," I teased. "You *are* the first hot nanny I've hired. And now look at us. Eating breakfast in bed after a night of hot sex."

"*Exactly*," she said, her eyes wild with a half-serious, half-joking rage.

Suddenly, Brynn pushed her half-eaten breakfast aside, snatched my breakfast plate away, and climbed on top of me.

"Hey! I wasn't done with that!" I said.

She didn't care. "Shea Ellis, you are *not* getting another hot nanny."

Her luscious lips melded to mine with a possessive heat. Blindly, she reached a hand between my legs and played with my package until I began to plump and lengthen. She threaded my cock through the hole in my boxers and stroked me until I was solid.

"I am *not* letting you go," she said between fierce, jealous kisses. "Understand?"

She angled my dick against her opening and leaned back. Her wet, blistering heat slid down my length.

"Oh my God, Brynn," I groaned, gripping two big handfuls of her tight little ass. "You're so tight."

She rode me wildly, her hips pumping and bucking on me, my mouth sucking at her tits, until I shot my cum inside her again.

Beaming mischievously, Brynn rolled off me. She let out a loud, contented sigh. She passed me my plate and, hungrier than ever, the two of us scarfed down the rest of our breakfast.

"This is the best morning ever," I said.

"Agreed," she said, laughing as she tore off a big bite of her bagel. "I swear I've never been like this with anyone before. I can't keep myself off you. This could be a problem."

"Might as well enjoy ourselves while we can ..." I said, my hand traveling up her thigh.

She saw the sparkle in my eye and shot me a warning. "Better watch it. We're not going to get *any*thing done today if we keep this up."

"Sounds perfect to me."

35

SHEA

It was hours past noon when I finally jumped in the shower and washed the sticky remnants of last night, and this morning, off my body. We still had a little time until Cynthia dropped the kids off at the house.

Technically, once we got out of bed, we agreed to keep our hands off each other. But that proved easier said than done. Brynn moved about the house, bopping around, humming to herself, wiggling her butt. She had such a youthful, vibrant glow about her after we'd fucked and made love all night and morning. It was way too hard *not* to give her ass a hearty smack every time our paths crossed.

"Shea!" she said, spinning around and holding an accusatory finger in my face. "You can't do that! Remember, when the kids are here, we have to act normal!"

"I know, I know," I grinned.

Guess I'm having a hard time keeping my hands to myself, too.

But the time finally came when we heard Cynthia's car pull into the driveway, followed by a series of car doors slamming. I went out to greet the kids at the door step.

"Hey Chloe," I said, giving her a hug. "How was school?"

"Fine! How was your night?" she asked with a coy grin.

"I had a good time." I patted her head. "Slick move to get us out of the house, by the way."

"Gee, Dad, I just don't know what you mean," Chloe said, slathering it on *real* thick.

"Uh-huh. I bet."

Nick and Cam were next, and I greeted them both with big hugs.

"Hey there boys," I said, adopting my gruff Dad voice. "How was the weekend at your mom's?"

"Good," they said.

"You guys gotta beat Tampa tomorrow, Dad!" Cam said.

I ruffled his hair. "I hear ya, bud. It's not over 'til it's over."

Nick tugged on my hand excitedly. "I don't have any home-work, Dad. Can you come shoot some pucks with me in the rink?"

"Yeah, me too!" Cam said.

"Sure thing, boys." I glanced up and noticed Cynthia's car still sitting in the driveway. "I'll meet you two down there in a few. I need to have a quick chat with your mom first."

"Okay!" they said, running off.

I walked over to her car and the window rolled down. Cynthia regarded me with her barely-contained disdain.

"Hey, Cynthia. I think we need to have a chat."

"I was going to say the same thing." Cynthia launched into her rant, without pausing to hear what I wanted to say. "I don't know what ideas your nanny put in Chloe's head while they were home alone this weekend, but Chloe has it in her mind now that she should go to *therapy?*"

I nodded. "Yeah. And?"

"My daughter isn't *crazy*. She doesn't need therapy. Abso-lutely not. I'm putting my foot down on that."

"She's open to it, Cynthia. You can't stop her from going."

Futilely, she huffed and puffed. "But—but!"

"Look, Cynthia. I don't know if you realize it or not, but our daughter has been carrying guilt for *years* over the thing with Buddy—"

She rolled her eyes. "Oh, lord, here we go again—always throwing *Buddy Parker* in my face. I make *one* mistake and you'll never let me forget it, will you? No wonder Chloe's always bringing it up! You're stuck in the past and you won't let your daughter move on, either!"

I shook my head. "You couldn't be more wrong. All this time, I've avoided talking about it with Chloe because I figured it was better if we moved on and left it in the past. Now I'm realizing how wrong I was. I had no idea it was eating her up inside. All along, Chloe thought that *she* was the reason we got divorced."

"Well ...?" Cynthia raised a palm, begging the question.

My nostrils flared. "I seriously hope you're not suggesting that she was."

"It's just funny, that's all. I mean, you *did* find out about the affair because of her, right? And then you went and filed for divorce immediately after. So, in a way, she *was* the reason."

Blood boiled in my veins. "You're unbelievable. Listen to the words coming out of your mouth, Cynthia. *You* put our daughter in that position. She didn't want to be there. What a horrifying thing for an eight-year-old—to be the first one to find out that Mommy is cheating on Daddy."

"Here we go, time for the guilt trip." Cynthia rolled her eyes, and then her window began to roll up, too.

"Wait. Wait," I said, measuring my voice. "I'm not trying to guilt trip you. I'm telling you, very simply, that as long as Chloe is willing to go to therapy and talk to a professional about this, I'm going to support her."

"Sounds like a threat to me," Cynthia said.

"Only because some part of you is scared that Chloe will learn the proper tools to sort out her issues."

"Deep, Shea. Deep. Maybe you should become a therapist yourself?"

I ignored the smart remark. "I know you won't believe this, but I actually don't want you to have a shitty relationship with your daughter. I want you to figure your problems out and have a healthy relationship—because I want our daughter to be well-adjusted and have a happy life."

"Oh, and since you have all the answers, I suppose you know just what I should do?"

Her comment might've been bait, but I took it anyway.

"Look. You *have* to stop blaming Chloe for the divorce. Because she's picking up on the fact that you blame her, consciously or otherwise. She's a smart girl, smarter than we realize, and she's perceptive as hell. And once she starts therapy, it's just a matter of time before she figures all this out. She's too smart not to, Cynthia. I just want *you* to figure it out before she does, so you can help her—and not be a roadblock to her healing."

Cynthia looked as if she couldn't decide whether to scream at me in a rage or break into tears. In the end, she chose neither. Without a word, her expression went stony and solemn, and she turned her gaze away from me. Her window whirred as it rolled up.

I watched her car race off, an emptiness inside me. It was an awful feeling, that my daughter might not ever have a healthy relationship with her mother. I knew in my heart that it would cause Chloe a lot more pain and anguish in the coming years— and I felt terrible, knowing I'd played a big role in causing that pain. I was just a kid when I met Cynthia. A dumb kid, high on fame, and with a million-dollar contract burning a hole in my pocket. I hadn't known what to look for in a woman. I just hadn't known.

I walked back inside and saw all three kids gathered in the kitchen around Brynn. She was busy chopping vegetables for the night's meal. The twins, engaged in a frenzy to tell Brynn about their weekends, wrestled and jostled and shouted over each other. Chloe, the wise and elder sister, stood at Brynn's guard and kept her brothers in line—while she herself updated Brynn on the latest gossip from her day at school.

It was chaos, but a loving chaos, and Brynn flourished in it. She cared about those kids as if they were her own. It was no wonder they were so magnetically drawn to her, why they did what she asked without arguing or sneaking off to do something else. They respected her, looked up to her, they *loved* her.

I walked in and gave my kids one more big hug.

I hadn't known what to look for in a woman before, but I do now.

———

Two days later.

I strolled into the dressing room, my bag slung over my shoulder. The two days off—away from hockey and sneaking out with Brynn at any chance we got—had done me well.

But stepping into that room was like walking into a funeral. The mood was tense, the faces nervous, the usual jokes and laughs nonexistent.

The Boston Brawlers had lost their swagger.

"Chin up, boys," I said as I took a seat at my stall. "It's way too morose in here. Why isn't anybody talking or having fun in here?"

Their defeated eyes looked at me like I'd lost my mind.

"Down 2-0 in our series, Boomer," Brooks grumbled. "I'm

not finding a whole lot to laugh about right now. Unless *you* got something to cheer us up?"

"Sure do." I chuckled as I slipped out of my suit jacket. "Guys, I admit it. You were right all along."

Everyone peeked up at me, eyes big and curious.

"About what?" Ilya asked.

"Brynn. The nanny. I've fallen head-over-heels for her."

Note: yes, it was way too early to talk like that. But I was only putting on a show for the boys. Anything to drag their spirits out of the gutter. They needed something to laugh at. They needed to forget about the hole we'd dug ourselves and have a little fun.

And oh, it worked like a charm. A buzz immediately gripped the room:

"I fucking knew it!"

"Are you serious, Boomer?"

"He finally comes clean!"

"And I actually have you idiots to thank for helping me realize it," I said, tearing off my undershirt and trading it for an athletic compression shirt.

"What do you mean?"

"Voting us King and Queen at the gala. Sneaky move, guys, but smart."

"So something happened?!"

"I kissed her later that night. I'll be honest, I sorta made a mess of it, too. But boys, we've been trying to figure things out since then, and things are looking good for me. For the first time since the divorce, I'm actually feeling a little optimistic about a girl. So, I guess I owe you all an apology. Sorry boys. You read me like a book."

My teammates went wild and launched a sortie of follow-up questions: how far had we gone, when was I going to pop the question (*"quick, Boomer, do it before you retire and she realizes that you're just a boring nobody!*"), what the hell we were going to tell my kids …

I shook my head. "Listen, guys. I don't know the answer to a lot of those questions. All I can say is that I like her a lot. And once this hockey thing is over, I can't wait to spend even more time with her and find out what the future holds. That said—as excited as I am to start the next chapter of my life? I don't want to do it a loser. I want to go out on top, I want to go to Brynn with a Cup. A champion for life."

"Get Boomer a Cup," Radar said, coining what would later become the team's rally cry, "so he can ride off into the sunset with the girl."

"That's some real Boomer thinking," Brooks said. "But hell, I can get behind that."

Lance, the Brawlers' future captain, took center stage in the room. "It starts here, boys. It all begins tonight. We walk out of here with a win tonight, and we start building from there."

We roared, hyping each other up for battle.

36

BRYNN

In the mirror, I could see Cam's face turning as red as a tomato. He'd just hit depth on a ninety-five-pound squat—his heaviest attempt yet—and was trying to grind his way out of the box.

"Push, push, push!" I yelled from behind.

Cam growled, legs and core trembling, as he summoned the strength to push through the squat. There was a loud metal clang as he racked the bar, followed by an excited *whoop*, and I gave Cam a high five.

Nick, psyched to match his brother's physical feat, took his place under the bar.

"You can do it, Nick! C'mon!" I cheered as I got ready to spot him.

I understood now why Shea had asked me to train the boys —it wasn't a given that they'd be blessed with Shea's tall, wide frame. On one hand, it was so sad that Shea didn't know who their father was—was it another teammate of his? Was it someone else? On the other hand, it was sort of beautiful in a sad way that Shea chose to raise the kids as his own and made sure they had every opportunity to have the success he had.

Shea was right. My ex, Michael, was a boy. Shea? He was a man. A great man.

He hadn't even blinked at my crazy speech about adopting. Well, he didn't exactly sound *enthralled* about having another kid ... but I could tell he meant it when he said he'd do it for me. Obviously, it was too early to think about that kind of thing. But then again, like I told Shea and the other guys I've tried to date—I just didn't have the time to waste on uncertainty.

Nick matched his brother's squat. Cam, of course, was ready to throw more weight on the bar to prove he was stronger.

But I pointed at the clock. "Dad's game is about to start, boys!"

We left the gym and headed for the man cave.

———

Halfway through the game, neither team had scored, but it was obvious that the Boston Brawlers weren't going down without a fight. If anything, Boston had the upper-hand—though they hadn't scored, they skated with an intensity that Tampa was having trouble matching.

And the twins were completely immersed in the emotions of the game, jumping around on the couch and yelling at the top of their lungs:

"*Go Lance, go!*"

"*Shoot it, Radar!*"

"*Go, Dad! HIT HIM!*"

"*Great save, Ilya!*"

Chloe came down and joined us. "Geez guys, what's with all the screaming down here?"

"Uhhh, we're watching Game 3!" Nick shouted. "Duh, Chloe!"

"Yeah—*duh,* Chloe!" Cam agreed.

Chloe rolled her eyes and plopped onto the couch, next to me. I could feel her gaze on me, as if she were waiting for me to glance at her before she opened up a can of worms. These past few days, I could tell she had something she wanted to talk me about ... and I was certain I knew what it was, of course; she wanted to know what had happened between Shea and I. And since I really didn't want to have that conversation, I wasn't about to ask her what was on her mind.

But Chloe had reached the breaking point. I could *hear* her gathering the courage to talk to me.

"So, Brynn," she began shakily. "I, uh, officially have a boyfriend now?"

"What? You do?!"

"Yeah," she said shyly.

"Who?"

"Adam."

"He finally asked you out? Awww, that's so cute!" I hugged her.

"Yeah, yeah," she said, embarrassed. "I'm worried Dad is going to get super pissed, though."

"Why?"

"He hates Adam. That one time Dad came home and Adam was over, he went psycho and tried to scare him off."

I giggled. "He doesn't hate Adam. He's just being overprotective of his baby girl. My dad was like that with me, too. I can break the news to your dad, if you want—and I'll try to keep him calm."

"Would you? That'd be such a huge relief ..."

"Of course, Chloe."

The twins leaped off the couch and started vibrating with excitement, arms raised in the air—they could see a play developing before it had happened yet.

"C'mon, Lance! Pass it to Dad, pass it to Dad!"

"He's open, he's open!"

I watched as Shea held his stick high in the air, calling for a pass. Lance sent a nifty cross-ice pass to the captain, and Shea stepped into the shot, hammering the puck with an intimidating *boom.* A crowd of players stood in front of the Tampa goalie, screening him—and the next thing the four of us saw was a little black disc snagging the back of the net.

The twins went wild, dancing around the room in celebration as their dad gave the Brawlers a 1-0 lead.

"Yeeeeeesssss!"

"He did it!"

37

SHEA

We had Tampa on their heels all night—but we just couldn't solve their goalie. Until Lance fed me that perfect cross-ice one-timer. Once we scored, the whole team let out this collective sigh of relief. That was the point when we knew, just *knew,* that we'd opened the floodgates and the game was ours for the taking.

Sure enough, that goal was the breakthrough we needed. Lance and Radar went to work in the offensive zone, both players lighting the lamp before the period was up. By the time the final horn sounded, we'd put Tampa down 5-0.

There wasn't anything quite like the thrill of victory to lift a man's spirits and get the adrenaline pumping through his blood. The dressing room after a big win like that was a sight to behold —everyone was in a great mood. Everyone was closer. The laughs were louder and harder. Sure, we were still down in the series, 2-1, but the boys *knew* we could come back and win this thing.

On the way home, I cranked up the radio and sang along as loud as I could, drumming my hands on the steering wheel. I raced from one red light to the next. I couldn't wait to be home. I couldn't wait to see my kids and be with Brynn—even if I knew I couldn't kiss her or touch her the way I wanted to.

When I finally pulled into the garage and stepped foot into my house at last, a surprise was waiting for me.

My kids, *even Chloe*, and Brynn. The hero's welcome that I hadn't had in years.

"Dad!" the twins yelled, mobbing me at the door with hugs. "You won!"

"Congratulations, Dad!" Chloe said, joining the group hug. "You guys really kicked Tampa's butt tonight."

My eyes met Brynn's, and right away, I felt a charge. She struggled not to smile so big. Inside, I felt the same way.

"Congratulations, Shea," she said once the kids broke away.

She didn't step forward for a hug. We had to play it cool, after all.

"Thank you, Brynn," I said.

I drank the sight of her in. Maybe it was the high of the victory, but I could've sworn I'd never seen a woman looking so beautiful in my life. I wanted to throw my arm around her and plant my lips on hers, claim her as *mine,* and let the kids think whatever they wanted to think about us. But I couldn't do that. I had to restrain myself instead.

"How, uh, how'd the night go?" I stammered—my eyes were on her breasts and I was having a hard time stringing together coherent sentences. Her spell over me was strong.

"Everything went fine." She folded her arms over her chest and leaned forward to quietly scold me. "Eyes are up here, big guy."

I grabbed her arm and whispered in her ear. "I want you *so* bad right now, Brynn."

"No!" she whispered back.

Grrr.

This was going to be a hard charade to maintain ...

Nick and Cam ran over, grabbed hold of my hands, and pulled me towards the basement.

"Dad, come shoot some pucks with us!"

"Okay, guys, but not for long. It's almost your bedtime."

———

After the kids took their showers and went to bed, I found Brynn in the living room, curled up on the couch with a glass of wine and a book. Pickles the cat was perched on her legs.

She peeked up at me and smiled. I sat on the couch, leaving plenty of room between us. I couldn't sit any closer, or else I might be tempted to do something dumb.

"Thanks again, Brynn."

She marked her page and set her book aside. "For what?"

"Everything, really."

"Oh, stop it."

"Seriously. You were a big reason we won that game tonight."

She laughed. "*Me*?"

"Yeah."

"What the heck did I have to do with that game?"

Quietly, I explained how the boys had zeroed in on an alleged nanny-crush since day one. I told Brynn how that rumor turned into one of the team's longest-running inside jokes of the year—one that drove me crazy at first.

"Mm," she said, sipping her wine. "So *that's* why they voted us King and Queen at the gala."

"Partly, yeah. But also because they like you."

She laughed. "They don't know anything about me!"

"Well ... um ... maybe I talked about you enough that they had an idea? They could tell that I liked you, anyway."

"Aw, Shea," she teased. "They knew you needed a little help getting the girl."

"Yeah, yeah."

"But what's all that got to do with your game tonight?" she asked.

"I walked into that dressing room tonight, and it was like we'd lost the game before we even set foot on the ice. So I said, fuck it. After months of denying it. I finally came clean."

Her eyes went wide. "Wait. You told them?"

"Yeah."

"But I thought you said it was a secret!"

"I'm sorry," I said, frowning. "You're not mad, are you?"

She shook her head. "Not mad at all. Actually ... I like hearing that. Makes it seem a little more real."

"Oh?" I started to scoot closer, just a tad closer, across the couch. But Pickles slowly turned his head and shot me a defiant stare: *back away, old man, she's mine.*

The cat was right. I didn't dare go any further, or I could make a mess of things.

"What a jealous cat." Brynn laughed and pet Pickles's head. "Oh! That reminds me. I'm supposed to tell you something. But first, you have to promise that you won't get jealous or overprotective or weird. Okay?"

My heart skipped a beat. How could I agree not to be jealous about something before she even told me what it was? Was this the part where Brynn told me something terrible? Was there someone else in her life?

"I don't like the sound of this ..." I said lowly.

"Relax. It's about Chloe. She told me she has her first official boyfriend."

Relief flooded my heart. *Whew.* But then—wait a minute.

"Chloe has a *what*?"

"Boyfriend, Shea, a boyfriend."

I glanced upstairs, in the direction of Chloe's bedroom. Brynn put her foot in my lap to keep me calm—or maybe to anchor me in place, so I wouldn't go running upstairs to have a chat with Chloe.

To stay calm, I squeezed her little foot in my hands and gave her a rub. "Who's the boyfriend?"

"Adam. The boy you met a few months back. I think you read him the riot act?"

"Yeah, I remember." I grumbled. "Adam, huh. I didn't like the kid when I met him."

"I know. But Chloe does." She gave me a smile. "And if you let it be known that you don't like Adam, you'll only drive him further into Chloe's heart."

"Damn. You're right." I gulped. "She's just so young."

"I know it's not easy to see her grow up, but she's not *that* young. She's in high school. The kids her age are all starting to date. And from what I hear about him, he seems like a good kid."

I sighed. "Well. As long as you don't think it's a bad idea. I trust you. I guess I'll have to be a little more welcoming to him next time."

"That's probably wise," Brynn said, smiling.

I stared at the ground and shook my head. "Chloe has a boyfriend. Whoa. She's really growing up."

Brynn giggled. "I'm sorry. Did that take all the wind out of your sails?"

"A little."

"Maybe I can blow a little bit of that wind back into your sails?"

I was determined to remain surly, but I'll admit it, I liked the suggestive note in her voice.

"Try me," I said.

"For one, you should feel great right now—your team won an important game tonight."

I shrugged. "Yeah."

"And you played a fantastic game."

"Eh," I grunted. "I did okay."

"You scored the game-winning goal."

"If I didn't score it, someone else would've."

"How about this one?" Brynn lowered her voice to a breathy whisper. "Chloe's not the only girl around here with a new boyfriend."

Okay—the last one managed to melt through the ice and put a spark in my heart. I didn't know that she was ready to think of us boyfriend and girlfriend, but I wasn't about to argue against it.

"You mean, a secret boyfriend?" I teased.

"You're not much of a secret boyfriend when you tell the whole hockey team about us, now are you?"

I snickered. She had me there. "You sure you're not mad I told them?"

"Positive. I love it, actually. Makes me feel like I'm yours."

I stared into her eyes. I knew it was a bad idea, that we weren't supposed to do anything while the kids were here, but ... I couldn't help myself. I crawled over the couch cushion that separated us. Mad that I was encroaching on his territory, Pickles let out a distressed mewl before he bolted. I slithered next to Brynn, wrapped a hand around her waist, pulled her under me and pressed my lips to hers.

In the stillness of the quiet house, the tell-tale sounds of our mouths, kissing and sucking, grew ever louder.

After a few minutes, Brynn pulled back, her brow heavy. "Shea, we shouldn't. One of the kids might hear us down here and wonder what's going on."

"You're right. One last kiss."

We shared one last kiss, soft and silent.

Then I told her goodnight, tore myself away from her, and quietly made my way to my bedroom.

———

It was a pitch-black night. I couldn't see a thing as I laid in my bed. And yet I couldn't sleep, so I stared into the darkness, thinking. Thinking how badly I wanted Brynn, how I *needed* to feel her lips against mine, how *close* she was—just a few feet down the hallway—and yet I couldn't have her.

This could drive a man mad.

Then I heard a sound at the door.

Not a knock, but a gentle twisting of the knob.

The door cracked open, almost without a sound. It was followed by the shuffle of a body sneaking through the open doorway with the grace of a cat. Just as quietly, the door was shut.

I grinned from ear to ear as Brynn's stealthy footsteps tiptoed across the room. The mattress dimpled under her weight as she climbed into bed without making a sound.

"Shea," she whispered as she crawled under the covers. "You awake? I can't sleep."

"Bad girl," I whispered. "You're not supposed to be in here."

"Oh? That's fine, I can go," she teased.

I heard her try to slip out of the covers and sneak away. In the dark, I managed to catch her by the wrist and pulled her back into bed.

"Nice try. But you're not going anywhere."

I climbed on top of her and kissed her. My hands went to her belly, and a hatched texture greeted my fingertips. A mesh fabric. Excitedly, I ran my hands up and down her sides, mapping out her outfit in my mind's eye—it was some sort of bodysuit.

"What's this you're wearing?" I growled in her ear.

"Something naughty. Do you like it?"

"I love it, but God, I wish I could *see* you in it."

Blindly, I reached out, waving my hand around for the lamp switch. But Brynn hooked my elbow and pulled me back in.

"No lights," she whispered. "I'm not supposed to be here, remember? See with your hands."

I grumbled—but the disappointment of not being able to see her was quickly replaced by the erotic excitement of running my hands all over her body, while she quietly sighed with pleasure.

When I cupped her tits, my breath hitched at an unexpected sensation: the points of her bare nipples, brushing against the palm of my hands. Her lingerie had peepholes, and she'd been *waiting* for me to discover her rock-hard nips, standing erect and out in the open. Roughly, I pinched and pulled at her bare nips until they grew longer and fatter, and her moans grew deeper.

"That was a nice surprise, Brynn," I said, snagging her earlobe between my front teeth.

"Good. I wanted to surprise you. I got so wet thinking about you."

"You are so bad," I whispered.

"And what do you do to a bad girl?" she flirted.

I let out a hungry snarl and yanked the bottom of her bodysuit askew. I ran my fingers over her silky folds. Brynn hadn't lied—she was sopping wet. And as I toyed with her pussy, she sank her teeth into my shoulder to keep from moaning too loudly.

I kicked off my boxers, shifted my hips, and positioned myself at her moist slit. She wrapped her arms and legs tight around my body. We locked lips. And, trying not to make a single sound, I pushed into her sweltering velvet grip.

In the dark and quiet bedroom, we made love, savoring every single inch of each other.

38

BRYNN

The next two months were a frenzied blur of the most important hockey Shea had ever played, and a fiery romance that the two of us struggled to keep under wraps.

For the Brawlers, the beginning of a heroic playoff run started with that first victory against Tampa. The Brawlers won the next game at home, knotting the series at two games apiece. For Game 5, Shea and the rest of the Brawlers traveled to Tampa. They won that game, too—and then they closed out the series by winning the next game in Boston, advancing to the second round of the playoffs.

With each victory, the Brawlers' confidence as a team grew. Each and every player started to hit his stride, blossoming like the spring flowers that were blooming all around Boston. Lance and Radar continued to click as a goal-scoring duo, leading the team's high-powered offense. Ilya looked unbeatable in net. Shea was the calm, reliable presence that the team needed on defense—calm, that is, until anyone neared his goaltender. Then, Shea possessively guarded his net like a rabid dog.

In round two, Shea and the Brawlers traveled to Toronto.

The hot and experienced Brawlers steamrolled the young Toronto squad, dispatching them in five games.

The kids and I watched every game during the playoffs. Shea had told me once that, when he was still married and his kids were still little ones, the family would be waiting for him at the door after every game. He told me how much he missed that, how that greeting always made him feel like a hero. So, when Shea returned home after every game, the four of us would be waiting for him. It was a small thing, but I could see just how happy it made Shea, so I made sure that it continued to happen.

When Shea was out of town, I began the search for a replacement nanny and started interviewing candidates immediately. It wasn't easy. I was *mostly* joking when I teased Shea about having a thing for hot nannies. But I'd be lying if I said insecurities never entered my mind when I interviewed the women who wanted to replace me. The thought of them taking my spot, forging relationships with the kids, *alone* in the house with Shea ...

It was almost enough to make me call the search off entirely.

The truth was, I'd been falling for Shea for a while. Sure, in the beginning, the two of us made more than a few missteps. But ever since he told me that the twins weren't his, and that it didn't make a difference in how he raised them, I knew he was a special man. He hadn't been scared off by 'the talk' that had sent every man I've tried to date since Michael running for the hills. I knew in my heart that I had to do whatever I could to keep him.

And in a strange way, that was exactly why I knew that I *had* to hire another nanny if I was serious about our relationship. It was great that we got along so well—but we needed healthy boundaries; we needed our own lives. I couldn't continue to live and work at the house.

With the parade of potential nannies coming to the house for interviews, it was no use trying to keep it a secret. I told the kids that they would have a new nanny, so they would have time to process the news. Chloe wasn't too effected, since she'd seen it coming—but the twins were crushed. They simply could not understand why I was quitting. *Why can't you stay forever?* they'd ask. I tried to reassure them that they'd still see me from time to time, but they didn't believe me. They never saw Estel or any of their other nannies, so why would they see me again?

Shea and I agreed that the replacement nanny wouldn't take over for me until after the playoffs were over. Part of that agreement was because hockey players were deeply superstitious by nature—and since the Brawlers were winning, Shea didn't want to mess with a good thing.

But another part of me had to wonder if there was more to it than just superstition: maybe, *just maybe,* Shea got an athletic boost from our forbidden romance? He said I made him feel ten years younger, after all. And on the ice, he sure played like it.

It was easy to understand, too. Our 'affair' was the most thrilling time of my life, and I might have felt a few years younger myself. On one hand, it felt so *wrong* sneaking around behind the kids' backs for our midnight trysts like we were. On the other hand? It was *so* exciting, and we never got caught. We knew we were being irresponsible, like a couple of insatiable teens that couldn't keep their hands off each other, but what else could we do?

The sex was frequent, whenever we could take it, and always sinfully hot. The fact that we 'weren't supposed to be doing this' only added more fuel to the fire. We were always inventing new excuses to be alone together. A quick run to the store for a gallon of milk might take us twenty minutes longer than it was supposed to. We always returned with our clothes looking slightly disheveled, my hair suspiciously messy, a fog lingering in the Bentley's windows.

One night, after Shea returned from the road and I was

feeling particularly pent-up, I was having a terribly hard time staying quiet for him. Shea tried cupping his hand over my mouth to muffle my screams, but even that wasn't quite working. So he whisked me to the basement instead, and we made use of the soundproof rink. Sometimes, I'll get a sudden reminder of the raunchy night we defiled the indoor rink, and a hot burst of shame rises to my cheeks—but then I remember how hard the two of us came, moaning and groaning at the top of our lungs while the rest of the house peacefully slept, and ... well ... I can't exactly say that I regret it.

When Shea was on the road, the kids stayed with Cynthia. It was a bittersweet time—we were *so* far apart. Yet, those were the only times when Shea and I didn't have anyone to hide from, when we could talk openly and without speaking in hushed tones. As soon as Shea got back to his hotel, he'd call me and we'd talk for hours. We could talk about everything or nothing at all. Just the sound of each other's voices kept us going. Inevitably, our phone conversations turned dirty, and we drove each other crazy talking about *just* what we were going to do to each other when we could finally be together.

And then, days later, we'd be back together ... only to remember that we *couldn't* do any of the things we wanted. At least, not until late at night, when the house was quiet and still and our hearts pounded in our chests.

All I knew was that I wanted the hockey player thinking about me *always*. As soon as he got home, I *needed* to feel his eyes all over me. I needed to know that he was obsessing over me, plotting out just when and how he planned to take me this time. As long as he wanted me, I knew everything was good, everything was right—in life and love and hockey.

My *only* complaint?

Shea still hadn't taken me out on that date. Yes, it was impossible with the kids around. And yes, he was very busy with his hockey schedule. I knew all that. But still, one *real* date—that was all I wanted, to know that this was really real, and not just some short-lived flame.

But I had to have faith.

And wait until hockey ended.

The Brawlers, meanwhile, continued their march through the playoffs. Their opponent in round three was a veteran Washington team. The winner of that series would play for the Stanley Cup. Both teams wanted it, bad, and it took seven games of back-and-forth action before Boston emerged victorious.

The Brawlers had one last team standing between them and the Stanley Cup.

Their opponent?

Nick and Cam's favorite team, of course—Chicago!

39

SHEA

B *oston, MA. Game 5.*

We led Chicago three games to one. If we won tonight, we'd hoist the Cup at home, and I'd finally accomplish a life's dream.

"*Boomer!*" one of my teammates shouted as I stepped into the dressing room for what I hoped would be my last NHL game.

"Evening, boys." I looked around the room and saw some nerves. A blank stare. A fingernail, anxiously chewed. More than a few bouncing knees. But it wasn't a nervous, frightful energy—it was a giddy sort of optimism. Like me, these guys had trained their whole lives for this moment. It was so close, and now that it was here, it seemed almost too good to be true.

Well, fuck that. I'd waited longer than anyone else here, and I wasn't going to let this one slip by.

"This is it, boys," I began. "This is what we've been working for. Everyone's got a job to do, and you already know what that is, so I don't need to remind you. Just don't overthink it. Sixty minutes of solid hockey. That's it, that's all we need, from top to bottom. Do your job tonight and we'll go home champions."

Twenty heads nodded.

We took the ice for warm-ups. I skated over and found Brynn with the kids, sitting front row. Brynn sat sandwiched between the boys—ever since she let them know that they'd have a new nanny once the playoffs were over, the poor boys had grown increasingly clingy around her. They thought that if the playoffs ended tonight, they'd never see her again.

I slid to a stop in front of the glass and waved at the kids. They pounded on the glass and smiled from ear to ear. Chloe was too cool to wear a "baggy, hideous hockey jersey," as she called it, but both boys wore their dad's name and number. Yup, that's right, Nick and Cam had renounced their Chicago fandom —at least for this series, anyway. That made me happier than I ever expected.

I winked at Brynn. I loved the way she smiled at me. How her eyes glittered, and she fought off a smile that threatened to spread across her entire face, and—

"Wow-ee, look at those bedroom eyes," Lance joked as he coasted by and whacked my butt with his stick. "You really think your kids haven't figured it out yet, eh? You two are so obvious."

I gave him a shove and chased after him.

———

An animal is most dangerous when it's cornered, and Chicago wouldn't go down without a fight.

From the moment the first puck was dropped, Chicago came at us, hard, fast, and heavy. Every loose puck was a dogfight, every hit was meant to hurt. Shots on both sides were rare and hard to come by—space in the defensive zone was too precious for either team to give up. Both teams protected their goalies. And if you wanted to go to the net, you had to pay the price.

By the end of the second period, neither team had scored. We returned to the dressing room for the intermission. We looked worn from battle: bruises, black eyes, a broken nose, more than a few fresh stitches, flushed cheeks, hair drenched with sweat, chests heaving for air.

There was something else, too. The boys were starting to get nervous that we hadn't yet scored. Everyone looked to me to say something, to say the magic words to rally the troops and lead them to victory.

I took a deep breath and did my duty as captain one last time.

"So we haven't scored," I said. "But neither have they. Boys, whatever desperation you feel right now, the other team"—I pounded my fist on the cinder block wall that separated our locker rooms—"feels a *hundred* times worse. Like a boulder on their shoulders. Because if they don't score the next goal, they know they'll fold. They *need* the next goal, boys, but they're not going to get it. Because it's *ours*. The next goal is ours."

A few heads nodded.

"The Stanley Cup is right there for the taking, boys. It's ours. Let's wrap this up tonight. Let's lift the Cup on home ice, in front of our kids and our loved ones. Finish it off tonight, and you'll always be a legend in their eyes. I promise you, you'll never forget this night for the rest of your life."

More heads started nodding.

I cracked a grin. "So let's get it done. Send me riding off into the sunset, so I can retire and spend the rest of my life with that nanny, alright?"

My teammates booed and flung an assortment of sweaty towels at me. I laughed, swatting the towels away, and took my seat at my stall. But then the boys began a cheer, "*For Boomer!*"

Lance nudged my shoulder. "One more period to go, Captain. How's it feel?"

I couldn't stop smiling. "Honestly? I can't fuckin' wait, Lance."

We returned to the ice for the start of the third period. I could sense right away that we'd loosened over the break—while Chicago had stiffened.

Right then and there, I had a good feeling the game was already won.

Five minutes into the third, we were staving off another Chicago attack. Ilya made a save, and the rebound bounced into the corner. I got there first and flung the puck around the boards, hoping my left wing could get there first. Lance and the Chicago d-man both raced to the puck, but Lance chipped the puck off the boards and past the d-man—and then turned on the jets to go streaking in on the Chicago goalie, all alone.

Lance doesn't screw up too many golden opportunities like that. The crowd jumped to their feet, ready to blow the roof off the building if the young star could score.

Lance deked left, then right, then placed a laser of a shot right between the goalie's legs and into the net. The building shook as eighteen-thousand roaring fans jumped up and down in revelry.

The next fifteen minutes of play never felt so long in my life. Every shift felt more important than the last, every shot more dangerous, as Chicago desperately tried to tie the game.

But Ilya kept us alive, making one great save after another.

With under a minute left in the game, Chicago's urgency hit a fever pitch, and they threw everything they could at the net.

The crowd started the countdown: *"ten, nine, eight, seven ..."*

Ilya tracked shots through traffic, snagging pucks out of air. The shots he didn't see happened to hit him—you have to be good to be lucky.

And precious seconds continued to roll off the clock.

"Three, two, one!"

Then the horn sounded and it was over.

We'd done it.

We'd really done it.

I raced over to Ilya and jumped into the goalie's arms—he toppled over and the two of us hit the ice.

"You did it, bud!" I yelled, laughing.

Our teammates weren't far behind. They hurried over and every last man jumped onto the dogpile, until Ilya and I were crushed under the weight of twenty of our closest brothers.

Next thing I knew, the Cup was being passed into my hands, and I hoisted it high into the air. Thirty-five pounds of silver held straight overhead, but to my arms, it felt totally weightless.

I skated the trophy right over to where my family sat. They jumped up and clapped, all of them, even Chloe, their expressions jubilant as they shared the moment with me.

"Thank you," I mouthed to Brynn.

I couldn't have done it without you.

40

BRYNN

When Shea skated off with that glistening silver trophy high over his head, Nick and Cam, sitting on both sides of me, immediately burst into tears.

"Aw, you guys!" I said, an arm around them both.

I figured they were tears of happiness—witnessing their dad accomplish a boyhood dream, one that was currently *their* boyhood dream, had to be a profoundly moving moment. Seeing the pure boyish joy on Shea's face made *me* tear up, too.

But Nick sobbed, his face mashed into my shoulder. "I don't want you to go, Brynn!"

Now that the playoffs were over, the boys figured tonight would be the last time they'd see me. After the game, I had to drive them to their mother's house.

"Me neither!" Cam wailed, his hand tightly clenching mine.

Gah. Their lamentations were like a knife to the heart.

Chloe did her part to try to cheer her brothers up. She wrapped her arms around Cam and gave him a big bearhug. "Hey, Cam, I don't want Brynn to go either, okay? But she said she's still going to visit us from time to time."

"Yeah but *none* of the other nannies ever visit us!" he cried.

"Well ..." Chloe locked eyes with me while she consoled her brothers. "Maybe this time it will be different. Who knows?"

I smiled at her.

I sure hope so.

———

The Brawlers' celebration left the ice surface littered with abandoned sticks and gloves and helmets. The athletes took turns with the Cup, each player skating a lap around the rink with the trophy held high above his head.

When the last player had taken his turn, the team gathered at center ice for a team photo. The Boston crowd sent their team off with an ovation, and the athletes gleefully skated off the ice, taking the party to the locker room.

The twins were still wiping their eyes when one of the Brawlers' team reps—a young man in a suit with plenty of room to grow into—found us at our seats.

"Mrs. Ellis and kids, right?" he asked.

"Oh, no," I chuckled. "I'm the nanny, not Mrs. Ellis."

"*Not yet, anyway,*" Chloe joked, loud enough that only I could hear it.

"Oops. My mistake," the young man said. "But if you'll come with me, the team will be accepting guests soon."

The team rep escorted the kids and I to a VIP waiting room, where we milled around with the other Brawler family members. Ella and Paige were there, both brimming with huge smiles, and they went around the room handing out hugs to all the other Brawler 'WAGs'—wives and girlfriends.

Down the hall, the locker room door was locked, as the boys were having a team-only celebration. We could all hear the wild party underway: hoots and hollers, shouts of euphoria, howls like a pack of coyotes, *awooooo!*

And then, finally, the locker room doors were thrown open.

We rushed with the other VIPs to see our champions.

The kids and I raced down the hall and ran into the locker room. The players were still dressed in their game gear, and they were soaking wet—not with sweat, but alcohol. The sweet smell of champagne and yeasty scent of beer hung in the air. One of the Brawlers emerged with a bottle of champagne, which he shook furiously before popping the cork, aiming the spray at his buddies and showering them with champagne.

Elsewhere, a Brawler poured champagne into the Cup, and the players took turns drinking from the trophy's chalice.

We found Shea sitting peacefully at his stall. While his teammates went crazy, the captain leaned back, content to soak in the moment, a sweet and humbled smile on his face. He lit up when he saw the kids. Chloe and the boys jumped into his arms and he held them tight.

"You did it, Dad!" the twins cheered.

"We sure did, guys."

"Congrats, Dad!" Chloe said.

"Thanks, sweetheart."

And then, the athlete set his eyes on me.

Shea stood and reached for my hand. I gave it to him, not knowing what to expect. He pulled me forward—surprised, I stumbled into his arms. Shea caught me, bent me over, and planted his mouth right onto mine.

In front of everyone.

The team, the wives, the kids, *everyone*.

And not a single person missed it. The Brawlers let their approval known with a manly roar—

"Get it, Boomer!"

"Aaaaaaw, yeah!"

—while the WAGs cheered and clapped with delight.

With Shea's lips pressed firmly into mine, I shot a worried

glance at the kids. The twins looked just as stunned and confused as I did. Chloe, on the other hand, watched us with a smug grin.

I put a hand on Shea's chest and pushed him back. "Shea! Everyone's watching!"

"I know!" he said, smiling. "Brynn, will you be my girlfriend?"

My heart pounded in my throat. Shea, the twins, the Brawlers, *everyone* seemed to be waiting for my answer.

"Of course I will ...!" I panted.

The locker room exploded with a second round of celebration. Nick and Cam turned to us with giant, twinkling eyes.

"Brynn's your *girlfriend* now?!" Cam gushed. "That's awesome!"

"Does that mean you'll still come by the house, Brynn?" Nick asked.

"Of course! I told you all along you'd still see me!"

Lance neared and ruffled Chloe's hair. "You're awfully quiet there, Chloe. What do you think about all this?"

Fighting off a smile, Chloe let out a sigh. "I'd say it's about time."

Lance, and all the other Brawlers, burst into laughter. "You and me both, sister."

———

After I dropped the kids off at Cynthia's, I headed to *Peasant,* a restaurant where Shea said the team was gathering to celebrate. I'd never eaten at *Peasant,* but I'd read the restaurant's glowing reviews—in fact, I'd mentioned the place to Shea in passing once upon a time.

I thought it seemed like a strange place to take such a raucous party, since the restaurant was known for its warm ambiance and cozy atmosphere—but hey, whatever. I was just excited to eat there.

I walked into the dimly-lit restaurant, candles romantically glowing at every table. There was a distinct lack of shouting from drunken, bawdy athletes. Had the Boston Brawlers already gotten themselves kicked out?

But no: I spotted Shea, waiting for me at a table, all by himself.

He stood as I neared, looking sharp in his suit and still wearing that unshakable smile.

"Shea ...! Where's everyone else?"

Like a gentleman, he helped me into my chair. "They're not coming. They're going out to the bars."

"But don't you want to celebrate with them?"

"I want to be with you, Brynn. Our first real date."

———

After a dinner that was every bit as romantic as it was delicious, Shea and I walked a few blocks to a shop that he swore had excellent gelato.

"It's amazing that no one's spotted you yet," I giggled to Shea as Brawlers fans, decked out in their black-and-yellow jerseys, pushed past us. In a city full of drunken revelers partying in the streets, the captain of the Boston Brawlers *somehow* managed to go unnoticed.

"The captain's retired now," he joked. "I think I've already been forgotten."

I stayed glued to his side, licking my gelato as we walked back to his car. "Maybe. But you'll always be *my* captain."

His Bentley came into view.

"What do you want to do now?" I asked as we neared his car.

He wrapped his giant hand around my waist, his fingers clenching at my sides. I loved it when he squeezed me like that.

"I want to get you home," he whispered into my ear. "And get you out of this sexy little dress."

"And then what?" I flirted.

He held the passenger door open for me with an ornery smile. "I want to feel you from the inside."

"*Fuck*," I muttered, as I climbed, weak-kneed, into his car.

Shea turned the key, and the Bentley's powerful engine growled to life. Shea set his hand in my lap, and my legs parted ever-so-slightly for him.

"Anything else you want to do to me?" I asked, hoping he'd get even filthier.

Eyes on the road, Shea nodded as his massive hand crept under my dress and slowly inched up the insides of my thigh.

"Oh, yeah," he said.

"Tell me."

"I want to come inside you. Again and again."

"*Shea*," I sighed, an eager warmth pulsing between my thighs.

The hockey player's fingers found the crotch of my panties, and I let out a loud, breathy moan.

"How's that sound?" he asked as his finger entered my wetness.

I can't wait.

EPILOGUE
BRYNN

Two Years Later

I flew down stairs as fast as I could on a lazy Sunday afternoon.

Chloe, now sixteen, had her head resting on Adam's shoulder while they watched a movie on her iPad on the living room couch. Pickles had joined the couple, too—the cat was a leg-sitter, and he was happily sprawled across both teens' thighs, loudly purring.

The two teens had been a steady couple for two years now. Chloe had really spread her wings in the time since I first met her. Not only does she *enjoy* going to her therapy sessions (imagine that!), her grades have improved, she's got a job waiting tables, and she seems to have a really healthy relationship with Adam.

The only thing that *isn't* perfect in Chloe's life is her relationship with her mother. Cynthia was extended an invitation to attend therapy with Chloe—but she refused. Sad to say, their relationship is somewhat rocky, but Chloe at least seems to understand that it's not her fault.

And although Shea initially claimed that he 'hated' Adam, just *try* to remind him of that fact today—he'll huff and puff and deny it and insist that you're remembering things wrong. Because Shea *loves* Adam now. It helped that Adam took Shea's ground rules for dating Chloe seriously—he always addresses Shea as 'Mr. Ellis,' he always has Chloe home by curfew and, most importantly, he's always treated Chloe right.

I stood before them, panting for air. "Chloe!" I shouted.

Chloe paused the movie and looked up at me. "Uh, what's up, Brynn?"

"Where's your dad?"

"I think with Nick and Cam."

"Where?!"

"The garage, probably?"

"Thanks!" I spun around and raced off to the other end of the house.

"Hey, Brynn!" Chloe called after me. "Is everything alright?"

"Yes! Everything's great!"

I hurried through the house, ran outside and found Shea and the boys lying beneath his black 1981 Corvette. The car was as old as he was, and he'd bought it as a retirement project two years ago. And talk about a project—it was a major one, since the car was badly rusted and needed to be totally rebuilt, inside and out. But every weekend Shea had the boys, the three of them got under the hood, and Shea taught his sons how to work with a wrench.

I walked over and tapped my foot against Shea's. He was lying on a mechanic's creeper seat, the kind with wheels that glide under a car, while the boys laid on the garage floor.

"Shea!" I yelled.

There was a mechanical cranking of a ratchet and a series of Shea's manly grunts before he answered. "What's up, honey?"

"Got a minute to talk?"

"Sure. Just give me one sec." Shea addressed his sons. "Alright, boys. The spec on the rest of these bolts is 480 inch-pounds, got it?"

"Got it, Dad," Cam answered, his voice just beginning to deepen.

"Then go ahead and set your torque wrench and tighten her up."

"Okay."

Shea glided out from beneath the car. I didn't wait for him to climb to his feet; I knelt down instead and planted my lips on his, surprising him with a full and deep kiss. The metallic tang of motor oil only made his salty lips taste even manlier and better.

"What's this about?" he laughed, wiping the sweat from his brow with the crook of his elbow. "Normally, you won't let me anywhere near you when I'm this oily."

"I know. But right now, I don't mind one bit." I smiled at him.

His eyes narrowed. "So what's this about?"

"Come. I'll show you."

His big, rough hands were black with grease, but I didn't mind. I reached for his hand and he clasped it and I hurried him into the house.

"You're not going to tell me what this is about?" he asked. A smile was quickly spreading across his face—I figured he knew well enough what the surprise was, but I wanted him to see it in person.

"You'll see soon enough," I said as I led him through the living room, past Chloe and Adam, and upstairs to our bedroom.

... But I guess, before I tell you what happened next, I should tell you what happened in the days and months *before* that!

———

After the Boston Brawlers won the Stanley Cup, Shea officially retired from hockey as a champion. About a week after the team's big victory, the Brawlers general manager actually came to his front door with a contract in hand, trying to lure the captain back for *one* more year to try to repeat their championship season.

But Shea didn't even need to think about it. He'd already announced his retirement, and he didn't want to be one of those guys who went through the whole retirement ceremony, only to come back a year later. He didn't mind that he still had some gas in the tank when he left the game—as Shea put it, there wasn't anything worse than seeing an aging guy's body break down until he couldn't keep up anymore. He didn't want to go out like that. Plus, he said Lance was more than ready to lead the team.

Besides all that, Shea was ready to start his journey into retirement and, really, a new life. But Shea only stayed retired for two weeks before he started to go stir crazy. His job search was short—he found a job coaching hockey at Chloe's high school. You'd *think* she'd be embarrassed over it, but she had apparently outgrown that phase of teenage rebellion. Anyway, the twins were sure excited—once they started high school in two short years, he'd be their coach.

Speaking of new jobs, after the playoffs were over, I officially quit as the Ellis family nanny. I reached out to Eloise's parents and found out that not only had Mr. Gibson found a new job, they wanted to bring me back on board!

But while I went to work for the Gibsons, Shea never hired my replacement. He said he didn't *need* a nanny now that he was home instead of always traveling. He also told me that he hated the idea of putting someone else in my place. Not because he was afraid he'd make me jealous or worried that he might actually fall in love with a new nanny—but because he said he knew no one could fill my shoes, and he didn't want to be disappointed when someone tried and inevitably came up short.

If I had any worries that our relationship might flame out once we weren't living in the same house and sneaking around together, they were quickly put to rest. We might not have lived in the same house anymore—but we ended up seeing each other more than ever before.

Shea was always texting me sweet nothings, always seeing what I was up to and trying to make plans and take me out to dinner. He pestered me to ask for more time off work, so he could take me on vacations to other countries and 'enjoy retirement' ... I had to keep reminding him that *I* wasn't retired!

When Shea had custody, I made sure to come by the house and visit with the kids, and it was as if nothing had ever changed. The only difference was that Shea and I were boyfriend and girlfriend now, and at night, I went home to sleep at my own apartment—which was something Shea and I agreed on, so we wouldn't confuse the kids.

When Shea didn't have the kids, we spent a lot of nights at my tiny apartment after I got off work. I loved those nights more than anything—I don't know why, it just made our connection feel so *real,* that the famous hockey player wouldn't turn his nose up at my cramped apartment or complain about sleeping on my shitty, creaky mattress.

Day after day and night after night, I fell deeper for Shea. Our lovemaking never slowed—it only grew more intense.

And one year ago, on a regular day, I went to the bathroom. When I wiped, I saw a spot of red.

Never thought I'd be this happy to have my period.

I quickly booked an appointment with my doctor and underwent a barrage of lab tests. The longest week of my life ensued while I waited for the results. The whole time, I never said a word about it to Shea—partly because I couldn't believe it was real. And partly because, if it *was* real, I wanted to surprise Shea.

Finally, the lab results came back, and the doctor gave me the best news of my life: my body was healthy and finally working again.

I called Shea right away and gushed that I had great news to tell him—but he told me to wait. He said that he'd arrange for a dinner date at my favorite restaurant in town and I could tell him later that night.

I thought it was a bit strange, and I was a little disappointed because I wanted to tell the good news *now,* but I agreed. We met, and over dinner at *Peasant,* I told Shea the news.

"That's fantastic, love," he said. "You were so excited. I just figured it had to be."

I could feel my expression straining. This was the hard part, where we had to figure out what came next—and if Shea really was serious about being a father again.

"So ... er ... what do you think?" I stammered.

Shea's smile grew. "I think we've got some work to do, Brynn."

Then, suddenly, Shea stood from his chair, sidled next to me, and went down on one knee. He held up a box, popped the lid, and a giant diamond sparkled with the candlelight.

"Will you marry me, Brynn?"

"Shea—oh my God! *Yes!*"

Our wedding was six months later. The whole Brawlers team was there, and my brothers finally got to meet *their* childhood hockey hero, Shea Ellis. My husband.

The Gibsons were sad to see me leave a second time—but moving back in with Shea was like going home.

———

With his oil-slicked hand on mine, I led my husband through our bedroom towards our bathroom.

"Is this what I hope it is, Brynn?" he asked.

"I don't know," I sang, "what do you hope it is?"

He didn't say. He only smiled. "Brynn ... you're getting my hopes awfully high ..."

I took him into the bathroom. "Before I show you, I want a kiss."

He pressed his mouth against mine urgently, impatiently.

"Now tell me," he growled. "I need to know."

It'd been a year of trying-to-get-pregnant sex—which was always so raw, so hot, so emotional and so loving. But in the end, it always ended up disappointing, because our efforts hadn't been unsuccessful.

Until now. Finally, *finally*, I had something to show him.

I held the pregnancy test up to his face—or rather, all *three* pregnancy tests, because I couldn't quite believe the first two.

"Oh my God." Shea laughed a pure and joyous laugh. His rough hands gently went to my stomach and reverently held my belly. "I can't believe it, Brynn."

"Me neither! That's why I took three of 'em!"

"You're gonna be a *great* mom." He leaned his weight against me and kissed my mouth again. "I love you so damn much, Brynn. I can't wait."

I melted in the arms of my first-ever crush. The man who was now the father of the life growing inside me.

"I love you too, Shea."

THE END.

ABOUT THE AUTHOR

June Winters believes every romance is hotter on the ice. Born in Minnesota, June grew up knee-deep in hockey and quickly learned to love the sport – but especially its strong and sexy heroes, who will do anything for their teammates ... and the women they fall for.

Keep your eye out for more hockey romance from June!

If you'd like to be the first to hear of June's latest releases, sign up for her private mailing list!

A NEW SERIES ... AND A NEW TEAM!

Date with a Devil

(Dallas Devils Book 1)

Austen Marlowe learned all she needed to know about jocks back in high school: they might be tall, muscular, and hot as hell ... but you can never trust 'em. Valuable experience for someone who **dates hockey players for a living.**

As the host of *Date with a Devil*, the young journalist is called into action when the captain of the Dallas Devils insults the team's few remaining fans. Austen's mission: save the athlete's beleaguered reputation.

But **Dane DeHardt** doesn't give a damn about his reputation -- and his one-man war against the media threatens both their careers. Worse, "The Big D" can't keep his eyes off of her. *Doesn't he know these dates aren't real?*

But DeHardt isn't the dimwit she's been led to believe -- and when the sinfully sexy hockey star isn't trying to talk the rookie reporter out of her clothes, he's pushing her to get to the bottom of a story she was ordered not to cover.

Can Dane make Austen forget why she swore off jocks in the first place? Is she willing to risk her job because it's the right thing to do? *Or is she being played by The Big D?*

EXCERPT FROM DATE WITH A DEVIL
CHAPTER 1

Austen Marlowe

"This is *way* harder than it looks," Robert Thomas said. The athlete's pizza dough was a chunky blob that became a patchwork of holes the second he tried to stretch it.

"Right?" Austen said with a giggle. As the host of *Date with a Devil,* Austen went by 'Austy.' Austy was a lot more charismatic and confident than her real-life persona. "It really gives you a newfound respect for the guys who can just fling it into the air, doesn't it?"

Journalist and hockey player stood side by side, wearing flowery aprons, while Austen's two-man crew filmed from across the counter.

"Yeah." Robert threw his pizza dough next to Austen's with a *plop*. "Yours looks *way* better than mine. People are gonna watch this and think I'm a pigeon."

Ever since she'd started this job, Austen had learned that 'pigeon' was one of the many strange words in the hockey player lexicon—it meant something similar to stooge.

"Relax!" Austen bopped the athlete's shoulder, leaving a

flour imprint of her fist on his shirt. "Looking like a pigeon is half the fun. People like to watch you pros get out of your comfort zone. It makes you athletes seem human for once."

"Hm. I guess," he said. Robert played wing and, at only eighteen years old, was one of the Devils' several rookies this year.

"So, Robert." She paused. "Y'know, it feels weird calling you 'Robert.' Do you go by Rob or Robert?"

"Robbie, actually."

"Robbie." She giggled. "I like that. That's cute."

"Cute ...?" He made a noise like he was disappointed, despite a toothy grin.

"So, *Robbie,* you're a young guy playing second-line minutes in the NHL. You have to be pretty happy with your six goals and eight assists so far this year."

"Yeah, it's okay," he said. "I wish we were winning more, though."

"We all do," Austen said, ready to breeze right along into happier subjects. "So, who has helped you out the most this year, adjusting to life in the NHL?"

"Oh, that's easy—The Big D. He's been amazing. He's really taken all of us rookies under his wing. I don't know what we'd do without him."

"Really? Dane DeHardt?" Austen might have accidentally scoffed. "That's surprising."

"Yeah. I thought so, too. I was intimidated when I met him, but he's a really good guy. Not at all like what you read about."

Austen briefly glanced up at the camera with a slight frown. She knew that this part of the interview would probably end up being cut. She changed subjects again.

"So, Robbie, I asked some of the guys on the team about you."

"Uh-oh." The rookie nervously tensed. "What'd they say?"

"They told me you're big into music."

"Yeah."

"In fact, they told me that you're the team DJ—the guy whose phone is always pumpin' the jams in the locker room to get the boys amped up before a game. I'm told that's a pretty big honor for a rookie to have."

"Yeah," he said. Robbie was soft-spoken and didn't have a lot to say. Poor kid was painfully shy.

"Your teammates also told me your nickname in the locker room is 'Matchbox,' " Austen said.

"Yeah," Robbie grumbled. "But they won't tell me why."

"Your name is Robert Thomas and you wear number twenty. I thought the whole 'Matchbox Twenty' thing was intentional. Are you telling me it's not?"

He looked at her as if she were speaking in hieroglyphics. "Matchbox Twenty? What does that even mean?"

"Oh, sweetie." Austen covered her mouth and laughed. "Matchbox Twenty. They were a band. And Rob Thomas was their front man. Which is why your teammates are calling you Matchbox. Get it?"

"I get it now." He rolled his eyes like a moody teenager. "But I've never heard of them."

"Seriously?" Austen panted. "I thought you were big into music!"

"Yeah, music from *today*. Not whatever era Matchbox Twenty is from."

"They're from the nineties, Robbie." She scooped up a pinch of flour and dusted the rookie's cheek. "And P.S., I'm only five years older than you are. Don't make me feel so old."

He laughed and wiped the flour from his peach-fuzzed cheek. "Whatever."

"You kinda look like a younger version of him, too," she said.

"Who?"

"Rob Thomas! From Matchbox Twenty. You've even got the same curly blonde hair. You're cuter than he is, though."

Robbie stared at his pizza dough. His cheeks began to blush.

Aw, Austen thought. *So innocent.*

But with The Big D apparently taking him under his wing, it was only a matter of time until Matchbox turned out like all the others—bawdy, foul-mouthed, and promiscuous.

It was a shame, really. But all those jocks ended up exactly the same.

———

Both pizzas came out of the oven piping hot. It was time to sample their creations. Austen's *pizza margherita* was surprisingly tasty, but Robbie's goopy pepperoni and pineapple monstrosity was, er, hilariously *not*. Austen was sure her *Date with a Devil* fans would get a kick out of the shy guy's creation.

Then it was time to wrap up the interview. Austen shook his hand and thanked him for his time.

Most times after an interview, the athletes rushed out the door. Sometimes, their posse picked them up and whisked them away to wherever it is a young millionaire and his tag-along friends hang out.

Other times, the athletes lurked behind to test the waters. To see if Austen was 'DTF,' as one of Robbie's teammates once phrased it—'*down to fuck.*'

Did they *really* not understand that her jokey-flirty banter was all for the show? Or was it just in the jocks' DNA to try to 'smash' everything that moved?

Austen was *sure* Robbie was too sweet and innocent to be one of those guys. But lo and behold, while Austen and her crew packed their equipment up and into their SUV, Robbie lingered behind like a lost puppy.

"Hey, Austy? I uh, I wanted to talk to you in private," he said, pulling her away from her camera crew.

Oh no, not you, she thought. *Don't ruin it. You were so shy and polite.*

"Oh, uh, okay. What's up?" she asked.

"I just wanted to say hey, I had fun."

"Me too," she said, suspiciously. "And?"

"And, um, I was wondering what you were up to after this?"

Guh. This was like pulling teeth.

"I'm going on a date, actually," she said. "A real one."

"Oh." Robbie toed at the floor. "With your boyfriend?"

"Just some 'pigeon' from Tinder," she said, with a warm smile.

"Oh! That's cool. Well, if it doesn't work out—I was just, y'know, thinking that maybe you could give me your number. So we could maybe do something like that for real, someday?"

Her heart filled with a mournfulness. She hated to let a guy down—or at least, she hated to let down a young, clueless guy like Robbie, who clearly didn't know what he was doing.

"Oh, Robbie. I had fun hanging out," she said, beginning to frown, "but this is just my job."

He stared at his shoes. "Yeah, that's what I figured. Sorry to bother you. I'm such an idiot."

He started to walk off, but Austen grabbed him by the arm and pulled him back.

"Robbie. You're a really nice guy." She didn't have the heart to tell him that he had a *lot* of growing up to do before she'd consider dating a guy like him. "But we work for the same company, understand? The Devils have a fraternization policy. I could get fired for something like that."

"I know." He shook his head. "I wouldn't even have asked you out in the first place, but ... well ..."

"But what?"

"Big D challenged me to get your number at the end of the date. He said I should try to extend the night and see where things go."

"Is that right," Austen said flatly.

Why am I not surprised?

. . . to be continued!

BOOKS BY JUNE WINTERS

Dallas Devils:

Date with a Devil (Book 1)

Comeback (Book 2)

Bad Teammate (Book 3)

Keeper (Book 4)

Just Friends (Book 5)

Best Man (Book 6)

Boston Brawlers:

Forbidden Puck (Book 1)

Ice Daddy (Book 2)

Crush (Book 3)

Colorado Blizzard:

Hooked (Book 1)

Grudge Puck (Book 2)